Totally Bound Publishing books by January Bain

Brass Ring Sorority
Winning Casey
Chasing Lacey

The TETRAD Group
Racing the Tide

I0607520

Brass Ring Sorority

ROMANCING REBECCA

JANUARY BAIN

Romancing Rebecca
ISBN # 978-1-78686-389-8
Copyright January Bain 2019
Cover Art by Melody Pond ©Copyright February 2019
Interior text design by Claire Siemaszkiewicz
Totally Bound Publishing

ROMANCING
REBECCA

Dedication

This book is dedicated to the real Rebecca Fairfax — *thanks* is not a big enough word for the amazing inspiration you've brought to my life.

To my white knight, my beloved husband Don — one lifetime will never be enough…

A special vote of thanks to all the wonderful people at Totally Bound Publishing — you guys are the best at what you do.

And thank you, Nancy, and Sierra Brave, for encouraging me to write by reading all my stories.

Chapter One

I saw that you were perfect, and so I loved you. Then I saw that you were not perfect and I loved you even more.
— Angelita Lim

"Oh, my God. I'm driving the wrong way!" Rebecca Fairfax quit staring at the lovely wildflowers growing in profusion by the side of the country road and hit the brakes — hard — skidding the back wheel of her cherry-red Honda Gold Wing motorcycle to an abrupt halt.

"Damn it, why can't everyone the world over commit to driving on the same darn side of the road?" she muttered from under her safety helmet, using her foot to help rotate the heavy bike around to face the correct way. *Running late, check. Needing to use the bathroom, check. Losing my bloody mind, as evidenced by my accepting the Ringers' dare to kiss a duke, check and mate.*

After backtracking for a mile, she noted the brown tourist road sign she'd missed the first time. Castle Piers, next exit, with an image of a castle outlined in white. Sixty seconds later she made the turn, loving the sensation of the huge bike vibrating between her thighs while the world lived close, the air sweet with the aroma of honeysuckle, the wind caressing the bare skin of her cheeks. Riding a bike made being human different, somehow more raw and real. No other form of travel could compete. And, thanks to Lacey's William James Thornton III, the powerful bike had been waiting at the five-star hotel when Rebecca had arrived in glorious London last night.

Then Castle Piers came into view and the *oh my God* stuck in her throat.

Perfection. Surrounded by a vast moat stippled with water lilies and swans a-floating? She half expected the Lady of the Lake to rise and present her with Excalibur. Mesmerized, she rolled back on the throttle, bringing the bike to a standstill, bracing it with her feet and turning off the motor. She kicked out the back stand, and, with one booted foot outstretched to add stability to the motorcycle, leaned back in the leather saddle, determined to take the time to drink in the awesome sight. The sweet, fresh fragrance of early summer assailed her senses and she tipped her head back, eyes closed.

Then a new idea hit, making her reach for her notebook from under the elastic cord on the seat behind her. She began scribbling down her first impressions, afraid she'd regret not getting this moment back for posterity if she let it go, whether she was running late or not.

Xaviera St. Clair, her alter ego and the superheroine of Rebecca's *International Intrigue* series, was scheduled to visit a castle during her next adventure. Rebecca's skin tingled with ideas for the fun plot she'd dreamed up. Xaviera was going to learn how to handle the wiles of one Pierce Knight, art thief and man of a thousand faces. The steamy story included a definite proclivity for over-the-top escapades in the bedroom. Rebecca's body heated further as she imagined the twists and turns of their delicious romps before switching her attention to capturing the view in front of her. This was her last book to finish out her contract before she began writing in her new genre, historical literary, and she wanted it to be the best one yet.

Okay.

Centered in the middle of the water, above the soft gray mist, stood a castle right out of myth and legend. Its sheer gray stone towers rose skyward, with only a narrow causeway across the lake giving access to the gatehouse with the great nail-studded oak doors. A pennant flying atop one battlement snapped and fluttered briefly against the pale sky before changing direction, and a barely visible rainbow, leftover from the early morning drizzle, floated in a semicircle, caressing the tops of the trees with their lace of leaves. *Wow. Just wow.*

The mythology rushed over her, tugging at her soul. She could write here in her spare time. Research more about Samuel W. Piers, the founder of the Hermetic Order of the Rising Sun, a Freemason and ousted ancestor of the Piers family, until the cows came home. The expression amused her, and she gave a soft chuckle, remembering summers spent on her adopted grandparents' farm helping pluck eggs from under irate, territorial chickens. The dusty smell of the henhouse sprang instantly into memory and she sneezed aloud in sympathy for her childhood self.

Time to quit dawdling, Rebecca. She tucked the slim journal back under its elastic holder, then gave a booted kick with her right foot to release the stand keeping the bike upright, pressed the starter and hit the gas. Maybe she could catch up with the tour yet.

Down the causeway she drove at a somewhat more circumspect speed, careful not to spill the motorbike over the steep sides and into the lake. *Ha, imagine arriving covered in trails of green foliage like a water sprite rising from the mists.* Not the first impression she'd want to make for the Piers family, hosting her this summer while she researched their ancestral home's secrets.

Okay. So they don't know my full agenda, thinking me here just to help run their social affairs. And, I might add, paying for the privilege, thanks to my Brass Ringers' wish package. She snorted. Who else would get away with that bit of cheek but a family living in a castle right out of Camelot?

A second later, she had the oddest sensation of leaving her old life behind when she hit the halfway mark of the land bridge, a sense of being at a crossroad so unusual that she slowed down again, shaking her head to dispel the disquiet.

"Help! Thief!"

The frantic words surged into her brain, thrusting away misgivings. She gunned the bike, driving under the portcullis and into the courtyard. Catching a blur of a figure out of the corner of her eye, she slammed the bike to a stop, sending the back wheel spinning into a semicircle before the machine ground to a jerky halt. She jumped off, asking forgiveness for the mishandling. She hated to take the time to kick the stand into place, but she couldn't bear to see the bike take a tumble. She ran full pelt toward the spot where she'd spied the furtive action.

Where did they go?

She swiveled her head, trying to catch another glimpse of movement.

There.

The perp vanished between two stone pillars in the courtyard. No one followed on her heels, though she strained to catch any sounds of pursuit. She ran full tilt. *Thank goodness I memorized the layout of the castle before I left Canada.*

Her heart beating too rapidly, her boots slapping noisily on the pavestones, she dared a glance backward. A small group of tourists hovered about what looked like the tour guide in a yellow safety vest, pointing in the direction she was running, as if to direct her. *No help there.* She turned and ducked under a narrow overhang, wondering if she were nuts. If something had been stolen, it wasn't hers, after all. *But, damn it, it's the principle of the thing.*

Cooler inside, the massive stone castle pressed in around her, causing a sense of dislocation. Footsteps echoed hollowly, making her run faster, down the length of the corridor.

"Damn it anyway! Who steals from a fortress surrounded by a moat?" The map she'd pored over didn't show any way out in this direction, though it could be missing some key features kept secret.

Her lungs burned. *Note to self—up the workouts. Far too easy to beg off and write another scene for the current manuscript and skip the less fun part.*

She glimpsed the culprit taking another turn. There were damn fast, she'd give them credit for that. They'd been up and down so many passageways her head was spinning.

Dashing around another corner near the kitchen, she tripped, catching herself with one hand pressed against a sharp stone edge. Dank, cooler air assailed her nostrils. An abyss lay dead ahead with steps leading downward and out of sight. She teetered on the edge, jerking her body backwards at the last possible second. *Great. Just about ended myself before my overseas adventure begins. Second thought, looks like it has begun. This is right out of an action movie set.* She made light of what could have been a critical error, sweat trickling down her spine, her guardian angel hissing in her ear about the cost of being careless.

"Yeah, I know," she muttered.

She clambered down the stairs, holding on to the cold stone sides. *No handrails, of course.* Down, down she went, moving into uncharted territory she had no mental map for, making the going a whole lot riskier. She swore she could hear a bell tolling, upping her apprehension.

The tunnel narrowed, pools of water appearing on the floor. She gave a quick look to check out why. *Oh, boy.* Tiny waterfalls were following the path of narrow crevices worn into the walls. The water level deepened, more than could be explained by the trickles. Where was it coming from? She splashed through water up to her ankles. It flowed over her boot tops, soaking her feet and chilling her to the bone. *Oh, my God, I'm under the goddamn lake.* The thought made her breath freeze solid, two lumps of ice for lungs. This was a whole different enchilada. What if something above was just about ready to give way? Her fear of drowning reared, nearly stopping her heart.

To up her courage, she began to sing an old Johnny Cash song. *"How high's the water, papa? Sixteen feet and rising. How high's the water, mama?"* Her voice echoed off the walls. If the deluge got as high as in the song suggested, she would mostly likely drown, trapped in the tunnels under the castle like a sewer rat. She shuddered and kept up the singing, louder now to drown out the fear and the voice of reason.

She stopped mid-tune at an odd thudding sound very close by. Rebecca pressed on, far more frightened than she'd ever been before during her quarter century on the planet. *I don't want to die, not before I've lived. Think about something else. Anything else.* At least a few sconces lit the way, some kind of portable device someone had rigged up. Maybe the thief?

She stopped mid-stride. Her peripheral vision had caught a glimpse of symbols carved into the rock, something man-made. An eye within the compass and the square, forming a partial pentagram. Not large, but distinct, and old, centuries old, Freemason imagery, found in many locations the world over. But it was the addition of another symbol nudged up against it that sent a shiver of excitement racing through her bloodstream. *King Solomon's seal.*

She swallowed hard, her heart pounding as she stared at the marking, taking it all in, never having thought that her research would lead to so powerful a find so early in her journey to England. It boggled her mind what it meant, what it stood for. The threads of time were staring her in the face, and not many could make the connections her feverish brain could.

The pentagram within a double ring with an Egyptian ankh housed inside was a secret symbol known only to a few souls who didn't mind spending time in musty libraries. The pentagram was also an alchemical symbol, the intersecting triangles representing the elements of fire and water or the elements of male and female. The symbols had later been adopted by a group of like-minded occult seekers, one of the Hermetic Order of the Golden Dawn's splinter charters, the Order of the Rising Sun. And the reason she was at Castle Piers.

The Piers family tree included a black sheep, the leader of the splinter group, one Samuel W. Piers, who'd run the Osiris-Sun Temple for the Rising Sun Order more than a hundred years ago. The mysteries of his leadership, the missing artifacts and the secret knowledge he was said to possess called across the ages, fascinating a small band of researchers, of which she was one — though she left the magical demonology part of the practice to others.

She reached out a hand with awe. She was about to touch her Holy Grail. Her fingers traced the ancient carvings, steeped in such mysterious history and beauty, and she shook her head in disbelief. *Gobsmacking.* Rudyard Kipling could not have been prouder, the storyteller behind *The Man Who Would Be King,* the tale of a pair of Freemasons looking to be kings of Kafiristan. He'd borrowed the imagery of that order, and now here she stood, tracing the stardust of that mythology connected to King Solomon.

Chapter Two

Nothing is ever as simple as it appears. — *Terrance Bridge*

Dragging footsteps pulled her abruptly into the present. *No time to waste.* She ran again, pushing herself harder, and turned a final corner. She spotted the thief, a thin, slight male, not twenty feet ahead, close enough she could hear his harsh breathing. Was it from pain? She could only hope he was in some discomfort after he had led her to the brink of demise on the stone steps.

"Stop! You can't get away now! Might as well hand back what you stole." At least her voice didn't give away her terror. She reached in her pocket and withdrew the Leatherman she always carried — a handy weapon in a pinch. *Damn shaky fingers.* She jerked the knife out with a fingernail from its steel housing, breaking the nail off to the quick in her hurry.

"Damn it!" Pain shot up her forefinger and she stuck it into her mouth to soothe it.

"Fine. Take it. Just let me go." He tossed a wrapped package toward her, about the size of a bumpy plastic football. *Odd.* It sprayed a little water on touchdown, landing with a plop. Whatever he had stolen didn't weigh much.

"Sorry. No can do." She shook her head for emphasis, realizing at that moment she still had her helmet on. "You just took someone's property."

"Hey, lady. Can't you give a bloke a break?" he whined. *Just a skinny kid.* And his having a British accent wasn't the usual bonus.

"Why should I?" she asked, narrowing her eyes and drawing closer. She looked him over for weapons. He didn't appear to have any. Thank goodness she had a canister of mace in her pocket, compliments of the good friend who had provided her sweet ride. Of course, she'd also taken a few self-defence courses, but nothing beat pepper spray in the eyes for a quick end to things.

"What's going on here?" a new voice roared out of the darkness.

She started at the unexpected noise, slipping on the wet rough-hewed ground. Pinwheeling her arms about, she went down with a splosh, hitting the deck awkwardly. The pain reverberated through her right hip before the water soaked through her jeans. She gritted her teeth with frustration and scrambled to her feet.

"That woman stole your Fabergé egg," the thief accused, pointing a rigid forefinger at her, one she instantly wanted to bite off.

"That's not what happened, and you darn well know it!" Adrenaline flooded her system. *The unmitigated gall.* "I was chasing *you!*"

"She's lying!" he said.

She took her eyes off the obnoxious pants-on-fire thief for a second, glancing around to see who had finally shown up to help, expecting perhaps the errant tour guide. But it wasn't him. He hadn't looked at all like a legendary ruler such as Uther Pendragon or King Arthur in his yellow safety vest. But this man did. *Oh boy, does he.* As though he had walked straight out of *The Mists of Avalon* or *The Once and Future King*, standing there with his arms crossed, glaring at the two of them as if they were in cahoots. From his thick brown hair falling forward onto his forehead to curl just right, to his chiselled facial features that spoke of centuries of good breeding, he would make the perfect lead in *any* movie that required a hot, over-the-top-sexy hero.

Oh. My.

She swallowed hard, her mouth suddenly too parched to be able to speak a word. *Xaviera, we've got the guy to play your hero in your swan song, that's for damn sure.* He was also the perfect protagonist for the historical literary book she envisioned using this castle location for, now that she was preparing to make the break from writing steamy romances. *Finally.*

"You can both come with me. I'll need to get to the bottom of things." His fine British accent tugged at something deep inside her.

"You don't believe this lying sack of sh — this idiot," she said, clearing her throat, self-correcting at the last second, with how cultured the man sounded and not her wanting to make a poor impression. He offered her his hand and she took it. *Whoa. Nice strong hands, too.* He helped her to her feet, blessing her with a stern look. *Fine, play it that way.* Anger rose at the unfairness of his accusations. At least it ratcheted down her libido.

"I just got here. How am I supposed to know who's lying and who's not? Are you okay?"

"Let's see. I jumped off my motorcycle nearly taking a spill, raced through these oppressive tunnels in an effort to rescue *your* freakin' treasure, and all I get for my trouble is suspicion. So, to answer your question, no, I'm *not* okay!"

"She's just trying to cover up," the thief said in a know-it-all tone of voice. She just wanted to smack him one or, better yet, kick him where the sun don't shine.

"You shut it! We both know the truth of things. Not two minutes ago you asked me to let you go in the most whiney voice imaginable. Weren't such a tough guy then, were you?" She'd dropped her favorite Leatherman in the bruhaha and gave a look around for it, using her foot to splash the water, ignoring the annoying pair.

"Oh, thank goodness!" She spotted the weapon stuck between two flat rocks, handle side up. She leaned down to pick it up, but her head swam from the effort and she swayed dizzily. The tunnel's sides squeezed in like the aperture of a camera shutter in a silent black and white movie. Perhaps the freight train was about to run over the heroine tied to the track by the devious villain?

His Hotness rushed to her, taking her arm to steady her. She leaned against him, breathing in the fresh-from-the-woods fragrance that lingered on his wool coat. *Yes. I'll just cuddle here all day. Please take my messages. I don't want to be disturbed.*

Another arm slipped around her waist, drawing her to his side.

"Perhaps I should carry you?" he inquired, his plummy voice tinged with concern.

"Perhaps that would be best."

She looked into his eyes. *Oh my, what a lovely shade of melting chocolate.* Then she caught sight of the thief from the corners of her eyes.

"Stop him! The thief—he's getting away."

"I thought the matter had not been decided yet?" He raised a sardonic eyebrow, his mouth twitching. Strange, he seemed less worried about the real thief than she did.

"Your tour guide can vouch for me. He pointed the way before I gave chase. Plus, *this* guy" — she pointed at the slippery culprit still moving with obvious discomfort down the tunnel, holding onto the side while hopping on his one good foot — "gave the game away by announcing what was in the package. The Fabergé egg. How could he know that if I was the one to steal it?"

Hmm, those melting pools of chocolate. Are those flecks of gold? Hard to be certain in the dim light. He paid her words homage and his expression softened. "Of course, that does make a great deal of sense. Though he still might have seen you take it."

"Duh, of course, it does." She slipped into defensive mode. "And I did not take it — I'm not the one trying to sneak away."

"Right you are."

"You can let me go," she said with reluctance. "And nab the guy."

"Are you certain? I don't want you falling and suing us."

"For goodness' sake, I'm not going to sue your ass. Though, on second thoughts, perhaps I should consider suing you for slander."

He pulled away from her, leaving her instantly colder and bereft of the lovely sensation of being in La-La Land. She tugged off her helmet, letting her fair hair spill out over her shoulders. She fluffed it out with one hand for added emphasis.

"You wouldn't happen to be a duke of something or other, would you?" she asked at his recoil, praying it

19

was so. That would even make up for slugging through water and ruining her best pair of motorcycle boots.

"No, just an earl. The Earl of Craigmere to be precise. My father's the duke, so I don't inherit until he's gone, which I hope is a long way off — at least most days. He can be a real ballbreaker about my life at times, though perhaps he has reason." He ran a hand through his hair, disheveling the arrangement and only managing to look even more fetching. "Excuse my language. Ash Piers at your service. Why did you want to know if I'm a duke?"

He'd turned back around to converse, ignoring the distant sound of the thief's dragging footfalls. He stared at her now without her helmet, taking in the thick waves of hair she prayed were framing her face in a flattering manner and not sticking out awkwardly from being confined.

"Nothing, I was just wondering — this being a castle and all. I'm Rebecca Fairfax, by the way."

He gave her a charming smile that nearly melted her panties clear off. Then his forehead knit, as if he was trying to figure out a puzzle.

"And all the way from Canada, I see. I can hear it in your speech patterns. Quite different from an American accent. I quite like it. Though I sense I've met you somewhere. Ever been to England before, Rebecca Fairfax?" His eyes locked on hers, and she could almost see him racking his brain for answers. *Oh please, don't let him be a reader of erotica. The chances are slim, right?*

"No, first time. And, perhaps you might want to stop that thief?"

"Ah, yes, of course."

This time he hurried away, leaving her — yeah, breathless. And worried.

The package lying abandoned on the ground aroused her curiosity. *I'll just peek. I deserve to for having done what I did, right?*

She picked up the parcel. It dripped water and she gave it a gentle shake to remove the last drops. She shivered, cooler without the headgear.

With shaking fingers, she pulled away the bubble-wrap cover that had appeared so weird when the thief had tossed the item away. The action made some of the bubbles pop as the sticky tape loosened, startling her further. She tore the final layer out of the way, holding on to her shattered nerves with more effort than she was prepared to admit. And stared, just *stared* at the discovery. This was no ordinary egg, but the 1903 Royal Danish Egg, also known as the Danish Silver Jubilee Egg. One of the largest ever made, it was recorded as 'lost'. *Ha, I bet my bottom dollar this is no replica. It looks authentic.*

Made of gold with light-blue and opalescent white enamel and watercolor on ivory — according to credible reports she had read doing research for a novel — it was surmounted by a Danish Royal Elephant, Denmark's ancient Order of the Elephant, and supported by three Danish heraldic lions. Was the surprise still inside? It was said to have contained a double-sided miniature screen on a stand, showing portraits of King Christian IX on one side and Queen Louise on the other, each surmounted by a diamond crown and initial.

I have to peek inside to see if it still holds the treasure. Making her numb fingers locate and open the egg took extreme focus, but she was rewarded a few seconds later when the top popped open just like it was supposed to. It did indeed contain the prize. But how on earth had the Piers family laid their hands on such an awesome treasure? What was the connection to the Danish Royal family?

The sound of footsteps approaching woke her from her thoughts. She hastily tucked the prize back inside the egg and rewrapped the treasure in the bubble wrap. The tape wouldn't hold now, of course, ruined from having been in water. It would have to do.

The Earl of Hotness was alone, looking quite pleased with himself.

"Where's the thief? You didn't dispose of him for daring to steal the royal jewels?" She couldn't resist.

The man's look of horror was priceless. "Do you think I'm a barbarian?"

"No, of course not." She shook her head vigorously, making her hair dance around her shoulders. "I've just always wanted to use that expression."

He seemed quite mesmerized by something, keeping his glance locked on her for a bit longer than called for. "My royal jewels have not been stolen. Quite intact, in fact."

"Ah, good to know." Her gaze moved of its own accord, slipping down his fine frame, from his extra wide shoulders to his trim hips, checking out his package. Fortunately, his pea jacket ended in a shorter style. *Yes, quite intact.* She glanced back up, caught in the act.

Chapter Three

Just when I think I have learned the way to live, life changes.
— Hugh Prather

"Are all Canadian women like you?"

"I have no idea what you mean. Like me in what way?"

"Enjoy a good double entendre with an earl?"

She snorted, the heat rising in her face. It had been years since she'd blushed. What had gotten into her? *Good grief, I've just met this man.* "I'd prefer an earl who nabbed the culprit. What happened?"

He shrugged. "Such a pathetic story really. He shared that he needed the funds to buy drugs. I had to let him go. He was on the brink of going into withdrawal shock. Bloody awful condition, I've been told."

"*What?*"

"Sorry, just wanted to tease." He ran his hand through his hair, giving the most appealing expression. "No, the guy pulled a Keyser Söze. Gone without a trace. I waited too long."

"Ah, I see. Now that was kind of both our faults, eh."

"So, Rebecca Fairfax, what on earth made you chase a suspected thief through a castle when you can't possibly know where you're going? You could have been badly hurt, you know." All traces of humor had vanished.

"Well, it wasn't as bad as all that. I do know the layout of this castle. I researched in preparation for my summer job here."

Now it was his turn to look flummoxed. For a second. "Ah, the new summer events coordinator. You're off to quite a spectacular start."

She snorted again. "And I seemed to have missed the tour I booked getting this back." She handed him the poorly rewrapped package.

"What did you think of the Danish Jubilee egg?" His casual expression belied the sharp look in his eyes when he took the treasure from her.

"Well, I know it's not a reproduction, if that's what you mean."

He sighed theatrically. "Now, you know, housing such an important state secret, you can't *ever* be allowed to go home again."

"Excuse me?"

"Forgive me, just my British sense of humor." He did not appear to be one tiny bit sorry.

Her heart hammering madly, she heard more footsteps coming. *Now what?* Ash straightened when a man came into view, the half-smile vanishing.

"Father, what on earth are you doing down here?"

"Father? As in the Duke of Piers?" Rebecca asked, her brain taking in the silver-haired man who bore a distinct resemblance to his son. Same handsome features, same strong yet elegant build. And the same haughty expression that they both shared at that moment.

"Yes, why?" He gave her figure a once-over, then turned back to his son. "What's going on? The tour guide's in a tizzy, saying that a thief has stolen something very valuable. Is this her?"

"What? No! I'm the one that rescued the darn egg."

The duke's expression cleared when his son added his affirmative nod. His Grace looked from his son to her again, and Rebecca was careful to keep her expression neutral. She chanced a peek at Ash, but he was staring at her intently.

"Now I recognize you!" Ash's expression changed to one of horror.

"What do you mean? I just got here."

"You're *that* writer. The one that writes those — those steamy stories. You're not just here to be our events coordinator. You're here under false pretenses! Admit it."

"I'm here to practice my chef skills and help you make money this summer. That's all. I just happen to also write. No crime in that."

"There is if you're thinking of using anything to do with us in your stories. Father, we have to sack this woman immediately. She's not being totally honest with us."

He glared at her, and she returned it in spades. How dare he disparage her profession? Sure, she aspired to become a writer more like Hilary Mantel or Simon Sebastian Montefiore, and write rich historical books based on factual research by living in a castle with an intriguing mystery. One she planned to solve on the sly and get major kudos for the summer, and one she just been handed an important key to. But it was her business, and hers alone. Plus, she had been damn good at the erotic genre too. Took pride it doing it well. The idea of writing hot and bothered – it worked.

"I'm not being dishonest. I am a darn good chef and I will do my job to the best of my ability. You have my word on it. And I did save that family trinket." If he was going to disparage, so was she.

"Trinket!" Ash's voice rose a satisfying octave.

"Now, now, Rebecca should be rewarded at the very least, Ash, for saving the treasure." The older man appeared far less threatening now, giving her a second and more friendly looksee. He'd seemed to enjoy their heated exchange far more than she or her new nemesis had. She gave *him* an extra steely-eyed glare for good measure.

"It's true all right. And yes, I will have my reward." And with that she did something she would never have thought possible. Something entirely spontaneous, something she was not known for back home and one of the reasons she was on this journey of self-discovery. Since she was about to be booted out, at least she would win the dare. And a part of her wanted to flip the bird to his son for being such a pain in her ass.

She went right up to the duke, stood on tiptoe and tugged his handsome silver-fox head down by grasping the back of his neck. Which was when she planted a huge kiss on his lips. His lips were rather stiff at first, but quickly, very quickly, he got into the spirit of things, and tugged her closer to him, obviously enjoying the moment. He did a very thorough job of it. And it was not unpleasant, his lips tasting of sweet sherry while the fragrance of rich tobacco smoke emanated from his jacket.

I wonder how it would be to kiss his son instead? What would he taste like? Would he be all-commanding, pushing his tongue into my mouth, caressing and tasting me? The thoughts appeared as if by magic in her brain, further surprising her and making her stomach flutter with anticipation.

"What the hell!" Ash exclaimed in anger or horror — she wasn't sure which — behind them and when she finally managed to pull herself out of his father's embrace and turn to him, she found him with his hands tightened into fists at his side. *What's his problem?* She was the one who had stepped out on a limb, not him. Besides, he was just waiting to throw her out.

"Ah, my Cinderella, you've come back for me," his father said with satisfaction, obviously taking the innocent kiss rather well.

She grinned. *Think I'm a thief and dishonest, eh, your Hotness? There, I've also won the bet.* She pulled out her phone from her jacket to send a text. *Hmm, terrible reception, no bars.* She'd send it later. She needed to credit the right Brass Ringer with the win. She hoped she'd beat the last official time for a Ringer getting the dare completed, getting the kiss in so fast. *Well done, Rebecca.*

"Well, well, this calls for a huge celebration." The duke had a rougher voice than his son. She looked up to see what he was referring to. He was appraising his son, seeming to be making some kind of decision. The younger man still stood stiffly, staring at him, his expression tightly controlled.

"What are you going on about?" Ash asked, his voice lacking any sense of humor.

"Why, this young woman has gotten our Danish treasure back, and, by her very favorable actions this fortuitous day, is consenting to be mine with a kiss! I knew this would happen. That the right woman would just appear at a propitious moment and take matters into her own hands. I've long dreamed of this. And now, we are engaged! So much to celebrate, I hardly know where to start. I warned you, Ash, if you won't give up your philandering ways and guarantee succession with an heir, then it's my duty to marry again and have another."

Wha – Rebecca's phone slipped from her nerveless fingers and into a puddle of water at her feet.

"No!" she shouted, leaning down to fish it out. The electronic device was her most vital possession in England next to her laptop, hooked up to an international plan to save her funds. Cold and drenched, her fingers sleuthed the lost object under the frigid water. She brought it up sopping wet and hurriedly unzipped her stiff motorcycle jacket with the built-in armor to get at the softer shirt underneath. She pulled the fabric away from her body and dried her iPhone off.

"Oh, thank goodness, it's all right." She looked up to find both men starring at her intently. Why? She looked down to find she had exposed a great deal of toned flesh. Then she remembered what had just transpired.

"Ah, that kiss didn't—"

"Yes, sweet beyond belief! I look forward to many, many more in the future, sweetness."

"But, you don't understand—"

"Ah, but I do, your actions give you away. You wish to marry a duke. I'm a duke in desperate need of a wife. Could it be any clearer? And the timing, beyond belief. Why, just this morning I was told my ticker—well, you know, not so perfect anymore. But this, *this* is exactly what the doctor ordered."

"What about your heart? What did the doctor say?" Ash's expression instantly changed to one of concern.

The duke waved his hand in dismissal. "Nothing important. I just want to think about the amazing thing that's happened here today. A fine young woman appearing in our midst with the courage of a lion. And proving herself with a kiss. Spectacular start, don't you think, son? Bodes well for the future progeny of my loins."

Blink.

She looked from one outraged son to a very satisfied-looking father.

Say, just a sec, maybe this is my golden ticket to stay here and not be thrown out on my butt.

She could hardly admit she'd kissed the man to win a bet. Even in England, where eccentrics abounded, she might look certifiable. And surely this whole mess would be cleared up soon? But it did give her a way around being booted out right now. *A bird in the hand and all that.* Play along until she'd made herself indispensable and they wanted her to stay all summer. Fair dues, with everyone getting what they wanted? Well, maybe except for the Earl of Craigmere. His expression was priceless. *And totally worth the deception.*

Chapter Four

Keeping the British end up, sir. — *The Spy Who Loved Me*

"We need to get you out of the damp, father," Ash urged. He looked at Rebecca, giving a slight shake of his head to keep her from protesting further. It was all show anyway and damn obvious what she was up to. His father's unorthodox behavior could be explained by his weakened state—hers, most definitely not. But they could sort this debacle out later. Much as it went against all he had been experiencing in these last few minutes, certain that he'd shared something rather special with the charming, witty and oh-so-sexy Rebecca, he had to face facts. She wanted a duke, not an almost duke.

He shook his head, trying to forget how perfectly she had fit into his arms. Her light floral fragrance mingling with the leather of her jacket was a potent combination, sensual and like nothing he'd experienced before. Anger flared, which he fought to contain. She just had to go and expose her true colors. *Gold-digger.*

He'd only came down here today to check that the tunnel flooding had not worsened. But yes, it was becoming obvious that they needed to make repairs or it just might collapse. And how much was that going to cost? Keeping Castle Piers in a good state of repair was straining finances.

Okay, his father's accusation held merit. Ash admitted his playboy status was well-deserved. Something he and Dad had begun to argue about rather regularly. But this damn castle was expensive to keep up, a far more important concern. So maybe it was time to hand some of their treasures over to an auction house? But marrying for money or prestige, like this Canadian upstart was doing? *God damn it, but that rubs me the wrong way. And what makes me even more annoyed, my damn cock doesn't agree with my assessment.*

"I guess I'd better ask the name of the woman I'm engaged to?" his father prompted, taking her arm and directing her down the tunnel, toward the stairs and exit.

"Ah, yeah, it's erm—Rebecca. Rebecca Fairfax." She sounded a bit blown away, as if her name had nearly escaped her. *Probably can't believe her good fortune.*

"And what do you do, sweet Rebecca Fairfax?"

"I just finished taking a cordon bleu course back home so I'm hoping to hone my skills while I'm here, and I wanted to try my hand at being an events coordinator, before your son complained and put the kibosh on it. And, as mentioned, I also write." She gave him another glare which he gladly returned with a bonus attached.

"You haven't been fired from the job. My son overreacted. What kind of stories do you like to write, my dear?"

"Ah—novels."

"And I take it, from the exchange, you want to change genres?"

"Yes, I do. I did write a series of novels about a heroine, Xaviera St. Clair, with superpowers, but I've just got one left to write to fulfill my contract, then I'm going to change gears to historical novels with its rich traditions. More like Simon Sharma or Philippa Langley?"

"Commendable. But your first novels sound interesting as well. What kind of superpower did the heroine have?"

In spite of himself, Ash listened. And why wasn't she mentioning how much erotica was contained within those pages? The heroine had superpowers in and out of the bedroom in those over-the-top stories. Why, just the idea was enough to get him hard. *Focus. Think of something else.* And no way would he ever admit he'd read a large part of *Hijinks in Netherland,* standing in a bookstore, because he'd barely been able to put it down. Her back-jacket photo did not do her justice though. She was much prettier in person.

"Extra-sensory perception. Telepathy, to be precise. She can read the minds of people, find out all their hidden secrets."

"That would be quite the advantage in real life. Reading other minds. I'd like that, though being able to turn invisible was always my idea for a perfect superpower. Just think of all the havoc that could create."

"Invisibility. You've never mentioned that, father." *Who is he, talking to Rebecca?* Someone must have highjacked his real father, left a virtual clone. *Can they can do that now—leave a replicant?*

"You don't know everything there is to know about me, son. I've always liked to keep my cards close to my chest. It would be good for you to learn the skill. You're far too obvious with all your womanizing."

"Damn it—"

"*Tsk, tsk,* show more respect for your future stepmother, son. She's obviously deserving of it."

Ash gritted his teeth so hard they began to ache. It was only by the barest of margins he didn't launch into a tirade that would shake the very foundations of Castle Piers, and probably result in it falling down about their ears. *Serve them bloody right.*

"Your grandmother has invited us to tea. It will be the ideal time to present Rebecca formally to her. She's going to be so very, very pleased."

"Isn't that carrying all this a bit far?" Telling the dowager would add another layer of complication. "I mean, you hardly know this woman and she's already proven herself a gold-digger. Actions speak louder than words. Isn't that what you're always saying to me?"

"Now hold on a cotton-picking minute! I am *not* a gold-digger. I paid to come here, to spend time in your flooded castle, not the other way around. And not only that, asked to be a non-paid employee."

"Calm yourself, Rebecca. My son is just being a donkey's hind end. I will explain it in terms even an imbecile can understand. And that matters, that she might want to marry up a bit? Look what she brings to the table. Beauty, charm, talent. What else could I ask for? I think it's more than a fair trade."

What else could he ask for, indeed? Such an intriguing woman. Too bad she was willing to marry for money or prestige. Likely both.

"I'm in favor of a very long, long, *long* engagement," Rebecca spoke up again, her voice sounding a bit strangled. *Thank goodness someone has some sense.*

"Nonsense. No time for that. Three months, I think. Just in time for my fiftieth birthday. My half-century milestone. Too perfect to begin the second part of my life in this amazing new journey with a beautiful new second wife on my arm."

"Just what did the doctor say, father?" Maybe Ash should schedule a psychiatric appointment as well? And how on God's green earth could so many life-altering events be happening in the dreariest tunnel imaginable?

"All confidential, son. I didn't want to worry your grandmother. You know her fragile condition. So the less you know, the better. And I don't want you worrying her about *any* of this. Understood?"

Complete madness, but he found himself nodding. He ignored the look of disbelief that Rebecca shot him. *You helped cause this, beautiful. You can help me fix it when the time is right.*

The stone steps to the main floor finally appeared at the end of the tunnel. He sighed with relief before realizing what a steep climb it would be for his father.

But his father managed it, albeit one step at a time, only stopping once to point out a rather large crack that appeared to be widening in the granite wall. In short order, their little party made its way to his grandmother's apartments.

He took note of Rebecca, who seemed to be too busy taking in the castle's grandeur to make simple conversation. *Sure. Adding up the totals, I'll bet.* His stomach twisted in complaint. He'd just get this damn tea with his grandmother over with and he could get on with his day. He wanted to be anywhere but standing next to a woman he equally wanted to bed and teach a lesson to.

Rebecca froze. An odd sensation of being observed come over her. She turned from admiring a seventeenth-century French tapestry masterpiece of knights on horseback likely produced at the Royal Factory of the Gobelins to come face-to-face with a wicked gleam emanating from Ash's chocolate-brown eyes. She couldn't seem to look anywhere else and their eyes locked in an intense glare, well beyond the usual moment of politeness before both parties glanced away. *What was he thinking about? And what have I let myself in for?*

The insane antics of the past hour came flooding back, thoughts she had been trying to dodge by studiously observing the castle's furnishings. *Certifiable.* No other word suited. A plot right out of a romance novel. A crazy charade. Though, come to think of it, Lacey, her fellow Brass Ringer, had gotten fooled by her best friend, Will, one fine masquerade party in Manila when he took on the persona of a rake to nab a sword she'd always coveted. *And look how that turned out. Married a week later.* At least Rebecca didn't have to worry about that. She'd never marry either of these two men, and especially not this one, even if he was the last man on earth and she was the only hope to save the human population from extinction.

Okay, maybe she'd kind of asked for this by going overboard in the kissing. *But my goodness, not the father.* A man twenty-five years older than her, for heaven's sake. Why couldn't His Hotness have been the duke? Then she wouldn't be suffering under this fake engagement scenario. Though she would be out on her ass if that were the case, so fate had handled it correctly. How old was he anyway, the almost duke? No more than thirty for certain, otherwise the math wouldn't work.

And the friggin' irony, the coup de grâce, the urge to write erotica is back again. Best guess, she desperately needed to let loose all these new sensations somewhere, and the safest place was on the printed page.

She stuck her tongue out at Ash. She had to do something — she didn't have the grace under pressure her characters were known for. *Huh. A little easier for them, with time to think things through with my help.* His eyes smoldered with enough heat to catch the damn tapestry in a flash fire. And he was making her throat dry, and her panties soaking wet. She swallowed hard. *Yes. I'll need to see this as research, only way to get through it.* And it was the only way he'd let her stay — that was fairly obvious — and the drive to remain in Castle Piers for the summer was strong. She had plans. But engaged to the father and wanting to jump into the sack with the son? *Oh boy, this is going to be some friggin' summer.*

She kept her eyes averted, following her old fake fiancé into the dowager's apartment after a polite rap on the oak door with a brass lion knocker. *Are those bells tolling in the distance again?*

The dowager's suite was scrumptious, if a bit hot and stuffy. All three tugged off their jackets, leaving them in a heap on a French provincial embroidered satin damask chair. Ash placed the rescued Fabergé egg atop the pile.

Then, out from behind a lovely embroidered screen of an English garden at sunrise, came a handsome woman of a certain age. Silver hair perfectly groomed, lustrous pearls in place, navy lace suit tailormade, she graced them with a beaming smile before sailing across the room to greet them.

"Edward. Ash." She accepted a kiss on the cheek from each in turn. What was the duke whispering into his mother's ear? Maybe he was just reassuring her that all was well. *As if.* "And you've brought company. How delightful. And so pretty. Tell me, who are you, child?"

"Mother, I'd like you to meet my fiancée, Rebecca Fairfax, just arrived from Canada. Very timely. She rescued the Danish Jubilee egg from a scoundrel."

"My goodness! Really? One of our most beloved treasures too. Handed down from a fortuitous liaison between the first lady of Russia and a long-dead scoundrel lurking in our family tree. I thank you, child. Let me take a good look at you."

She came closer, her bright blue eyes missing nothing. Rebecca wished she had a mirror and a comb, perhaps a bit of powder. All that sweating and running about could not have done much for her appearance.

The older woman squinted her eyes, peering into her face. She was almost Rebecca's height. Rebecca gave her a quick smile of greeting, thinking this intelligent woman would make a great ally. Get her son to back off now it was apparent they'd just met, and an engagement was out of the question.

"Excellent choice, Edward. Very lovely, good birthing hips. She's got that beautiful blonde hair you love, too. And the most unusual eyes I've ever seen. Deep green with a starburst of bright gold. Beautiful and rare. Perhaps she can whelp a better grandson than this rascal." She raised her eyebrows, giving His Hotness a pointed barb.

OMG. Did she just say that...?

"And now we *must* have a party. Don't we have an events coordinator arriving this week who could take care of all the fuss and bother for us? Good call. Getting the pigeon to pay for the privilege." The older woman gave a half-chuckle.

"Mother, this *is* the new events coordinator. She arrived early, for some reason."

"Oh, dear, I had no idea. Well, doesn't that make the whole process easier. Rebecca will know *exactly* what she wants and can plan it to boot. I say, very clever, Edward."

I can see where her son got his allotment of marbles.

An odd sound from His Hotness made her swing right around. He seemed to be choking on something.

"Are you okay?" she asked. He was either trying to hold in a good belly laugh or strangling on his tongue. She hoped it was the second option. He had been not one bit of help so far, going along with all the shenanigans like it was business as usual. *Unless this is business as usual?*

"I arrived a day early to take the castle tour. I wanted to experience it first hand as a tourist before I moved in. You know, reconnoitre things. I left my luggage back at the hotel."

"Quite right. My grandson can help you retrieve your belongings later. Shall we gather around the table? No need to change, dear, we're quite informal around here."

The dowager placed a commanding hand, gaily decorated with a rainbow assortment of jeweled rings, on her son's arm, nodding at Ash to follow suit. He advanced toward Rebecca, his expression — She racked her brain for the perfect word choice to describe his look of bafflement that mirrored her own, and 'nonplussed' was the best she could come up with. *Well, Welcome to Oz, your Hotness.* Why was he not immune to the antics of his eccentric family by now?

She laid a hand on his arm, giving him a speculative look. "You down with this?"

He frowned, not catching her drift. However, at such close quarters, she caught his scent again. She'd read in a book on human attraction that a defining moment in meeting someone was how they smelled—right up there after appearance. She'd just never experienced its importance firsthand before.

"Do you have any other siblings or relatives about to jump out of the woodwork at me? Perhaps wanting something for free?"

He had the grace to look a bit abashed. "You're hardly the one to talk. Marrying for money."

She glared, her heart pounding. She hissed in his ear. "You have no idea what you are talking about. I would *never* do that." *Calm down, Rebecca.* "It sure beats being called a Lothario, a gigolo, a seducer, Don Juan, a philanderer—"

"How about *cocksman*? That has a pleasant ring to it." He leaned forward as he spoke, his breath warming the small channel before trailing down to her third favorite erogenous zone—her sensitive neck. The erotic experience made her tremble, followed by an earthquake of pleasure erupting in her loins. *Just keep going down, down…*

She closed her eyes, imagining how far he could go using nothing but his hot breath, and the heat and dizziness of her overactive imagination tilted her world sideways. She opened her eyes to find him grinning like a damn wolf.

"That remains to be seen. You might be one of those types—you know, all talk and no action." She even impressed herself with the crispness of her tone.

"Oh, I have more than enough action. In fact—"

"Are you two coming or not?" His father had turned back and was staring at them with a speculative look.

"Of course. We were just discussing Rebecca's luggage."

When his father strode away, Ash whispered in her ear, "Next time I see that tongue wagging at me, I just might have to grab it and not let go."

I'd rather go swimming with the fishes than break bread with these three. But she dutifully walked side-by-side with her assigned escort into the next room. At the very least, she'd gain fodder for a book. *Nah, no one would believe it.*

The dining room turned out to be a bit fancier than she'd expected. More like an intimate grand ballroom, if that made any sense. High widows framed by heavy silk Damask burgundy drapes tied back to let a bit of sunlight in, a table set with snowy white linen and engraved silver utensils with matching plate ware, and the final spectacular addition, a sparkling crystal chandelier setting off the spacious room and adding a touch of old-world charm.

Two uniformed footmen stood nearby, apparently ready in case someone invaded England, their burgundy jackets engraved with the crest for Castle Piers—an outline of the battlements above a lion— prominent on their chests. *And they needed to charge me for the opportunity?* Hell yes, to experience this firsthand, she'd have paid double, not that she'd admit a word of that to anybody. And if this was informal like the Dowager suggested, then she had a lot to learn.

She took the seat offered, wishing she could step into Clark Kent's phone booth for a second, despite her hostess' lack of concern over what everyone was wearing, and emerge in a flattering lace tea gown instead of her motorcycle attire.

The dowager rang a tinkling bell from the head of her table, her rings catching the light. A female server in a black and white uniform with a starched white cap, for heaven's sake, came in promptly, bearing an engraved silver soup tureen.

Everyone waited while she made her rounds, ladling the green soup into each bowl in turn. When the young woman exited, the dowager took up her spoon, apparently signaling the meal was to commence. Rebecca took a spoonful, then set her spoon back down beside her plate, pleased she had managed not to spit it out. *God-awful stuff. Cold. Green. And flavorless. Right, note to self, stock up on snack foods.*

"Maybe now would be a good time to discuss my duties. You know, hours of operation, what you expect of me, that kind of thing."

"But you just got engaged to my son," the dowager said, raising one finely drawn eyebrow. "Surely, just planning that party will be enough to keep you busy for some time?"

"Right. Well, I want to be of more use than that. I was thinking, perhaps a Teddy Bears' Picnic or a concert might draw a good crowd?" Was this woman really too infirm to hear that her son was a nutcase and that no way in hell were they engaged? She looked strong, a proper matriarch. Of course, Rebecca didn't want to be the one that made her take ill — that would be the worst thing. Ever. She'd just have to wing this for a while.

"Yes, I think a Teddy Bears' Picnic would fit the bill, if you have the time, dear?"

"I would love to arrange that." She nodded her approval, managing a few more sips of the bright green slime before it was whisked away — *thank you, God* — and a course of chicken and string beans was set before her. She tentatively picked up her knife and fork.

"Now, dear, I would like to learn a bit more about your life in Canada. Do you live in an igloo and have to manage those lovely big Husky hounds? We at Castle Piers are more partial to our Corgis, a wonderful breed of dog. Perhaps they could be adapted to pull sleds? Then again, perhaps not. Ours have become rather chubby layabouts. All due to tasteful snacks from our table, no doubt."

Rebecca choked on her chicken. Ash jumped up and raced around the table to her side, pulling her to her feet. He effectively used the Heimlich maneuver on her and the piece of white meat dislodged from her throat and flew across the white carpeted floor, landing near an antique Ming vase, where a footman discreetly disposed of it.

Ash kept his arms around her, giving her a moment to recover. Her eyes watering, she took a few deep breaths to steady her shattered nerves.

"Whew, tha — anks." Her voice was a tad unsteady, but it was darn wonderful she could still speak.

"You must be more careful, my dear. My mother had pearls of wisdom about this very thing. *Never speak with your mouth full.* She said it quite often. I was raised with three brothers."

"Good to know," she said, enjoying the comfort of Ash's strong arms more than she should and ignoring the slight slur on her eating habits.

"You can let her go now, son. She seems quite recovered."

"Ah, yes, quite right." His arms dropped from hugging her ribcage right under her breasts. Her nipples had pebbled at the contact, drawing her attention to the sudden disappearance of the strong, virile man at her back. She'd bet the boxful of loonies and toonies she kept near the front entrance to her condominium back in Winnipeg for tipping the pizza delivery guy that her areolas were visible through her tee shirt.

Fighting the urge to hug herself across her chest, she slumped back down into her chair, wishing she could just sink right out of sight.

"The chicken's a bit dry, mother. Not surprising that someone choked on it." Edward spoke out in her defense, giving Rebecca a look of sympathy.

Dry. Ha, it must have been left in the oven overnight to transform it into this stringy jerky. Three months of food like this and she'd be slimmer. There, one blessing to look forward to, considering she was always fighting the size of her annoyingly curvy hips. Considerably perked up, she sat straighter in her chair and took a sip of water to ease her dry, scratchy throat.

From across the table, Ash shifted in his seat, his eyes averted, moving his bits of chicken around on the fancy plate. She had the sudden urge to present them with a lavish banquet of all her favorites. Before she'd taken gone to university to study writing, she'd made sure she had a backup career, taking courses at Red River College's culinary school, and had just undertaken further top-level culinary training. She could whip up a five-course meal with the best of them.

"Perhaps I could treat you all to a meal tomorrow. I came armed with a plethora of recipes to share with y'all, courtesy of my sous chef instructor."

"And you would provide the ingredients, my dear?" the dowager asked, obviously thinking of all the money she'd save.

"Sure, why not."

"Splendid, a home-cooked meal by a professional chef. I do know how to choose them." Edward beamed at Rebecca, looking like he'd hit the jackpot.

His Hotness remained quiet, scowling at his plate. She didn't blame him. She wanted to toss hers right out the window. She could only imagine what was for dessert.

Ash adjusted his pants. The woman sitting oh so smugly across from him would make a saint howl or at least wonder if he had been a bit hasty in taking a vow of chastity. He had to get out of here and find a willing partner, work off some of the annoying cloud of lust she'd surrounded him with. But that looked to be hours away. First, he had to drive her back to the hotel and fetch her belongings. He sighed. *What I don't do to keep this family intact. And what's wrong with everyone today?* He'd been certain his grandmother would put the kybosh on the idea of her son and the interloper marrying, if nothing else to protect family interests. But no, the little schemer had only cemented her position even more, pulling his beloved grandmother over to her side.

But he did admire her quick recovery from nearly choking to death, and she had rescued the infamous Fabergé egg. But he abhorred the sneaky kissing bit. There was no way to explain that. She was a gold-digger through and through and he wanted no part of it. *Sometimes the devil comes wrapped in very pretty packages.*

"And what other interests do you have, my dear? Besides being a chef?" the dowager asked, signaling for the dessert to be brought in.

"I enjoy writing and arranging events, of course. I wanted to experience first-hand living in a castle, so I'm getting the best of all worlds by living here for the summer. It's an incredible opportunity to surround myself with the ambience, to make my writing have that certain X factor that doing so can bring it."

So she wasn't denying it, though that part of her secret was already out, anyway. What other secrets was she hiding? It was worrisome to have a writer in their midst with their checkered family history.

"Very wise. Do you write along the lines of *Fifty Shades of Grey*?"

Ash stared with astonishment at his grandmother, before turning to hear Rebecca's answer. This he wanted to hear.

"Ah, actually, I want to write in other genres, branch out. Novels based on real history intrigue me. And I'd love to turn a period piece into a screenplay."

"You'd do better writing *Fifty Shades*. Apparently, the author made *millions*." The older woman nodded her head sagely. "I thought it quite lively."

"You read that?" Rebecca asked, her expression priceless.

"Of course, dear. Who doesn't enjoy a good spanking from time to time? Does the body good. We had such a lively discussion about it at our Purple Hat Book Club meeting last month."

"Mother!" His father's face had changed color dramatically. His grandmother had better be careful, or Ash might be giving him the Heimlich next. The dowager was in outstanding form today, obviously enjoying entertaining and hopefully shocking their guest. He'd always admired her outspoken ways. Not behavior typical of grandmothers, from what he'd learned from his friends growing up, but it sure beat the stuffiness of some.

"Now come on, don't be a prude, Edward. This is two thousand and nineteen for heaven's sake. Surely it's time we all admitted our foibles and got on with things. And having sex is one of the more pleasurable things in life. Why, it even got us that lovely Danish Jubilee egg. I rest my case."

Chapter Five

We must be willing to get rid of the life we've planned, so as to have the life that is waiting for us. — Joseph Campbell

Dessert turned out to be the best part of the meal. A moist English trifle, rich and filling. Rebecca sighed. So, she wouldn't be losing weight after all. She had a notorious sweet tooth.

Everyone had an extra serving, and the table conversation died. Glorious peace washed over her, giving her time to reflect. She imagined Facetiming with her beloved Ringers later and telling them the events of the day. *No friggin' way will they believe me.*

"Well, if you're finished, perhaps I could drive you to town now?" His Hotness interjected, waking her from her daydream. She looked up, right into his eyes, and experienced heat's lash from across the table. *Oh sister, he has it going on.* Like a smoldering Heathcliff and a charming Rhett Butler all rolled into one glorious, stunning man. A scene from a movie, *The Postman*

Always Rings Twice, came to mind, with Jack Nicholson and Jessica Lange taking bread dough she'd spent hours creating and knocking it clear off the table in the effort to rip each other's clothes off, bread making long forgotten. *Oh yeah, baby.* She licked her lips, thinking of how exciting such a deliciously wicked thing must be.

"Sure, why not." She needed to get a grip if she wasn't going to give the game away. She cleared her mind of all things sex-related and stood.

"If you'll excuse me, I'll take His Hot—your son's offer."

"Fine, dear, then we can have a lovely chat later about the engagement soiree and the picnic. My granddaughter will be thrilled about the teddy bears. She's collected them for years."

She gave a noncommittal smile, wanting to duck and dive planning her own engagement party, and hurried to retrieve her jacket from the pile near the door, noting that the egg had vanished. Hopefully it had been stored in a safer place.

His Hotness opened the door and they fled the scene of the crime together.

Good job. She gave herself a mental pat on the back as they strode down the corridors together. *I didn't do anything more untoward than choke on that god-awful chicken.*

The lovely sense of being holier-than-thou lasted until they got to a cavernous stone area featuring large arches at each end. It looked as though it might have been fashioned to stable horses at one time in the distant past. Now it housed the family's various vehicles. A vast array of them. She spotted her cherry-red bike parked in line along with the others. She strode over to the motorbike to retrieve a personal cloth bag with their famous Ringers logo from one of the saddlebags, then hurried back to rejoin him.

"Wow, very nice," she said as he opened the door of a cream-colored Rolls Royce to usher her inside.

"Yeah, figured you like it," he said, with a grimace.

"Excuse me!" Seething, she turned on him, poking a finger right at his chest. He backed up, startled. She continued advancing, making her point, prepared to push him all the way to the North Pole if that was what it took. "I am not marrying anyone just for the money! If you like, I can leave right now, go home and never see any more of your zany family ever again. Not be here to help you throw events to raise extra funds for the obvious structural problems like you have in the tunnel."

She crossed her fingers behind her back. The last thing she wanted was to go home and miss out on the fabulous opportunity, but if they stayed at cross-purposes, who knew where that would lead? And she couldn't very well tell him about the suspected connections to hidden family treasure she was here to research. She'd been sworn to secrecy by a film company wanting to swoop in and reveal the results at the last minute. They'd promised her a chance at having a screenplay written by her make it to the big screen if she played her cards right. Just the thought of it nearly took her breath away. She couldn't imagine giving up such a fabulous opportunity. Or revealing the bet.

She stopped talking and he stared down at her, emotions racing across his face. The most obvious one was curiosity. *Ha, got him.*

"I apologize. I don't know what's gotten into me today. You're doing me a favor going along with all of this." He ran a hand through his thick curls, making him look boyish and far too charming. "This will get sorted out, I promise. Just give it time. Okay? Am I forgiven?"

Sincerity lingered in his expression, and she stopped advancing on him.

"Okay, truce for now. Pinky-swear."

She made him hold out his hand and she twisted her little digit around his, noting how much larger his hands were than hers.

"Repeat after me. I promise to be nice to one Rebecca Fairfax and not call her a gold-digger. At least out loud."

A deep chuckle greeted her directions, a wonderous sound that danced through her bloodstream and tantalized her nerve endings.

"You should laugh more often. Life's too serious to be taken seriously."

"So I've heard, though you'd best share that with my father. He's of a different mind — at least when it comes to his son. Shall we go?"

He went around the car, climbed in the opposite side and started up a motor that purred like a happy pussycat and off they sped.

He didn't buy her act for one second. He'd only apologized to save his family the public embarrassment of her running off and perhaps telling all. Or, worse, writing a tell-all book. And he had to admit she had depth, unlike the string of ready-to-bed women he'd been seeing off and on for more years than he cared to remember. Her ideas for raising money would be a godsend. But he would be keeping a close eye on her.

She was not going to get away with using his family for any of her devious schemes.

But she was right about one thing. The tunnel did need repairs, the sudden rise in flooding a worry. And rather surprising as well. Just the week before the tunnel had been damp, but now there were actual ankle-deep puddles to slog through, more than could be explained by a few trickles of water flowing in. Perhaps he should call an engineer? And how much would that bloody cost? He sighed. They were castle-rich and cash-poor. And no one in his family would hear him out on the subject, blithely figuring it would somehow all work out. *My burden to bear alone.*

"So, tell me. Do you have any ghosts living in Castle Piers? My fellow Ringer, Miranda, one of my sorority sisters from university, loves to debunk anything paranormal."

Ash winced. "Which one? The warrior-monk, the spectral horseman, the unfortunate Lady Charlotte or the Red Witch of Satanic fame? The Red Witch gives us the most grief, by the way. Every Halloween, a crew shows up in the graveyard and chants, leaving bits of black candles strewn about to be cleaned up by others — trying to raise the dead or gain some unearthly power through her blessing, I would guess."

"Really?" She turned her head to stare at him, the expression in her rare green and gold starburst eyes dazzling. Her writer's imagination was no doubt hard at work, giving her goosebumps and all sorts of chills running down her spine. *Good. Keep her on her toes.* Though he had a better idea of where he'd like to keep her.

"Yes, really. The oldest ghost we have is the warrior-monk figure carrying a flaming sword. Quite spectacular, according to the handful that have seen it. First documented in the fourteenth century. Perhaps he's the one who knows where some treasure is hidden? Help the current owners pay for repairs."

He glanced at her, noting her slight wince at his words.

"Have you seen it?"

"Me? No." He shook his head for emphasis. "When you don't believe in them, how can you see one? Or maybe I just wouldn't admit it."

"Makes sense. I don't know anyone who does believe in ghosts and will admit to it. The only experience with the supernatural was my friend Casey's experience on Oak Island when she was researching the Money Pit. The Devil Dog said to be protecting the treasure hidden on the Island showed up. Bright red devil eyes and all."

"And was it proven a hoax?"

"Yes. A regular dog wearing glowing red eyewear was unmasked. But not before it gave her and Truman — now her husband — quite a start. You know, deserted island late at night and you're racing through the undergrowth to find the source of unearthly howls and it leaps out at you."

"Our ghosts are far more civilized in England. They just float about for the most part. Though the horseman galloping toward some lucky onlookers and making the sound of thudding hoofs for special effect has frightened a few guests."

A heady scent drifted off Rebecca in waves. He breathed in deeply, enjoying it far too much. Like a fine wine connoisseur, he enjoyed the fragrances of women. But hers was special. *Quite intoxicating. And dangerous.*

"If everything is supposed to be more civilized in England, please explain your family. I'm dying to know exactly how you can explain that whole 'wide birthing hips' comment away." She turned hostile eyes his way, the starburst irises flaring brighter. She crossed her arms over her full breasts and he had a sudden memory of his arms pressing up against her ribcage. Not only large breasts, but quite perky. *Lovely.* He would so enjoy having them exposed to his expert caresses. He'd have her forgetting all about ghosts and goblins in no time. *Christ, get a grip, Ash. She's your father's fake fiancée. It can only lead to trouble.*

"Please forgive my grandmother. She can be a bit much, I know, but she means well. You have a splendid figure, by the way. The perfect sized hips, birthing or otherwise."

She narrowed her eyes at him. "Thanks, I think. You know, she didn't look exactly what I would call infirm."

He sighed. "She's very good at hiding it, I would imagine. Stiff upper lip and all that." It was strange, his father letting slip about his heart condition. Not at all like him, which worried Ash further. Maybe things were worse than even his father was admitting to? That would follow the family's MO of never giving in and acknowledging a weakness.

"Ah, we're here. We're lucky, it's the one day a week they're open late." He pulled into a parking spot in front of the farmers' market with its rows of stalls and turned off the motor. The drive had gone quicker than ever before. *Must be due to the lively conversation.* So different from most females, Rebecca talked about all sorts of subjects that had nothing to do with flirting. A part of him found it refreshing, while another part worried what she was up to.

Rebecca unbuckled her seatbelt, exiting the Rolls before he could come around to assist. He locked the vehicle, then hurried to catch her up. He discovered her inside the covered market, surveying the different stalls with their offerings.

"What do you need?" he asked, joining her.

"Okay, thinking of Crêpes Suzette for dessert, so I'll need a couple of oranges. Marmalade, honey and butter." She ticked the items off on her fingers. "And I would imagine you have flour and eggs?" He gave a nod. He had no idea, but it sounded about right. She gave a quick perusal of the area. "And fresh asparagus would be nice with the entrée. Chicken cordon bleu, I think, so that will take a good quality cheese to stuff it. And we'll need a high-proof alcohol for the crêpes, like an orange-flavored brandy or liqueur, to flambé them. Oh, and bread flour and yeast. I want to make my own dinner rolls."

"That's quite the ambitious meal, but it sounds delicious. Just don't be choking on the chicken, please. I don't think my heart could stand the shock."

"Ha ha. Here we go." She tugged at his arm to draw his attention elsewhere. "Bright green baby asparagus — good as it gets." She went briskly about her business. When she tried to hand payment over to the stall keeper, Ash stepped in.

"No. I insist. I pay," he said over her objections, gently pushing her aside.

"How many can I expect for the meal?" she asked, frowning at his intervention.

"I'd plan for my sister, Gracie — Grace — to join the four of us. She's away during the day taking ballet classes for the summer, but she's generally there for dinner. We tend to have our main meal late in the day."

"Grace — the granddaughter who collects teddy bears. What a lovely name. How old is she?"

"Twelve going on sixteen. Knows it all, but absolutely adorable at the same time."

"Oh my, I just realized she lost her mother. As you did as well…" Rebecca stopped her examination of the chicken, chewing on her bottom lip instead. He had to fight the urge to taste those plush pink lips. He cleared his throat before answering.

"Yes, well it was a long time ago. Gracie was only a newborn. Complications due to diabetes during the pregnancy. Gracie's been raised by our grandmother ever since. You'll find her a bit outspoken too. Our little-miss-know-it-all." He smiled.

"I look forward to meeting her," Rebecca said, choosing a selection of deboned chicken breasts. "I'll go with that number in case someone wants seconds or leftovers."

"She's going to want to know all about you. And once she sees your motorcycle, she's going to be enamored. Be prepared. You'll be hounded day and night to take her for a ride."

"Excuse me, Miss, would you like to try our new cheese?" a polite voice inquired from across the aisle, indicting a display of free samples on one of the stalls.

"Sure." They headed over and were each handed a cracker with cheese on it.

"Yum, very nice," Rebecca said. She smiled her thanks at the woman, then added Ash to the benevolence. *What a lovely smile she possesses, lighting up the room so effortlessly. Why did she have to kiss Father first? And why does she have to be a gold-digger? And a thorn in my side?*

"Hang on a moment. You've got a cracker crumb on your mouth." In spite of his better intentions, he trailed a finger across her warm lips, brushing at the invisible speck. She stared up at him, and he leaned in toward her, reaching to draw her closer. How would those luscious pink lips taste? He'd bet like sweet cherries...

"Hello, Ash," a sultry voice and a heavy touch on his arm interrupted, keeping him from following through with the action. He looked up to find Vanessa's hand firmly attached to him. He'd missed her arrival.

"Vanessa." Annoyance made him grimace. He had been so close to finding out if Rebecca tasted as good as she looked. *The forbidden fruit, does it taste sweeter?*

"Is that any way to greet me?" she teased, and leaned in for a kiss, sinking her fingernails into his forearm.

"Rebecca Fairfax, I'd like you to meet Vanessa Masters. A neighbor." He disliked being manhandled in public and stepped back. *Save that for the bedroom.* Vanessa was dressed to the nines as always, her dark hair secured in a sleek bun, her fringe grazing her dark eyes. Red lipstick screamed *siren*. It was usually his favorite shade. In his experience women who wore that shade knew the score, making his life a whole lot easier. Maybe too easy. His freewheeling sex life had grown tired of late. Even Vanessa's expertise in the bedroom, her use of unusual positions, potions and devices, had gotten stale. No fantasy left. Just precise ways of doing things that squeezed all the spontaneity from the moment. Something deep inside him wanted more. A connection he could not quite define. Did it even exist?

"What? Only a neighbor? I beg to differ, darling. We've become *such good friends*." A lowering of her eyelashes accompanied her words before she gave him a sweeter smile. "I didn't know you had any interest in shopping for food, Ash. I'd have guessed you a strictly takeaway kind of man. Leaving more time for the fun, bordering-on-illegal bedroom exploits you've become so famous for."

"Rebecca has promised to make dinner for the family," he explained, unhappy with the blatant innuendo. He glanced at Rebecca, noting the high color on her cheekbones. *What would she have done if I'd kissed her? Is she as passionate in the bedroom as she is her other pursuits? As her books suggest? Damn if I wouldn't love to find out. What if father gets that chance?* The horrid thought crept into his mind, setting off alarm bells. *Remember she's a gold-digger. Focus on that.*

"Oh, I say. How did that come about?" Vanessa asked. He absently noted her cooler tone and the strange way she was observing Rebecca, too busy considering what could be done about the dismal situation with his father. Surely, there had to be some way to stop things before they got right out of hand? A way that wouldn't upset him? Of course, Rebecca was just play-acting at wanting things stopped, and wouldn't be of much help. He was right out of his depth on this one. Life didn't come with an instruction manual. *Damn unfair.*

"She's staying with us for the summer." He gave Vanessa a quick check. Normally he'd use the opportunity to set up a future date with her. She appeared to be waiting for something as well. His good manners, drilled in since birth, clicked in on autopilot. "Perhaps you would care to join us for dinner?" he asked, uncomfortable with the whole situation. Then he immediately thought he shouldn't have done that when he caught the odd expression on Rebecca's face. Her color was higher, her eyes flashing with emotion.

"Really?" Vanessa's eyebrows were in danger of vanishing entirely under her dark hair. "Of course, darling. I'd love to join you for a meal anytime. You know that."

"Yes, I'm here for the summer to be the family's events coordinator. And apparently, now engaged to be married as well," Rebecca explained, her voice sounding tight. He gave her a quick glance. She looked quite uncomfortable, staring at Vanessa as if she were the devil incarnate. And his neighbor staring right back at her with a strange quizzical expression, as if trying to place where she'd met her before? *Odd. Oh right, read one of her books and recognizes her.*

Dead silence. *Damn, why did she have to bring that last point up?*

"Engaged to whom, pray tell?" Vanessa asked, her mouth looking as though it had tasted the worst sour grapes imaginable. A look she couldn't pull off.

"Why, the duke, of course."

"I say, that's brilliant!" The relief on her face would have been laughable if not for the repercussions sure to be coming. Now everyone within a hundred-mile radius would know their business. And it was not the kind he wanted known, damn it all to hell, before he had a chance to rectify things.

Chapter Six

Sometimes I'm grateful that thoughts don't appear as bubbles over our heads. — Anonymous

Why did I let that slip? Rebecca chastised herself. But the green-eyed monster had bitten her in the ass, right after Cupid shot a lustful arrow, and she had made a stupid decision not to think it through.

"Yes, well, it's rather unexpected," she added, wishing she could dive under a stall and not have to face Ash's recriminations that were no doubt coming next. And he had a right to them. She should have kept her damn mouth shut. And why hadn't she insisted on going to the hotel first and changing into something more appropriate?

"It will be so lovely for little Gracie to have a new step-mum, bless her heart. She's at such a good age, too, just beginning her teenage years, when having a mum is so vital. When will the formal announcement be?"

Oh. My. God. This was getting so out of hand. And this time, far worse. Her own damn fault. *And what do I know about raising children anyway? And could it come to that?* Her heart slammed into her chest.

"Not sure. It's so very recent. Might not take, you know," she said in a lighter tone, trying to sound worldly with a touch of *savoir faire*. Though the last thing she felt right now was indifferent. Instead, she was seething and upset and ready to pour her heart out to one of her fellow Ringers — any one of them — just to let this insane day be seen by someone in a hopefully better light. Surreal didn't even half cover it.

Vanessa frowned. "Okay. Well, congrats and all that. At the very least, you must be planning a party?"

"Apparently," she said in a dry tone of voice.

"Good. Maybe I can wangle an invite as well, Ash?"

"Of course. Now, if you'll excuse us, we're in a bit of a hurry," he said. He grabbed the bag of shopping from Rebecca and stood waiting for her to precede him out of the market. She rolled her eyes, then got a move on when she caught Vanessa hovering not far away, watching them with keen interest.

Silence reigned as they walked back toward the vehicle.

"So, what, you're never going to talk to me now?" she asked, buckling herself into the Rolls' front seat once more.

"What do you want me to say? That you made it worse? You do realize everyone is going to know about the engagement now?" His face was stiff with anger or disdain — she couldn't tell which. "Maybe you *do* want this engagement?"

She pressed her lips together. Things did look bad. *How to explain what I can't admit to? That I need to stay here longer. And damn it, he did make me so mad. Threw me right off my game.* She took a deep breath, trying to come up with the right words.

"Okay. I could have shown better judgment. I screwed up and I'm sorry about it."

"Too little, too late, lady. The proof is in the pudding, as my grandmother would say," he muttered the words, giving her a stormy look from his devastatingly intense brown eyes. Even mad, he looked good. *Too good.*

"What's that supposed to mean? I'm not a damn pudding, you know!"

He gave a harsh chuckle, starting up the vehicle. "No, but if you were, I'd think you be a sweet cherries jubilee kind of dessert. With the odd sharp-tasting bitter bit of truth hidden inside as the damn prize for the unsuspecting victim."

"Well, that's just plain weird. However, if you were a pudding you'd be a dark chocolate one with gritty coconut that would get stuck between your teeth and give one grief all day long!"

A slight quirk lifted one side of his lips. The tight knots in her stomach relaxed and she leaned back in her seat for the drive to her hotel.

"Tell me more about yourself. You mentioned something about belonging to the Brass Ring Sorority at uni. What's that about?"

This was a subject dear to her heart and far safer. "Ah, my favorite group of women. There are eight of us. Lily and Lacey, twin private investigators," she said, counting them off on her fingers. "Casey — a professor of archeology at the University of Manitoba, Elin, ufology expert and awesome Swedish goddess. Ava's the lawyer and helps keep us on the straight and narrow. And Tessa. She's still finishing her graduate studies in music. Oh, and Miranda, the pixie who loves to debunk the paranormal. We came together to support one another and ended up sticking together afterward. Now we help one another make one dream each come true. You know — reach for the brass ring?"

"I find that very admirable."

"Well, they're not going to be too pleased about my current predicament," she said with a snort.

"Really?" His skepticism grated. "Do you have to tell them just yet?"

"Maybe not. Things do have a way of sorting themselves out, right?" But a frisson of worry snuck up on her, something telling her it wasn't going to be as easy as all that. *But hey, no one can make you marry them if you don't want to, right? Arranged marriages are a thing of the past in Canada. Surely the same rules apply in Britain?*

"What about family?"

"I was one of the lucky ones. Adopted by a good family as a newborn." Something about Ash invited sharing a confidence. The fact of her adoption didn't normally spill out so soon.

"Have you had any contact with your birth parents?" He gave her an interested look as he maneuvered the car through the narrow streets — driving on the proper side of the road, thank goodness. Maybe she'd get the hang of it with time.

"No, none."

"You didn't want to?" he pressed before pulling the Rolls Royce into a parking spot at the All Seasons hotel. She was itching to collect her things and change into something more flattering. The memory of Vanessa Masters made her flinch. Now, that woman knew how to maximize her best assets. And had even found the perfect shade of red lipstick for her coloring, something Rebecca had never managed to do. She always ended up looking like a damn vampire with her fair skin.

"Sure, but it's not as easy as all that. My birth mother didn't put down the name of my father. And she's deceased. All I have is a locket given to me as a baby and said to have belonged to my father's family. It was discovered in my receiving blanket with a handwritten note. The only clue mentioned in the letter is that she'd been a nanny in England for some time before I was born." She touched the talisman through her clothing, the metal warm between her breasts. "Maybe that's why the interest in the British Isles. I think she may have gotten pregnant over here, then gone home. I can't verify it one way or the other. No living relatives I'm aware of."

"I am sorry to hear that."

"Thanks." She swallowed around the lump that tightened her throat, unshed tears filling her eyes. She blinked them away, wishing she wasn't such a softie about it all. Facts were facts and there was changing them. Not that she hadn't been blessed, having a good family who loved and cared for her and who she loved back unconditionally. She fumbled undoing the latch on her seatbelt, her fingers uncooperative.

"Would you like me to help you?" he asked, unbuckling his.

"No, no, I'm fine." She hurried out of the car and across the parking lot to the front doors into the lobby. She scurried into an elevator, hitting the button for the second floor. She'd insisted on it. Never stayed anywhere above the fifth floor. Statistics said that she'd have a better chance of surviving a shark attack than an emergency above the fifth-floor level. Just another odd fact she'd gleaned researching her novels. She wasn't sure which she loved more sometimes, researching or writing.

The doors were about to close when Ash stepped on, giving her a nod. She pressed her lips together, wishing he had given her time alone. He seemed to take up all the space and oxygen in the confined area, like some kind of sex god. No wonder he was considered a heartbreaker. Any lady would be certifiable if she turned down the opportunity to jump his bones.

"I'm sorry if I upset you."

She shook her head, not trusting herself to speak. She gave a weak smile, not wanting him to think she was at all perturbed.

The door opened and they exited, Ash waiting politely for her to do so first.

"Do you have your key card?"

"Yeah, it's here somewhere." She rummaged in her jean pockets until a sharp edge of the plastic stabbed her under a fingernail.

"Damn," she said, sucking on the offended digit. Then pulled it out of her mouth to open the door with the card.

"You're bleeding," he said with concern, taking her hand and turning it over to inspect it.

"It's nothing." She tried to pull away to close the door to the suite, but he would have none of it. He closed it with his foot and hauled her ass to the bathroom. He held her hand under the cold running water.

"Sit," he commanded. He rummaged around in the vanity drawers to find a first aid kit. She dried her hand on a towel and sat on the edge of the tub.

"It's nothing, just a little cut."

"You can never be too careful. Germs are lurking everywhere."

"You a germaphobe?"

"No, just a safeaphobe."

"I don't think that's a real word."

"Probably not," he said with a chuckle. "But isn't that how words enter our lexicon? Someone comes up with something that makes sense and it's added after enough people agree?" He dabbed her finger with an antiseptic ointment and applied a small bandage, wrapping it tightly around the tiny wound.

"Ouch! Not so tight."

"Don't usually hear that complaint. Most women like a good, tight fit," he said with a smirk.

"I'll just bet you don't hear enough complaints. All that flattery has gone to your head."

"Well, it's been said one does better with honey than vinegar."

"Sure, if you want to collect bar flies," she shot back.

He chuckled softly, then leaned down, capturing her lips with his. Something he had been waiting to do for hours. *Oh my.* She tasted of wild strawberries and cream, exotic and arousing. After a slight hesitation, she returned his caresses. Her lips moving gently against his, their soft plumpness an invitation, she teased the seam of his mouth, nibbling.

Her fragrance stirring all his senses, he thrust his tongue deep inside her mouth. She met him with passion, teasing him, enticing him. She moaned, a sound that stirred his senses, made him want to have her spread before him, a slave to his every desire.

She slipped her hand around his neck and stood up, tugging him in close in the process. *Yes, green light.*

Fiery heat filled his body, all his attentions diverted to his insistent need to possess her. To win her.

With her curvy body pressed tight against him and her lush breasts pushing into his chest, he placed his hands around her waist. He caressed the bare skin just above her waist where her T-shirt had ridden up. It was soft and warm and oh so smooth. He slipped his hands up inside her shirt, then around to fill them with her breasts. A deep primal moan vibrated within his body and escaped as a growl in his throat when her nipples pebbled through the fabric under his touch. He ached to take them into his mouth, to taste all of her.

He grabbed the hem of her shirt and yanked it up. He reached around, preparing to undo her bra. He couldn't wait to have her naked body spread under his, have her scream his name as she came all over his cock.

"Hey, wait a minute. What are we doing here?" She pulled away, giving him a startled look, half indignant and all woman. *So beautiful.* And so responsive to his touch. With a bed close by. What else could they ask for? He watched with dismay as she pulled her T-shirt back down over her perfect breasts.

"Let's see. Two consenting adults with a hotel room at their disposal. *Carpe diem,* beautiful." He gave her as charming a smile as he could manage, thwarted from what he most needed. To make love to her and keep her all for himself. *Where in the hell did that thought come from? Remember what happened with Samantha the night before the wedding? Women can't be trusted. Use them before they use me* had become his motto of recent years. Not nice, but it kept his heart safe, even as it left him cold and unsatisfied.

"No, this is all wrong. I'm sorry. Too much is happening too quickly." She reached up with a shaky hand to push away a lock of hair from her face and tuck it behind an ear.

"I didn't hear any damn complaints a minute ago." All his blood had rushed to his cock, not leaving much for his starving brain cells. Besides, in his experience, the woman would be undressed by now and encouraging him take *her* to bed. It had worked every time in the past — why not now?

She narrowed her eyes at him and he wished he could take the words back. Frustration always brought out the worst in him. *Rein it in, Ash. This woman is different, obviously has a higher moral code than you're used to.*

"Sorry, that came out all wrong. You're right of course. Please excuse my actions." He stepped back and ran a hand through his hair. "I'll wait for you downstairs."

She nodded.

Exit stage right, Ash, before you step in it any further.

* * * *

Rebecca stared at her flushed face in the mirror, unable to meet her own eyes. *What the hell was I thinking?* No excuses came to mind. For once in her life, she had no idea of how to fix things. She'd always prided herself on her self-restraint, now, gone in a flash. And for what? A man who thought he was God's gift to women. Expecting her to fall into bed with him just because he was the hottest man on the planet. Well, it wasn't going to happen.

She shook her head vigorously. She had higher standards than that. But at least she'd had the common sense to stop herself, even if a little late. He was an admitted womanizer, for heaven's sake. And how on earth had she agreed to go along with the crazy plan of being engaged to the father? She groaned aloud. She'd only managed to get herself into a deeper hole when meeting Vanessa, with all that wink-wink-nudge-nudge-nonsense.

She straightened up. *I need to pack up and pretend none of this happened. Maybe I should just go home?* But the idea held no pleasure. So much more waited her at Castle Piers than spending time with the Looney Tunes family. The incredible discovery on the tunnel wall, not to mention researching more of the family history and finding out first-hand what it was like to live in such amazing surroundings, now and back in medieval times when the castle had been built. It was something she'd planned for years. And damn it, no hot Lothario was going to get in the way of the opportunity of a lifetime. Even if he was the most exciting human she'd met to date. Because he was also the worst kind of man for her. He'd break her heart in a second, and move on to the next woman. A pattern of behavior usually proved itself out.

Determined, she set her jaw and exited the bathroom. In a whirlwind, she finished packing her things, still wishing she'd had room on the plane for her guitar, music being her favorite way to reduce stress. She didn't even bother to change, and was rolling the suitcase out of the hotel in no time. There. *I'm off to meet the wizard, the wonderful wizard of Oz...*

Chapter Seven

So it turns out being an adult is mostly just Googling how to do stuff. — Anonymous

An awkward moment in the lobby was followed by an awkward ride back to the castle. Thirty minutes later, she took her first free breath of the day. *Was it only one day?* It seemed more like a whole week. Some kind of time warp thing had been going on.

His Hotness had finally left her alone to unpack, and she stood still surveying her new lodgings, chewing absently on a fingernail. *Not too shabby, eh.* At least one thing had worked out today. A bedroom fit for a princess greeted her inquiring mind. The perfect wide window seat for writing and viewing the courtyard, the perfect canopied bed for sleeping and dreaming and the perfect furnishings, including a fireplace to curl up in front of. Lush fabric in royal blues and golds further enriched the large space. Three months of this and she'd not want to go home to her more austere surroundings of the ubiquitous and dull Canadian beige.

His Hotness had told her to join him in the solar when she was ready for a bit of supper, and he'd give her a tour of the castle, promising to have the groceries seen to. She looked over her wardrobe, not certain what to change into after having a quick shower.

She dithered, surveying the slim pickings. She'd thought she buy clothing in England, when she'd better understand what she should wear. And it had kept her luggage dealings at the airport easier. But now, staring at the dismal choices, she wished she had toted along less conservative pieces. Something swishy and cut down to expose a bit of flesh would be so much fun with this screwball crew.

Perhaps a pair of scissors and a needle and thread was in order. Born and bred in rural Canada, she had a variety of self-sufficiency skills that kept her world in order, sewing being one of them. Even stitching up small wounds, though that hadn't been called upon too often, thank goodness. But she kept the special curved needle in her kit bag just in case. *A girl can't be too prepared.*

Twenty minutes later, she surveyed her changed appearance in the mirror with a great deal of satisfaction. Her little black number revealed a daringly low neckline that exposed just the right amount of creamy flesh. Why she was doing such a thing she wasn't exactly sure, but the devilish side of her nature had come to England to play, and she was going to live fully while she had the chance. Besides, it was hardly a crime for a girl to look good. *Flaunt it while you got it, sweetheart.* Her grandma's words, not her own.

At the last second, her hand on the doorknob, she stopped. She marched right back around and opened a dresser drawer, took out a light cardigan and shrugged it on over the dress, doing the buttons up over her ample breasts. She sighed, irritated. It seemed she could take the girl out of the prairies but couldn't take the prairies out of the girl.

She stomped up to the solar, curious. It was a lengthy stomp. She had calmed down considerably by the time she reached the top of the long spiral staircase leading to the separate tower that held Ash's private apartments. She remembered such a stairway was also referred to as a vice. *Puntasitic. Ascending the vice indeed, eh. How apropos.* She snorted, pleased with her pun, then sobered at how that knowledge rubbed her the wrong way. She continued onward, focusing instead on her environment, a far safer subject. Castle Piers was said to feature a spectacular solar that would have been gloriously sunlit during daylight hours, but the night had fallen by the time she turned the corner and entered the intimate space.

An inlaid onyx, hand-planed hickory-wood floor, intricately painted ceiling with gold filigree on the detailed rose-crown molding and a stone work and hand-carved beam fireplace excited her senses, drawing her in like a mosquito to exposed skin. It made her fingers itch for a pen and paper or computer keys, though none more than His Hotness sprawled on one of a pair of matching wingchairs in front of said fireplace like he owned the castle, his dark broodiness obvious in his body language and frowning countenance. *What's he have to get all moody about?* She was the one who'd landed feet first in the quagmire.

"Looney for your thoughts?" she said on impulse, using the Canadian name for the gold-colored coin representative of a dollar.

His deep brown eyes locked with hers, making her knees wobble and knock together. She swallowed and sat herself down on the matching wingchair a fair distance away, chewing on her bottom lip.

"Looney?" he asked, raising one eyebrow.

"Poor joke. It's a Canadian coin. Worth a hundred pennies." She drilled her fingernails on the arms of the padded chair, crossing her legs first one way than the other, unable to get comfortable.

"Hmm, well, I was just sitting here considering the weirdness of this day myself." He shrugged. He'd changed too, his well-fitted black suit with the open snow-white shirt collar the perfect foil for him. Pure sexiness. James Bond paled in comparison.

"Would you care for a drink before we eat?" he asked.

"Yes, please." A drink would calm her. "Whatever you're having will be fine."

He got up and headed for a side table with a small bar. He poured a good amount of an amber liquid from a decanter into two crystal glasses and handed her one. Her fingertips touched his and the static electricity sparking between them nearly made her drop the heavy glass. As it was, she spilled a touch on the back of her hand and quickly brought the offending drops to her mouth before they could stain her dress.

"You've had quite a day. This should go down well." *Christ, didn't he feel that too?* Her body flooded with heat and anticipation. Or was she as divorced from reality as everyone else around here? Their eyes locked again and she knew. *Damn right he felt it.* Vindicated, she sat up straighter and took a swallow of the excellent, quite potent scotch that slipped down the back of her throat, its smoke and fruit fragrance delicious. It rested well in her stomach, sending delicious waves of heat zinging into her veins.

The alcohol continued to slip down easily, too easily, and soon the room had a pink hue of contentment softening its fancy edges.

"Another?" he asked. His glass was empty too.

"No." She shook her head. "Not if we're heading out on tour soon."

"A bit of food is in order then." He rose and strode to the sideboard, picking up a covered dish and bringing it back to set in front of them. He took off the lid to reveal a plate of sandwiches. "We need to make up for the rather tough chicken, I'm sorry to say."

"It wasn't that bad, if you fancy jerky."

He chuckled, handing her a small plate with a linen napkin tucked under it. "Please, go ahead."

"Thanks." She helped herself, realizing she was hungry and needing to replenish her energy. In short order, she polished one off, then a second one.

He served himself, munching on a cucumber and cream cheese offering. They ate in silence. When they'd finished, he took her plate from her and set it aside. *Now for the interesting part.* She sat up straighter, in a hurry for the tour to begin.

His lips twisted, reminding her how amazing they had felt pressed tightly to hers. "You've seen a lot of the castle already. Few have ventured into the underground labyrinth and you managed that on your first day. Though, of course, it's so massive it would take weeks to see all the rooms and caverns. Some areas are even bricked over—I would love to check what's behind them one day."

"I would like to explore more down there, if that's all right?" She had a hypothesis to test and access to the area was essential.

"Well, it's not the safest area. Especially since it's begun to flood of late."

"Is the water coming from the lake or the moat? Have you had engineers in to check?"

"Recent development, the water pooling so quickly." A shadow crossed his face.

"When I was down there earlier, I noticed ancient carvings in the wall. What can you tell me about them? I don't recall there being any press about any find."

"Not important. Just some hoax. Come." He stood and offered her a hand, pulling her to her feet, ignoring her question. She shivered.

"Do you need a jacket?" He slipped off his suit jacket and swung it over her shoulders. Immediately his fragrance cocooned her in a heady state of arousal.

For the next two hours they tramped through Castle Piers. Ash was a good tour guide, explaining the history of the various features the castle possessed. She found it fascinating, his voice mesmerizing in its deep baritone, thrilling and enthralling her. And breathing in his essence made it all the more memorable. She could tramp just about anywhere listening to him talk. He'd called her find in the tunnels a hoax, but she knew better. She'd research more now that she'd seen the evidence with her own two eyes. There was nothing she loved more than a riddle or a mystery. Her writer's imagination always thrilled to any and every *what if*?

"I came across the information that this castle was originally built at the intersection of two powerful ley lines. What can you tell me about that?"

"Hmm, yes." He rubbed along his jawline that had just begun sporting a five o'clock shadow. It gave him an even more virile appearance and did some sweet things for the butterflies dancing with abandon in her stomach. *Imagine that slight scraping along sensitive areas of my anatomy. Oh. My. Yes.*

"Important ley lines have been assigned to this location. I think that's why black sorcery is attracted here and why the numerous graveyard visits during specific dates of the year—not just All Hallows' Eve. The possibility of spiritual power intrigues them—those who venture to come here. Perhaps they hope to find the legendary Solomon's ring." He gave a light chuckle. "They'd better not be digging on our property if they know what's good for them."

"The Ring of Aandaleeb. The legendary artifact that commands and controls seventy-two demons. That would be some find." Her heart stilled. Did he know anything about it? She didn't think so—it looked as if he was just joking.

"In any case, we'll leave that to posterity." He leaned over and plucked a loose thread from his jacket which she still wore, bringing him too close.

"Of course." If a mate could be chosen by the appeal of his or her fragrance and by the intensity of their presence, she was doomed. Maybe she needed to research magic spells herself? Find one that would overturn Ash's hold on her damn senses.

His hand lingered on her shoulder, then he swept back her hair which had fallen over the side of her face, tucking it behind her ear.

"You have such lovely hair." He caressed the back of her head, running his hand through the thick locks, sending delicious chills racing down her spine.

"You don't look so bad yourself." *That* was the best she could do as a writer of romance? *Turns out it's a lot harder to navigate the stormy waters in real life.* He tied her tongue in knots by standing too close. And now she had ruined any chance of their even having a relationship, by agreeing to marry his father. The surreal day overwhelmed her, aided and abetted by this impossible-to-ignore man.

She stepped back from the spiraling spell, standing straighter. "I need to check in with my friends. And perhaps call it a night. Been some day." She gave a half-laugh that came out rather strangled.

"I understand. Sleep well, sweet Rebecca."

She nodded and turned around with a muttered goodnight, scurrying back to her cave as if there was not a second to waste. Shut the door behind herself and took a deep cleansing breath.

Facetime with the Ringers. Now.

She glanced at the clock on the mantlepiece. It was early evening in Canada with the five-hour time difference, but she desperately needed to see whoever was available. This whole day needed sorting.

"Hey, babe, how's it going?" Miranda asked, the only one found at home, her pixie face coming into full view surrounded by its precise frame of glossy dark hair, which she'd cut short in recent months.

"Oh, Miranda, you have no idea what I've done! The trouble I'm in for kissing a duke and an almost duke. I should *never* have accepted that bet."

"What on earth are you talking about? You just kissed a guy. Well, two if we're being exact. And in one day. But, hardly the crime of the century."

"You won't believe it. I don't believe it!" She filled in her friend, watching her eyes grow larger and wider by the second until she looked under a bewitching spell.

"Unfuckingbelievable!"

"Yup," Rebecca said, her voice trembling with spent emotion, "And it's only been twelve hours. I don't know if I can take any more, let alone three months' worth."

"*Nonsense.* Of course you can. You're our Rebecca. Think of this as the most awesome research imaginable. *Wow.* Wait till I tell the others. Too bad they weren't here for this. And this time, *I* win the bet. Not sure what it's going to be just yet, but I hope it creates something as exciting. You do know you don't have to marry him, right? Just go along for the ride and end it when it's the right time. No harm done."

"Yeah, sounds good." Then why the queasy feeling it wasn't going to be quite as easy as all that? No, Miranda was right. Of course, she had the power to end it. Any time. "Thanks. Say hi to the others for me."

"Will do. Catch you later, babe."

"You bet. And thanks, you were a great help."

"Let me know what you find out more about the Solomon connection—didn't see that one coming."

"I'll keep in touch. Love to you all."

* * * *

"Rebecca Fairfax. I want a thorough dossier on her entire life history. Not one stone left unturned. I'm certain there's connection between her lineage and the Hermetic Order of the Golden Dawn, after what Sloan has reported. I want proof in my hands before I proceed. There's no turning back once I do." The sorceress gave the order into her cellphone, her tone neutral, her fingers drumming against the top of her antique office desk.

"Anything else, my sorceress?"

"No."

She hung up and leaned back with satisfaction, staring at the online photo of Rebecca Fairfax on her Facebook account which had popped up during her online search. She had to be the one. The birthdate matched precisely. She resembled him with her central heterochromia irises that went back generations, and tending to hold her mouth in a way reminiscent of him in certain photographs. *Strange, finding his bloodline in Canada. But these days, with travel so common, it's easy enough to send DNA anywhere.*

She shrugged. *Doesn't matter.* Once she had her proof, plans could be set in place. Plans that would bring her great power and wealth, if the woman was found to be a direct descendent. And she was so close to finding the Seal of Solomon she could taste it, following the precise trail of clues in her research that had recently led to the Piers family tree. In the meantime, a blood ceremony would suffice. But the end result of years of hard work and research would be everything she'd ever dreamed of. *Power beyond the human imagination.*

Her mind drifted back to that fateful day she'd been called upon, an image seared into her mind for all eternity. The moment when the angel had announced herself during the meditation hour she set aside each evening as the clock struck midnight.

The entity had come to her in a dazzling display of light. She'd stood on a silvery crescent moon, holding Mercury's winged staff with two serpents entwined around it, her head bearing a crown of twelve stars.

Exactly as predicted in the *Book of Revelations*. She had spoken, her voice seeming to be everywhere at once.

'I have come because thou hast desired it. Though art chosen to be the one. Many incantations I have followed you, watched your soul be clothed in a new body, over and over again. I am all things, and I tell thee now, you will find what you search for. The power will be yours. The power of Horus will come through me to you. Blessed with the wisdom of Solomon.'

She looked up and caught her reflection in the huge gilded mirror that hung opposite her desk, noting her high color and glittering eyes. She smiled and got up, smoothing one hand over her sleek hair, checking that her long scarlet gown lay properly over her slim hips. She never looked better than when she was excited about an upcoming ceremony, powered by the innate knowledge she was the chosen one. *Hmm.* Who should she choose for a lengthy marathon? She mentally ran through the candidates, before selecting one and sending off a quick text. There was an almost instant response, which was highly gratifying.

High heels clicking on the inlaid marble flooring, she walked to the wet bar and poured a stiff whiskey into a silver chalice. The chalice was one of her favorite artifacts. Dating from the eleventh century, it featured the intricate scrolling of a Latin inscription around its bottom edge. Running a long red-painted fingernail over the lettering, she murmured the powerful words that never failed to stir her imagination, "*Sanguis de carne mea.*" *Blood of my flesh.*

She tipped her head back and let the fragrant nectar flow down her parched throat, its aroma and warmth slithering into her empty belly to her satisfaction. Not that she was celebrating just yet, but her gut agreed that she was on the right track. And her gut never lied.

Chapter Eight

All I'm armed with is research. — Mike Wallace

Touch me, Ash, make me yours.

Her breasts tight and heavy, craving his touch. Her rubbing herself against him. The friction providing some relief, the invitation spurring him to action. The kiss starting soft and gentle, spiraling out of control in a heartbeat, his hands all over her. Seeking. Caressing. Insisting. A burn inside about to burst into an all-out flame. So raw and intense, pushing her limits, to forget all but this moment. He ground his hard length against her, seeking entry.

Yes.

She opened for him. Wet. Swollen. Needy. Like someone had flipped a light switch, she became alive. Every nerve ending, every cell, every fiber of her being wanting him inside her. *Brand me. Make me yours.* She reached down and grasped his shaft, marveling at the velvety texture covering a rigid core. Ready, insistent, she spread open her thighs, inviting him in. She stared up into the warmth of his *enveloping gaze as he positioned himself over her body, pressing against her wetness.*

In an instant the scene changed.

Alone. Cold and shivering. Deprived of Ash's warmth, dark shadows creeping along the edges of her consciousness, the unknown sending a frisson of worry through her trembling body.

She sensed another presence. Something or someone out there, wishing her harm. A growing evil. Fear restricting her throat, her eyes burning from trying to see through the haze. Who could mean me such harm? And why?

A strange voice called out to her in the darkness, horrible in its chilling calmness, sending ice shards through her bloodstream. She shivered uncontrollably with fear, unable to swallow or move. Frozen in terror. The singsong voice was like none she had ever heard before.

"Re...bec...ca, come to us. Re...bec...ca, we need you."

She forced herself to wake up and face the truth. She was losing her freakin' mind. No way could she ever act on her lustful instinct. All she could do was keep it hidden inside as best she could, because it looked like her guilty conscience had turned against her, sending her a night terror in retaliation. A shower partially drove away the dream-turned-nightmare, at least enough to allow her to turn her mind to research.

At least she found out exactly what she wanted to know by getting up so early. She confirmed the exact connection between Castle Piers and the former monastery that had been built on the site originally. A high-ranking Templar knight had overseen it, long before the Freemasons had come along to guard the site, and when the knights of the Temple were arrested in France at dawn on October the thirteenth, 1307 – a Friday and the origin of the aversion to any Friday that lands on the thirteenth day of any month – he'd had ample time to hide the accumulated treasure. Treasure existed somewhere in the bowels of this castle, the secret location lost to the annals of history.

The Templars had accumulated more treasure than any other organization during their brief two-hundred-year period, acting as money lenders for powerful people, including kings and queens, and starting the first recognizable banking system in the modern world. But this success was also ultimately their downfall, a double-edged sword. Sending warrior-monks to be tortured and put to death in one of the vilest of ways— burned at the stake. All because they helped a French king, the ironically named *Philip the Fair*, who preferred to welch on his debts. *Bastard. Accusing innocent men of horrendous deeds.* It riled her to the core of her being. Misuse of power always did.

After the Templars were dissolved, along came the Freemasons, of which the Piers' ancestor, one Samuel W. Piers, a black sheep of the family tree, was a more recent one. When the man began his own Hermetic Order of the Rising Sun, splintering off from the Golden Dawn order, he'd been given the secret knowledge, the cypher manuscripts that she, Rebecca Fairfax AKA modern sleuth, had also decoded and confirmed. *Follow the bloodlines, the truth will be told.* And now that she'd found the cryptic symbols that masqueraded as the tree of life in the Rising Sun order with their Osiris-Sun Temple, she knew what she was on the lookout for.

Rebecca got up, too antsy to sit, and began to pace the floor. With what she now knew to be true, then the Piers family could very likely be coming into unimaginable wealth, having unknowingly guarded an artifact long thought lost to the mists of time. Money that could be used to reinforce the tunnel system at the very least. She shuddered. If only it held up for her searches, she'd be happy. The worst thought imaginable was those catacombs flooding. Trapping her. *Don't think about it, or I won't be able to be the heroine of my own adventure. The very reason I came to England. And please let my finding this out for the family make up for my deceptions in allowing a fake engagement. I might have some reason for gold-digging, just not in the way Ash is thinking. Never in that way. I only want the best for the family.*

A brisk knock at the door startled her, making her spin right around and hurry to open it. Thank goodness she had already showered for the day and looked presentable. She smoothed down her cotton skirt and turned the doorknob.

"Good morning, miss. The family is asking for you to join them for breakfast in the main dining room if you are quite ready?" An attractive thirty-something female, dressed in a crisp white and black uniform, her dark hair tidy under a white cap, gave her a brief smile.

"Sure, I'm famished. What's your name? I'm Rebecca, by the way."

"Sloan. Nice to make your acquaintance, miss. If you'll follow me."

"Of course." It would take a bloodhound to follow the breadcrumb trail to the new location otherwise. At least she would be getting ample exercise built in to her day. Finally, after many twists and turns, the woman waved her into the dining room.

"There you go. Enjoy your breakfast."

"Thanks."

His Hotness glanced her way when she entered, his jaw tight. Thank goodness he would never know of her lustful dream. She was certain Freud would have something to say about the ending. It was impossible to miss the tense vibes swirling about the room, the trio appearing at loggerheads. *What were they talking about?*

The grandmother sat at the head of the table, the duke to her left. Food in silver engraved dishes lined a sideboard, steam escaping around the covers. The fragrances wafting into the air made Rebecca's stomach rumble. Loudly.

"Come, join us, dear." The dowager looked the most composed, not a hair out of place in a becoming bouffant style. She appeared to be enjoying herself this morning, her mouth slightly turned up at the corners as though life was a lark she truly embraced. Rebecca found herself grudgingly liking her more. The attitude was infectious. She returned the smile, the disturbing dream slipping even further away.

The duke stood, holding out a chair for her. She sat, murmuring her thanks.

"Before we eat, I want to present you with this small token of my affection."

In complete bafflement, Rebecca peered at the ornate, heavy looking ring he was holding out to her between his forefinger and thumb. A massive square-cut emerald dead center surrounded by an array of diamonds, it caught the light, nearly blinding her. *What the hell!* He slipped it on her finger without warning, then kissed the back of her hand before sitting, looking very pleased with himself, while she sat, too stunned to speak a word.

"There, now it's official. Thank you, Mother, for allowing us to use your engagement ring. I hope you like it, Rebecca. If not, we can go to London today and pick out a new ring. Just say the word."

What word? That this is certifiable? And why so soon? Sure, she intended to go along with it for a while, but she didn't need a ring yet. Or maybe *never* if she found the treasure and gave it to the family, which would surely make up for everything? The whole situation was beginning to confuse her more and more. And guilt at the deception bit hard. But if she didn't do this, the alternative was a castle falling into ruins around them.

"Uh-huh," was all she managed. She gave His Hotness a desperate look, hoping he could read it and help. *Please, say something. Anything!* But he wouldn't look her in the eye. So, this was what they had to have been discussing. *Well, blow me down and tie me to the train tracks – this is completely, utterly and entirely nuts.*

"Bacon, miss?" the servant inquired. Rebecca jumped, rising a few inches off the chair seat. He had appeared suddenly at her side like a helpful ghost.

"Uh-h – sure." She swallowed at the delectable odor, saliva flooding her mouth. Starving. *Maybe this whole thing can be sorted better on a full belly.*

But the family just took it as a matter of course, eating and drinking and conversing as though things were now normal. The soft clink of silverware on china, and the grandfather clock chiming the quarter hour as the perfect foil. All except for His Hotness, who only picked at his food. Rebecca was embarrassed to realize she was consuming food like an out-of-control maniac, and gave a small hiccup.

"Excuse me." Heat rose in her mortified cheeks. Stress always made her hungry. *Should have seen that coming, eh.*

"I adore a young woman with a hearty appetite. Good for you, dear." The dowager nodded her head sagely.

"And we are to be blessed with a meal of your own creation today. I do look forward to that."

Rebecca nodded, thankful for safer ground. The ring felt oddly heavy on her finger, a reminder of what she had gotten herself into. Or, more precisely, what the Ringers had gotten her into with the damn bet. She'd tear a strip off them later. "Me, too. I love to cook for others. Very satisfying."

His Hotness got up and came around the table, confronting her. She eyed him suspiciously. *What now?* He grabbed her left hand, yanking off the ring.

"Ow!" she squawked.

"It needs sizing. I'll take care of it." He jammed his fist that held the ring in his jacket pocket and strode from the room, a man on a mission. *Well, at least the damn heavy thing is off my finger for a while.*

"I say. That was rude. You must speak with him, Edward."

"He's just trying to be of service. Wouldn't want such a valuable ring to go missing, Mother, now would we?"

It had fit perfectly. *What is that about?* She shook her head. One more loose thread. Tug on it and the whole fabric of this existence would unravel. But what would it reveal? Her writer's mind quickened, imagining the possible scenarios.

* * * *

Ash parried with his epée against the expert onslaught of his fencing partner, sweat dripping in his eyes. He needed this workout like a greyhound needed a run.

His fencing master came at him again, their swords connecting in a series of ringing clashes and scrapes that echoed in the gymnasium. Deadly as sin today, he hit another valid touch with his sabre, the electrical connection to his conductive vest counting and scoring the win. *Sweet revenge for yesterday's loss.*

Rebecca's image filled his mind as he made the requisite bow of respect toward his opponent, pulling off his protective mask. Her inner beauty was even brighter than her physical. That had been obvious yesterday during the ensuing craziness, and today at breakfast when she'd put up with his nutty family. It was driving him crazy with frustration. How could it have been just twenty-four hours since they'd met? And last night's dream. Unfuckingbelievable. She had been so hot, proving responsive to his every need. His every desire. He wanted her. And he couldn't have her.

"Good match, Ash. Want another? Give me the opportunity to square things off," Arthur, his closest friend who also doubled as his fencing master, pushed his mask up to reveal his flushed face. Bright blue eyes, eyebrows raised in inquiry, bored into his. Arthur hated losing. He'd go at it all day until he was ahead, given the chance. Ash didn't have time to spare today.

"No, I'm finished. I like stopping while I'm ahead." He gave an evil grin. "Besides, I promised Vanessa I'd stop by the university and meet her for lunch."

Arthur frowned. "You know that woman's using you, right?"

"No more than I'm using her." Ash snorted, not wanting to admit to a growing reluctance to meet with her. Perhaps it was time to end things? No more clandestine hook-ups sounded far better to him at the moment. Give him time to clear his head.

"Just be careful. She's the kind of woman who has a hidden agenda. I'd bet she wants to be Lady of the

Manor someday. Wouldn't be surprised if she got herself preggers just to force your hand. You do know the dowager would come down on her side? Always talking about you settling down and providing the next heir in line."

"Well, apparently *dear old Dad* wants to provide another." Ash's gut roiled, making him unable to keep the sarcasm at bay. He just couldn't go there, the thought abhorrent to every fiber of his being. At least he now had the damn engagement ring locked away for good. No way was Rebecca going to wear someone else's ring.

"What on earth are you talking about?" The red eyebrows climbed up to meet the fiery red hair, which was sweat-streaked and standing to attention. "I had no idea the duke was seeing someone, let alone about to remarry. And after all this time, too. That *is* something. Well, good on him. Still life in the old boy yet."

"*Phhht.* Going after a woman young enough to be his daughter. It's obscene."

"Who's the woman?" Arthur looked highly interested, and before Ash realized it, he had spilled it all. The chase through the tunnels and the woman responsible for all the uproar. Even the worry about his father that took the edge off his anger.

"She's an obvious gold-digger. And who knows what else she's up to? What if she's after some intel on our family's black sheep? What's going to happen if that all gets stirred up again?" Even as he said it, he hated his words, wanting to call them back. Rebecca had such a look of integrity to her. He just couldn't reconcile his image of a woman after a man's wealth with the woman who he'd enjoyed sparring with yesterday. And who'd featured so prominently in his dreams.

Maybe it was just wishful thinking on his part. Twenty to one, she'd mess up if she wasn't good at hiding things, and he'd be right there to call her on it. But another part of him hoped that she was who she appeared to be—a good person. And the most sexy, badass female he'd had the pleasure of meeting in his twenty-eight years of existence.

"That's ancient history, Ash. The woman's probably just here for the reasons she's given. Practicing her chef skills and learning about local customs. Isn't she planning a meal for the family tonight and helping to arrange an event already? Looks legit to me."

"Well, that better be all there is to it or I'll have her out on her ear so damn fast..."

"My best advice? Take it one step at a time. See what develops."

"Okay. I'll give it a few days. But she's on notice."

Chapter Nine

God save us from the people who mean well. — Vikram Seth

"Why would anyone in their right mind choose to follow the teachings of the Satanist Code, Professor Masters? Such people are vilified, seen as pure evil by the larger community. Seems kind of nuts to me to want to go there. It's *never* going to be accepted mainstream." The student asking the question, a frown furrowing his brow, halted typing up his lecture notes on his laptop long enough to look up at her standing behind the lecture podium. Vanessa paused, annoyed by the interruption to the smooth flow of her summer session presentation, a course she'd taken on as a favor to the university — she never knew when she might have need of the goodwill it created — but kept the displeasure from showing on her face. Facial expressions created wrinkles. But before she could respond, another voice spoke up, drawing the laugher and hoots of the entire student body filling the lecture hall.

"You do realize that it encourages all kinds of hedonistic pleasures? What guy in his right mind wouldn't go for that part? Lots of free tail." This even bolder student was a jock looking for an easy credit. *Good.* He was in the right place at the right time, taking the summer session course of *Demonology in Ancient History.* She often went easy on athletes, as they did wonders for her sex life. Helped keep her legendary sexual appetites satisfied. She loved sex, loved the variety of partners her lifestyle provided, even encouraged. She made no apology. If there was only going to be one time through this physical manifestation of life, she was going to enjoy every damn minute of it. And her university connections kept her from getting caught. Who didn't owe Vanessa Masters a favor? Or enjoy her favors?

"Yes, the Church of Satan does allow for free thinking, which leads to fewer restrictions on a person's life. The true rebels, you might say. But they also have a code to adhere to, the same as everyone else. They don't encourage stupid or foolish behavior and pretentiousness or self-deceit. But they value realistic, factual pragmatic actions. They wish everyone to achieve their potential, becoming wealthy and successful using whatever methodology works for them. Of course, not that I follow such teachings or suggest anyone else does."

She allowed herself a small smile of derision. *Best to keep them guessing.* The university, free bastion of thinking it held itself up to be, would not take kindly to one of its professors acknowledging her beliefs and ties to the occult. However, one could give lectures on its historical existence right up to present day. It was the best platform she could ask for. Lots of students took a keen interest in the one course she also wiggled into her program each semester. *Such devilish fun, teaching the dark arts.*

"But we do need to know as a society that such things exist. That demons are called upon by others to fulfill their every wish and desire. What these demons are called, and what their purpose is. Now, let's get back to learning about the seventy-two Solomonic Demons. As I've stated, the ring bearing his seal was purported to be able to call up and control a multitude of useful demons. And our next one is one of the most useful of all—Amy. A common enough name, but the gifts presented—outstanding. Arriving on a great ball of flame, he manifests as a man, giving a well-versed and powerful magician the secret path to finding hidden treasure of great value."

"Now we're talking! *'Show me the money',*" the virile athlete spoke up again, earning himself a constrained smile. *Smile lines also not encouraged.*

"Okay, that's all for today, people. I want you to study up on the purported Seals of Solomon for next class. Oh, and be able to explain the differences between a Conjuration and the Circle of Containment. Quite different things, you will discover. You don't want to mix those things up at the wrong time. A demon just might reach up and pull you down to hell if you aren't properly prepared."

This earned her a smattering of snorts and laugher which she acknowledged with a cool nod. *Too easy.*

She checked the watch she had added to the wide gold band circling her slender wrist, taking a moment as always to admire the elaborate engravings. One of an Egyptian Ankh, the symbol for life, surrounded the clock face, and the other, the image of the All-Seeing Eye housed within a triangle, an ancient Freemason symbol, decorated the back. *Ah, just enough time to put the final touches to a new grant application before joining Ash for lunch.*

She frowned with displeasure. Having to reconfigure the application to the new exacting standards recently adopted by the university had been a waste of many hours. *The old ways were best, always have been.* Vanessa smoothed out her expression when she realized what she was doing. She used her fingertips to press against invisible wrinkles. Though it was another administrative hoop to jump through, this one looked like it might prove to be worth the damn trouble for once—taking a select group of students to visit the historical site of Rosslyn Chapel to study the vast array of historic symbols it contained. Her thirst for ancient knowledge knew no boundaries. Nor did her thirst for a man's commitment to her passion. She'd also better step up her game with Ash. She had a sense she was losing him and *that* she could not, would not allow. She might be the most recent in a long line of lovers he'd had, thinking of his exploits in recent years, but she would also be the last. How else to gain full future access to Piers Castle?

* * * *

Ah, yes! The heavenly fragrance of freshly made bread. Rebecca breathed in as deeply as her lungs would allow, filling them with the arousing and satisfying aroma of baking the stuff of life. She pulled the first tray of dinner buns from the oven and used the back of her oven glove to push away a stray curl that had fallen out of her ponytail, surveying her creations with immense pleasure.

She'd made her grandma's cloverleaf style buns, placing three small dough balls in each greased muffin tin. The best was that it was easy to tear the sections apart for application of loads of whipped butter. Which she also had at the ready, along with the stuffed chicken breasts, savory with herbs and butter cheese. *Now, for the* crème *de* la crème, *preparing the flaming dessert.* She checked the clock over the stove. Right on schedule. Finish the dessert preparations, and she'd have time for a quick shower.

The day had been quite informative. The heart of most homes was the kitchen, and Castle Piers was no different. The few servants that kept the place humming along had been coming and going all day, happy to fill her in on anything to do with the family, especially when offered incentive in the form of freshly baked treats. Apparently, her sticky buns were to die for, according to Sloan.

It turned out that the two footmen from the dowager's apartment had been stage actors, dressed up. They came in whenever the grandmother wanted to entertain—just stayed for an hour or two and collected their wages. The upkeep on such a huge estate had to be tremendous, making Rebecca wonder how things stood. Not that it was any of her business.

Sloan had also mentioned the family secret—the dowager wanting her grandson to get married and have heirs. Something to do with a legal clause making the title of the land revert to another branch of the family tree if no direct heir existed. *So why am I being pressed to marry his father? Wouldn't it be better for the son to have the heirs now, continue the bloodline?* Not that she would *ever* volunteer to help.

Rolling out the dough for a final tray of sticky buns, the yeast squeaking from her heavy-handedness, she eased up before the roller flattened it too thin or full of holes. She lathered on the butter, a large amount of golden-brown sugar laced with cinnamon, cut them into sections and popped them into the oven.

There. Now for the dessert.

The main kitchen of the castle was a dream come true. Huge, with every conceivable device known to the kitchen gods, it was set up so well that one person could manage. Chrome appliances, tiled floors, ample working space... She'd love to bundle it all up and take it home.

She was just finishing cooking the last crepe, placing it on waxed paper to keep the large stack from sticking into a solid congealed mass, when a girlish voice interrupted.

"What are you doing?"

She turned around to find a young girl working hard to look older than she was with a lot of heavy makeup, and surveying her with feigned disinterest. Her brown hair was caught up in a snug ballerina bun, her costume of a gauzy skirt over a black leotard a dead giveaway.

She smiled at the pretty girl, who was twelve going on sixteen, as Ash had so aptly put it. "You must be Grace?"

"Yeah." She pursed her lips. "Are you the new cook?"

"No. Just volunteered to make a meal for the family. I'm Rebecca, by the way. I just arrived from Canada to help with arranging summer events."

"You're the one everyone's talking about." Grace squinted her eyes into a full-out challenge. "So, you want to be my new mother." The young girl crossed her arms over her chest.

Finally, someone with some sense in this family.

"Well, I'd say that's still up in the air at the moment."

The girl grunted and rolled her eyes, which were rimmed in thick black liner.

Rebecca checked the time. "I should shower and dress before the party," she hinted, not knowing what else to say.

Grace gave her another scathing glance. "Good idea. I hear Professor Masters is joining us and she *always* looks so chic. No one knows fashion like she does. She should be in fashion mags. She *soo* has the body for it."

"Good to know. Would you like something to eat?" Her sense of hospitality intervened, keeping her civil. Plus, the sweet child was only twelve. And she'd lost her mother. Sympathy welled up, easing down the stress and making her want to help.

"*Phhht.* Not bloody likely. I *never* eat carbs. They make you fat." She gave the pile of crepes and pan of sticky buns a disdainful glance, then looked back rather pointedly at Rebecca's curves.

"I would imagine that dancing would take care of any excess calories. Doesn't it take a lot of fuel to practice? Starve your brain and it's likely to cause personality changes. I've read that it can make a person feel cranky and judgmental. Lethal combo." She patted her own back for thinking of a decent way to suggest Grace try to be nicer. She understood all too well the trials and tribulations of becoming a teenager.

"My teacher says we have to sacrifice for our art."

But Rebecca caught the flash of longing as the young girl glanced at the baked goods.

"Sure, I get that. But the odd treat should be okay. If not, sometimes you go overboard when you do allow yourself to indulge. And that can lead to eating disorders."

"Maybe. My friend Julia has bulimia. She eats, then upchucks. Gross." The young girl made a face of disgust.

"Please, try one and tell me what you think. Did I use enough cinnamon in the sticky buns? You could help me improve my baking. Sometimes I think of entering contests, like MasterChef Canada."

When no objection immediately presented itself, she slid a half portion on a plate and added a fork. "Just try one bite and tell me what you think? I could use the feedback."

"All right. If it'll help."

She took a tentative bite, then polished it off in short order.

"So, more cinnamon? More butter?"

"Maybe a bit more cinnamon."

"Thanks. So, what do you do when you're not dancing?"

"Not much." Grace shrugged, her thin shoulders looking bird-like in her costume. "This drab old place is friggin' depressing. I mean, who wants to live in such a monstrosity?"

"Actually, I paid to stay here. I've always wanted to spend time in a castle. Spend time steeped in history. The sense of permanence speaks to me on such a basic level. Perhaps because I was adopted." She surprised herself with the revelation. She didn't normally share such information. But the girl had to be hiding a lot of pain, and sharing pain helped.

"How did you get engaged to my dad? You just got here, right? Did you meet on an online dating site?" Grace chewed on her lip, a frown pinching her eyebrows together.

"No. I just met him yesterday. It was on a dare from my sorority sisters to kiss a duke and he took it to mean a lot more than I intended."

"For real?" She pondered the information for a moment. "Then why haven't you told him that?"

I can't mention her father's heart condition because what if she doesn't know about it? It might devastate her.

"It's complicated." It was the best she could come up with on short notice.

"I get it!" The girl's eyes widened with understanding. "You're a gold-digger just like Sloan said you were."

Rebecca groaned. "No, that's not the case." *So the sticky buns weren't enough of a bribe to the staff. Good to know.*

"What other possible reason could there be? You come here, you don't know my dad from shinola, and voila, you're getting married. And you're what, twenty-five? And he's turning fifty. It's *disgusting*. Everyone is going to know what's going on."

She sighed. "Please, just take it up with your father. Maybe he'll listen to you."

"Ya think. After you threw yourself at him."

"Gracie, that's quite enough." Ash was suddenly in the room, his appearance heaven-sent. The almost-teenager immediately changed her expression, dropping about five years in appearance and a lifetime of attitude.

"Ash!" She ran right at him, catching him around the waist in a big hug.

"Hey, sweetie, how was your ballet class today?" He hugged her right back, his expression softening while interacting with Grace, who barely reached his shoulder. The love between the pair was obvious. A lurch in Rebecca's chest made her realize how much she would have loved a little sister, being an only child.

She scooted around the pair, preparing to exit the kitchen.

"Rebecca, I was wondering if I could have a moment of your time?" Ash asked, looking over his sister's head with an inquiring glance. His chocolate-brown eyes met hers, the boyish, open expression hitting her right in the solar plexus. God, what a fine specimen of a man. Tall, well-built, to-die-for handsome and good to his family. *I really need to take the next plane home if I know what's good for me.* And yet, she knew that wasn't going to happen anytime soon. *Suck it up, buttercup.*

"Sure." She waited while he gave his sister a final hug. Grace endowed her with a splendid look of disdain before dancing from the room.

"Grace has a lot of spunk." She suppressed a smile. It would take more than a displeased teenager to bother her now. Not with all she had on her plate since arriving at the castle.

"Sorry about that." Ash rubbed the back of his neck, giving a charming smile. She looked down at her socks, surprised they were they still on.

She swallowed hard when she caught his eye again. She sent out a silent prayer. *Please, God, I'm begging you to take this hex off me. I'm too damned attracted to His Hotness and it's interfering with* everything.

"It smells wonderful in here." He gave an appreciative sigh, making her heart flutter. "Not many women know how to bake and cook these days. You're some kind of woman, Rebecca."

The compliment sank deep. *So even prayer has failed me now. Perhaps I need to check out curse remover spells next?*

"Thanks. Would you like a sticky bun? They've been quite popular today."

"I'd better wait for dinner. But thank you anyway." He moved in closer while speaking, making her take a step backwards.

"Are you frightened of me, beautiful?" he asked, his voice low and throaty, barely above a whisper.

"No, of course not." *Duh, of course. You make me horny every time I see you.*

"You should be. The things I want to do to you…" He was close now, too close, and she was backed against a counter, with no place to go.

She swallowed hard, watching him follow the movements in her throat. He leaned down and kissed the sensitive spot where her pulse beat too rapidly in her neck, invading her space. His intoxicating essence filled her nostrils, making her want to lie on the kitchen counter, the floor — anywhere — while he backed up his threats with action.

"Your skin is so incredibly soft. Like a flower petal. And you smell so damn good." He pulled her up tight against him, bringing his full length into contact with her entire body, his arousal obvious. *Well-endowed too. Will the good things never end?*

"Smell?" she teased, her writer's mind scrambling to think of better synonyms in a last-ditch effort to keep herself sane. *Aroma, bouquet, perfume, scent, fragrance, incense, spice, tang…*

"A heavenly smell, most assuredly."

101

"Just our pheromones interacting. Nothing more. Perhaps we need to wear clothes-pins? Or become nose-blind like that commercial for Febreze Air Effects." Her arms slipped around his back and under his suit jacket without her permission, his muscles defined even through his dress shirt, making her mouth water. She wanted to lick him all over, taste everywhere, like a lollipop, a popsicle, an ice cream cone...

"I need another sticky—" The speaker stopped mid-sentence. Rebecca jerked away from His Hotness, managing to knock into the freshly washed pans from the baking, knocking them to the floor where they rattled and banged like a conspiracy of insulted ravens. *Ah ravens, the national bird of Bhutan.*

Her skin hot as though she'd been branded with an iron, she hurried to pick up the pans. Damn it, now she'd have to wash them all over again. She knocked heads with her partner-in-crime when he tried to help.

"Ouch." She rubbed at her forehead, giving him a full-on glare. She mouthed, *all your fault.*

"Oh, for goodness sake, let me help!" Sloan tsk-tsked, getting down on her knees to give them a hand. Damn it, now she knew more than she should.

Rebecca glanced at the clock, horrified. "I'll wash these later. I gotta change. Our guest will be here in fifteen minutes!"

"Don't sweat the small stuff, beautiful," Ash drawled, earning himself a second glare.

"Don't you *dare* think to give me advice, Mr. Almost-a-damn-duke!" She hurried from the room with as much dignity as she could muster, her face heated, and the low masculine chuckle following her giving her an inner thrill that defied reason.

She stomped to her assigned rooms, wishing she had the sense God gave a goose. If she did, she'd be flying to the airport and staying there, even if it took days, weeks, months — hell, even years — waiting for the next plane home.

But no, I'm in this freakin' stupid-beyond-words mess.

She hurried to change into her only evening option of last night's altered dress. She'd rinsed it out and left it to dry in the shower. It looked decent enough, with no wrinkles. She snatched it from the stall and hung it behind the bathroom door. *Now, for the fastest shower in modern history.*

Apply shampoo. Rinse. No time to repeat or condition. Towel off. Blast hair with blow dryer. Apply sixty seconds' worth of make-up. Pin hair in a sort of fetching up-do, leaving strands to suggest too cool to care. Pull on fresh underwear. Wiggle into dress. Ha! Not too bad. And mirrors never lie, right?

Shoes.

She rummaged around under the bed and found some four-inch heels that made her legs look awesome. *Damn the pain.* Professor Vanessa Masters was on her way over, maybe already there, and she didn't look like the kind of woman to worry about a little physical discomfort. Though she did look like someone who could cause some.

Hmm. No time to speculate. Get your buns in gear, Rebecca.

She raced back to the kitchen, worrying about popping the main course into the oven. On the way into the large room, she nearly smacked right into Ash.

"What are you doing still here?" She stood, hands on hips. "Don't you have a guest to entertain?"

"You look lovely. And you emit the most precious of fragrances. The delectable scent of flowers and sweet summer mornings. There, is that better?"

"What on earth are you talking about?" The man was certifiable.

"You don't remember the 'smell' incident?"

She had a hard time holding the grin in. "Yeah, maybe."

"Ash, Professor Vanessa Masters has arrived and is inquiring about you," Sloan exclaimed, rushing about the room, her hands filled with fresh flowers, giving the pair of them, *or more likely just me*, the evil eye. "And she's brought the most beautiful orchids. They smell heavenly."

Ash raised a sardonic eyebrow and she rolled her eyes right back.

"Go. Entertain your guest." Rebecca batted at his arm and turned to apply herself to final preparations.

"You're coming with me, beautiful. Sloan can handle the dinner from now on. You've done more than enough slaving away in here all day." Ash took her arm.

"No, please—"

"I won't accept no for an answer. You can handle this, right, Sloan?"

"Of course. Go. See to your guest."

"Well, okay, but I need to finish the dessert just before it's served. It's a flambé type."

"Never done a flambé," Sloan admitted with a frown, her interest obviously piqued.

"Until then you're all mine, beautiful," His Hotness said with a touch of smugness, keeping a firm grip on her arm.

"I think your father might have something to say about that," she snapped back, remembering the rabbit hole she'd fallen into. And now they were about to have a Mad Hatter's tea party. Though Carroll had never used the term in his book, he just might have approved its aptness for the shenanigans inside Castle Piers' heavily reinforced walls.

"That's his damn problem." But his expression clouded and he loosened his grip on her arm. A twinge of sympathy for what the family might be facing softened her thoughts.

"Sorry, I didn't mean to bring that up." She swallowed hard, upset to be the one reminding him of his father's health concerns. Problem was, the engagement and health issues had gotten tied up in one gigantic mess and neither of them seemed to know what to do about it.

"It's fine. Let's just have a pleasant evening and forget everything else. Do we need to pinky-swear to make sure no one breaks their word?"

She laughed out loud at the reminder.

"No, I trust you."

"Do you? Better not. I've got a terrible reputation. Well-earned, according to my father."

"Perhaps you just haven't met the right woman yet to help you walk the proper path." She wanted to get rid of the sadness and pain she'd glimpsed for a split-second in his eyes. Why did she care? He just wanted her out on her hiney, now or when he learned about the ulterior motive she had for being there.

"Proper path? Sounds awfully restrictive. No room to just be one's self." His tone had a harder edge, scoffing at the idea.

"Perhaps that's the wrong phrasing. Doesn't need to be a tightrope, you know. The path can be as wide as you like. And I would think being yourself should be at the top of the list. Being with the right someone should enable a man or woman to become the best person they can. Don't you think?"

"Maybe. In an ideal world. But real life is *not* a romance novel. It's hard work and family responsibilities. Sacrifice. No man wants to be corralled by those concerns any sooner than he has to be."

Dissing her happy-ever-after romance style fueled an instant anger. "Real love can overcome anything thrown at it!" she hissed. "But first one needs to grow up!"

They'd paused at the entrance to the formal dining hall. She didn't hear the duke join them in the hallway until he was suddenly right there. He'd obviously overheard a part of their discussion. "I say, well said, Rebecca. I've been trying to get my son to grow up for years."

Silence.

"Shall we go in?" With a beaming smile, Edward spread his arms wide around both their shoulders, pushing the pair forward to meet their guest.

Professor Vanessa Masters turned from the lit fireplace which was cheerily consuming thick logs of dry wood, the greedy flames busy cackling like an old hag of fairy-tale fame. The chill that the fire took from the damp castle was more than revived by Rebecca's first impression of their guest. The woman held a glass of aperitif in one hand, her expression guarded, taking in the advancing trio.

"Evening," she said, her smile cool, her dress impeccable. An off-the-shoulder red lace designer gown showed off creamy flesh, five-inch heels gave her a regal stance and a wide golden cuff on her forearm competed the perfect picture. Oh, and her hair was in a sleek French twist. *Mustn't forget that detail*, Rebecca thought, her head tilted sideways, cataloging the woman's appearance. *All in the name of research, of course.* The gold cuff interested her the most, the object catching the firelight which outlined the elaborate engravings with each movement of the professor's graceful arm.

"Hello, again, Professor." Rebecca was the first to move forward, and took the woman's outstretched hand, giving it a firm shake. First impressions weren't always correct. She needed to give the woman a fair chance.

"Please, call me Vanessa." Her hand was cool, despite the warming fire, but very strong. *Almost like a man's.*

His Hotness came closer, kissing the woman on the cheek. The interloper snuck an arm around his waist, leaning in closer, effectively blocking Rebecca from the scene. "You can do better than that, darling." She took the initiative of planting a full kiss on his mouth. *Wow. Taking quite a chance on smudging all that bright red lipstick.*

Of course, then she had to use her cool fingertips, running them over his plush lips to remove any evidence she'd laid down. *Grrr. What was that again about a fair chance?*

"Good evening." Heads swung around to catch the dowager making her appearance.

Vanessa hightailed it over to the woman, her expression fawning.

"Dowager, how lovely to see you."

"And you, my dear. I see you've met Ash's new step-mum."

Vanessa's expression became smugger, if that was possible. "Yes, she's quite lovely, Edward. You've done very well by yourself."

"I have, haven't I?" The duke beamed at all those assembled, as if he'd won the damn lottery. While she was stuck right in the middle of things.

"Yes, those lovely wide birthing hips and all. We can only hope for a new heir in a year's time." The dowager settled into a wing-backed chair, graciously accepting a glass of white wine from a servant. This time Rebecca had to fight the growl, tamping it down to keep it from escaping from her mouth accompanied with a string of profanity. *One, two, three...* A new thought edged out the anger.

Yes. Now I know what to do.

"I don't want children," she lied, shaking her head. "Never did. Sorry, if that nullifies our agreement. I *completely* understand, though." *Whew.* The words were cleansing. Freedom was at hand. She could barely keep herself from high-fiving someone. Not that there was anyone present who would understand how she was feeling, finishing the farce once and for all. She snuck a glance at Ash, but he seemed preoccupied. *Open your ears, your Hotness,* she wanted to shout. Surely even he could understand now that she was not a gold-digger? Oops, what if she got thrown out on her ass now that the engagement was broken? *Fingers crossed.*

"Women often say such things, then change their minds when the right man comes along. I promise you, I'm the right man for the job." Edward dismissed her objections.

"No, sorry. Won't happen. My mind's made up thanks to Mrs. Johnson's health class and a ten-minute video of a live birth that scarred me forever, seeing everything down there" — she pointed at her lower stomach for emphasis, shuddering with the memory — "open up to the size of a watermelon. Of course, I had skipped a couple of grades, so I was in the class earlier than my classmates. Best to end it now, save all the grief later." *There. Top that!* And partially true. She had seen the video, but the mental scarring was exaggerated.

"My dear, I have one word for you. *Kegels*. They'll put you back in fine form by your six-week doctor visit." The dowager outdid herself, beaming as though she had bestowed an answer of imperial import.

Her son continued with his own brand of looney logic.

"Nonsense. I won't hear of cancelling the marriage. We'll just whip my first born into shape. Make him step up and find a wife as well. Be responsible for a new heir." He gave His Hotness a look filled with warning before turning to Vanessa. "Are you free on my birthday, Vanessa? That will be our wedding day. Oh, did you get her ring sized at the jeweler's today, son?"

"No. I did not." His Hotness's face was inscrutable, his answer curt — hiding anger at the very least, she'd have betted. He struck her as a man who could not be pushed into anything he didn't want. *How about a little help here?* She needed to figure out a new game plan. Surely her fertile writer's mind could come up with something — anything — that would be objectionable to the duke? So that she could bow out gracefully and still be allowed to stay in the castle.

"What a lovely piece of jewelry," Vanessa remarked, coming closer and giving Rebecca's necklace a thorough check. "May I?"

"I guess." She could not keep the wariness from invading her tone. Something about the woman gave her the creeps.

The woman reached out, picking up Rebecca's locket up from where it was lying between her breasts. *Darn, her fingers are cold. Why did I lower the neckline of my dress?* If she hadn't played dressmaker, the woman wouldn't have been right in her space, would never have even seen the keepsake—though why that mattered was irrational at best.

"Unusual symbol. An Egyptian ankh. *The divine gift of bestowing eternal life.* Was it given to you? If so, it has so much more meaning to the wearer." The intensity of Vanessa's interest added to Rebecca's discomfort. The woman rubbed the locket as if she expected a Genie to appear and grant her three wishes.

"You have an interest in the Egyptian era?"

"Very much. The cradle of civilization. Fascinating era of history. I teach an undergraduate course on demonology at the university, and the ideas for many of our modern demons are thought to have originated from that time. The temple of Set being the most recognizable. And symbols are a particular passion of mine. Was it indeed a gift?"

"Yes, though I never met them. I was adopted at birth. The necklace was left to me by my father." She swallowed, unable to avoid the play of emotions the memory inevitably brought forth.

"Did he leave you anything else to remember him by? Do you know anything about him?" Vanessa pressed, still holding on to the necklace with a firm hand. *God, she sure can't read body language, for all her supposed intellect.*

"Just that he was born in England. My birth mother spent a year here as a nanny. Why?" What business was it of hers? She took an involuntary step backward, but the woman must not have expected the action, because she hung on to the locket and there was a momentary sting when the fragile chain gave way behind her neck, still clutched in the other woman's hands.

"My goodness! I'm sorry. I'll have this repaired and returned to you." She slipped it into her pocket. "And please, excuse my curiosity. My brother and his wife are considering adopting a child, and I'm consumed at the moment with helping them through the process. Anything you can tell me about it would be most helpful. Perhaps we could meet tomorrow in town for lunch? It's Saturday and I'm off from the university. My treat, of course. And I can return your locket at the same time."

Stunned at the sudden turn of events and dismayed with the way the woman had casually confiscated her treasure, Rebecca sought for the right response. But what could she say? If it would help, surely she could manage a couple of hours in the woman's company? And there would be others around. Not to mention it would be good research. The woman had to be a font of knowledge on many subjects, though demonology did not spring to mind as something Rebecca wanted to pursue. *Ever.*

"Sure, if I'm not needed for anything here?"

"Go right ahead, my dear. Do you good to get out and about. Meet the neighbors and all." Edward gave a happy smile.

Chapter Ten

Change is the end result of all true learning. — Leo Buscaglia

Ash could not stop himself from thinking about Rebecca, watching her interactions with the family and Vanessa. And damned if he could figure her out, figure the angle. Did she not want children or was it another ploy, a smokescreen to hide the truth? And yet another part of him wanted her to want children, for some crazy reason. He'd known her less than two days and she had upset his life to the nines. Yet he was reluctant to see her gone. Bloody confusing.

He caught Vanessa staring at him, giving him a look that made him wonder what her game was. All the women in his life were too damn complicated. And his grandmother wasn't helping any, mentioning Rebecca's lovely figure that he dearly wanted to get his hands on again. He imagined removing her dress, baring all that soft sweet skin. Making her as aroused as he was, kissing her all over, tasting her. *Oh. My. God.*

He breathed deeply in an effort to still his beating heart, to keep from getting up and announcing his intentions. That there was no damn way she was marrying his father until he found out what was going on between them. Who cared if it had been too short a time? A man just knew when something was up in his life that needed investigating.

He shook his head with dismay. The dinner party had become a blur of words and activity going on without him. Only when Rebecca looked his way did he sit up and take notice. Annoyed at how much she was affecting him, he had drunk more than he should have and found it difficult to break the connection, staring right back at her, the challenge clear.

"Dinner is served." *Thank Christ.*

"It looks delicious, my dear. A feast fit for a king — or a duke." Edward smiled at his little joke, raising a glass in Rebecca's honor.

"Thanks. It was my pleasure."

Polite murmurs came from all around. Ash squinted at Rebecca, sitting directly across from him. Vanessa was on his right and his father and grandmother were like bookends closing off the table.

"Sorry I'm late." Gracie came flying in, settling into a chair next to Rebecca.

"What kept you? You know it's impolite to keep people waiting," her grandmother reprimanded.

His sister bit her lip, flushing pink. "Time just got away from me, grandmother. It won't happen again, I promise."

The dowager nodded. "See that it doesn't. It's especially important to be on time when our Rebecca has spent a day in the kitchen preparing a meal for all of us. The very least you can do is to be on time."

Gracie looked across at him, rolling her eyes. He just about lost it, biting his lip to prevent a chuckle escaping. They'd heard it all before, many times. Gracie was habitually late. *Pretty much her MO.* Except for ballet classes. The problem was, she had pretty much been given her own way since she was a baby. *Not a good thing.* But she'd always had a trump card in having lost her mother so young. Maybe Rebecca was right, not wanting children. It could be dangerous, even in modern times. He'd never given much thought to such things before, and was surprised he was now. He was not certain he appreciated all this inner turmoil.

"Why don't you want children, Rebecca?" He had to know. Not that it mattered so much, but he wanted to know more about her. In truth, he wanted to know *everything*.

"Uh, well, I guess I've never thought about it much before."

"You seemed fairly certain a few minutes ago that it wasn't in the cards for you," he said with skepticism. Not sure why he was being so belligerent, he glared at her across the table.

"The decision does not need defending, Ash. Leave the poor girl alone," the Dowager intervened, adding in a brisk tone, "Rebecca, I must have this recipe. The chicken is divine. Edward, you have outdone yourself with this girl."

"Thank you." Rebecca swept her tongue over her bottom lip, making him feel hot and bothered at the same time. What else could that pretty little pink tongue do? He watched her consuming the chicken, hoping he was making her just as uncomfortable.

"You should try a taste, Ash," Vanessa urged, using her hand to nudge him on his thigh, then running it even higher, rubbing his bulge suggestively. He was already hard from watching Rebecca eat, tucking every tiny morsel into her mouth and chewing so girlishly. He wanted to master her. Make her beg for him. *Use those pink lips for a better cause.*

"Fine, I'll try it." He heard the churlish nature of his tone, reminding himself to take it down a notch, especially after getting a warning glance from his father. He wanted to say it was none of anyone's business if he partook of the food or not, but he needed to eat something. He cut off a slice of the chicken, popping it into his mouth after. He chewed, tasting it. *Yes, very good.* He tucked into his dinner, enjoying every morsel, then ate a few of the warm dinner rolls slathered with butter. Within a few minutes, his equilibrium was restored, bolstered by sustenance.

"Grace, I was wanting to ask you something?"

His sister looked up, a curious gleam in her eyes. "Yeah, what?"

"Your grandmother has filled me in that you collect teddy bears?"

Gracie shrugged. "So?"

"Well, I've been planning a Teddy Bears' Picnic event to be held here at the castle soon and I wanted your input."

"Like what?" Ash could see his sister was intrigued under the veneer of coolness that had become her MO of late.

"I want the usual things of course. You know, a parade, a bouncy castle, the boo-boo bandage station, food concessions and a face painting booth, perhaps a game or two of chance. But I was wondering if we should have a create-your-own teddy bear kiosk? You know, where a child can choose their own bear to be stuffed and put together right in front of their eyes. They would be personalized and custom-made that way."

"Oh, like Build-A-Bear." Gracie's eyes lit up at the idea.

"And I was wondering if you would be interested? I sure could use an extra pair of hands."

Gracie shrugged again. "Maybe I could help them choose a bear. We could even have rainbow bears, right?"

"Sure, why not?"

"I think that's a splendid idea," the dowager piped up, saluting Rebecca with her wine glass.

"I need to excuse myself now, prepare the dessert." Rebecca gave Ash a look he interpreted as being shy or worse, sly. *Yes, Virginia, there really is a Santa Claus. And the way to a man's heart can be via his stomach. Damn, she's good.* He'd give her that. Just enslaving his father and his family even further. He'd been right from the beginning, she had planned this. All of this. And now even pulling his sister in with the bear idea.

"Of course, my dear." The dowager gave a regal nod of approval.

He watched her leave the room. They would be discussing this later. If she wanted to discourage his father from the engagement, she was going about it the wrong way and she needed to hear it from him. Each day she stayed the family was getting in deeper and deeper and he felt helpless to put a full stop to it, given his father's condition. It all had to happen the right way. And now he knew the score, lose-lose. Sure, he'd miss her fresher, younger approach to life—it was affecting him more than he'd care to admit. There was a definite contrast between the Vanessas of the world and the Cinderellas. And Rebecca was a Cinderella, no doubt about it, while Vanessa and a long line of Vanessa wannabes came from darker stock, one he understood all too well. One where everyone knew the score and protected themselves from falling in love.

* * * *

What is his problem? Rebecca stormed into the kitchen, her high heels drumming her sentiments the entire way. Nearly refusing to eat a meal she'd slaved over, then giving her the evil stink eye when he had so obviously enjoyed it. *Bastard.* Then she felt bad for thinking the word. *Darn it.*

She hurried the final preparations for the dessert, fuming and finding it difficult to concentrate. Sloan was busy collecting the plates in the dining hall, giving her full rein to finish things her way.

It was a delicate process. Heating and lighting the brandy, then pouring the liquid fire over the warm crepes. She'd done it a few times for dinner guests and she did it gingerly now. She was just pouring the flaming alcohol over the tray of dessert when a voice rang out, taking her attention away.

"What are you thinking? Cook such a fine meal and enslave my father further?"

"What?"

The liquid fire slipped sideways, pouring slightly over the edge of the pan and onto the still lit gas stove. The brandy instantly turned into a larger flame, free of the confines of the warming pan. It raced across the stovetop, lighting her oven mitts on fire. She tore them off, throwing them a few feet away to land on a countertop.

Landing against the kitchen curtains over an open window, the fire lit the blue and white sprigged fabric instantaneously. A hungry beast, it consumed the curtains, charred pieces raining down around her. It began looking for more fuel, greedy fingers lusting over the ceiling, seeking entry.

"Oh no!"

A swift intake of breath, then Ash was instantly behind her, pulling her away. A loud whirling sound confused her, then water poured down from the built-in sprinkler system.

Immediately the fire began dying, giving up the ghost in mere seconds.

Drenched by the torrents of water spiraling from the nozzles in the ceiling, she leaned back against him, feeling the solidness of him. The depth of him.

She took a deep breath, dizziness threatening.

Soaked to the skin, he turned her around inside his comforting arms and held her close to his chest, saying nothing while she gathered herself. She trembled, fearing embarrassing herself. Her family had lost their home to fire when she was only seven, and it had taken years to get over it. She'd even learned to work with the enemy as part of her therapy. Until now, the demon had stayed away, becoming non-threatening. But now he was back, wanting his pound of flesh.

"It's okay, beautiful. That's what the sprinklers are for. Take some deep breaths — it will help, I promise." He rubbed her back in small circles, soothing her, helping her to recover.

"Thanks. I'm okay now." She went to pull away, not wanting to, but he would have none of it either, continuing running his hands over her back. *Very, very nice.* She could stay there all day.

"You know, if you wanted to get out of cooking for us, there are easier ways to go about it. One that doesn't involve setting the place alight."

She giggled nervously, hearing the tremors in her voice. "Yeah, that was the plan." She looked about. "Oh, my lord, the mess! It's going to take hours to set this right."

"*Phhht.* Don't worry about it. We've got lots of help. It'll be cleaned up in no time."

"But what about dessert? It's ruined." She glanced around, horrified at the dismal mess she had made.

"Nobody cares about dessert, beautiful."

"I hardly look beautiful! I'm soaked through and my hair's—"

"Are you kidding?" he scoffed. "You'd look beautiful in the proverbial gunny sack, Miss Rebecca."

She laughed shakily, finding comfort in Ash and his calm reassurances. It was a whole new side of him and she liked it, very, very much.

"You know when you're young, and you play those little games with yourself about what's the worst thing that can happen?"

"Sure."

"Well, mine was being burned. Then, when our house burned down when I was seven, you know what turned out to be the worst thing?" She punctuated her remarks with another shaky laugh.

"I'd love to know."

"Having to wear ugly donated Oxfords from the shoe guy down the street who just wanted to palm them off on someone and get kudos for giving something away to a needy family. And now look, ruined the best pair I brought." She held up one dripping foot, the black suede flattened.

"You'll never guess what mine was?" he said, a broad smile overriding the water drops sliding down his handsome face.

"Not a clue."

"Drowning. Now, thanks to you, I'm over it, allowing me to skip years of therapy."

"You're welcome, I think."

Another voice joined the conversation, startling both of them. The slight jerky movement of his body mirrored hers.

"What on earth happened in here?" Sloan asked, her expression horrified. They moved apart, leaving a small space between them.

"Sprinkler check. Working fine, by the way, quick response in an emergency. Wouldn't you say so, Rebecca?"

"Oh, yes, marvelous devices. Worked like a charm."

"What happened to the curtains?"

"Spot of bother. All under control now. But dessert's ruined, I'm afraid."

"We've got ice cream and those sticky buns Rebecca made earlier. Thank goodness they're in the pantry out of reach of the sprinklers. I'll pop them in the microwave and warm them." Sloan hurried about, getting things in order.

"We'd better get you out of those wet things. Follow me if you want to avoid the family and a thousand questions."

The pair squelched their way to the back staircase, Ash taking her arm for the journey. "Careful you don't slip, beautiful." He called over his shoulder to Sloan. "We won't be long, just need to change into dry things."

"No worries." She'd already pulled out a mop and pail and was hard at work.

"Good woman in an emergency," Ash remarked.

"Yes, she's very helpful." The stairs were steep, and by the time they'd reached the top landing, she was out of breath, either from his hand splayed on her back — hot even through her wet dress — or from what had just happened.

They continued the trek, arriving finally at her door. She shivered. The cooler air away from the heat of the kitchen played havoc with her soaking-wet clothes. Ash noticed, tucking an arm around her shoulders, bringing her in closer to him in an obvious effort to share his body heat. *Hmm.* He could share all his body, if she had anything to say about it. She took a deep breath. Funny how the fragrance of a man could be so stirring. She'd had no idea. She'd be a wiz at heating up that part of her writing now.

She sneezed. Loudly.

"A hot shower and right to bed with you. I'll make your apologies. We can't have you catching a chill."

"Yes, Doctor Piers," she teased, enjoying the care and concern. "You as well. I'd hate to see you catch something or suffer unduly on my account."

He nodded, going quiet.

The silence stretched for an uncomfortable couple of seconds. She bit her lip. If she opened the door with him standing right there she could not promise things would not go further. *Damn it, I'm human after all.*

Ash cleared his throat. "Sleep well, beautiful."

"Thanks, you too." She finally found the strength to pull away, fleeing into her room. Closing the door behind her, she leaned against it for a few seconds to orientate herself. *Day two barely over, and enough fodder for an entire series of bumpy-romance books.* Sudden sympathy for the characters in her stories who she threw willy-nilly into chaos made her grimace. Perhaps she should go a bit easier on Xaviera St. Clair and her new love interest, not send them reeling into the abyss? *Nah, why should they get off easy?*

Chapter Eleven

*If I had to live my life again, I'd make the same mistakes, only
sooner.* — *Tallulah Bankhead*

Rebecca directed her cherry-red motorcycle into a
parking spot in front of the Red Lion pub. She had
agreed to meet Vanessa at two, and it was now five
minutes to the hour. *Perfect.*

She tucked the key into her inside jacket pocket for
safekeeping and found she was under surveillance by
a group of teenagers. She pulled off her matching red
helmet, released her thick mane of hair, fluffed it with
one hand and gave the interested crew a satisfied grin.
It wasn't uncommon for teenagers to want what she
had, the freedom and adventure of the open road on a
sweet ride. For most, it would be the road not taken.

And just as predicted, one of the teenagers
approached, giving her a quick glance.

"Nice bike," he said, not looking at her, but keeping
all his attention directed on the Honda Gold Wing. She

did look pretty, gleaming chrome wheels and accessories freshly washed and buffed. Rebecca had even taken the time to detail the leather earlier in the morning.

"You in the market for one?" she asked.

"Yeah, maybe. Is the bike for sale?"

"Sorry, kind of partial to her, you know."

"Yeah, I get it. I'd never sell her either."

Rebecca nodded. "Well, got to meet my friend. Nice talking with you." An icy chill snaked down her back. *Is someone watching?* She glanced around and spotted a dark-clothed individual lurking in a doorway across the street. She squinted, sending her version of an alien death ray zinging at them.

"Yeah, thanks, you too." The young man, not more than eighteen or nineteen, slowly moved away, joining his friends. She glanced again at the unwanted surveillance, but the person had vanished. *Good.*

She loaded her helmet into a side saddlebag, removed her purse then used the rear mirror on the bike to check her appearance. *Not bad. Worth the crushed hairdo to ride the wind.*

"Get out and stay out! I don't want you to see you in here one more time today, Earl. Is that clear?" A man was being escorted from a restaurant across the way. He stumbled off down the street without a backward glance. *Pretty early in the day to be drunk.* She shrugged. *To each his own. Hard to judge when so many things in life can go wrong causing people to take the hardest path.*

She looked up at the Red Lion sign. *Hmm, a pub housed in a cellar with stone steps leading downward to the entrance. Unusual.* Though it kind of suited the vibes of the professor. She looked like she belonged underground. *Oh, not nice, Rebecca.* She strode down the steep steps to the heavy wooden door with the brass knocker and hinges.

Opening the door with a grunt—damn thing was ridiculously heavy for a business that might want regulars—she gave the place a quick perusal to get her bearings. Not easy. Management was into privacy. Alcoves and booths done up in black leather in a zig-zag configuration with even darker lighting. *Nice place, if you're a vampire. There, I rest my case.*

A man she took to be the host came up at a fast clip, all beaming smiles. "Good day. Do you have a reservation?"

"I'm not sure. I'm here to meet Professor Masters at two o'clock. She may have made one."

"Of course. Right this way, miss."

She nearly stumbled over an umbrella stand, the man righting it just in time when it threatened to topple over.

"Electricity expensive over here?" she asked, annoyed by having to rummage around in the near dark.

He gave another freaky grin, leading the way forward. "Ah, you joke. Are you an American?"

"No. Canadian."

"Ah, I see."

She was about to ask what he meant when he gave a wide flourish of his arm, stopping so short she nearly ran him down. "Professor Masters, your guest has arrived."

"Thank you, Raoul." Vanessa sat in one of the booths, her alabaster skin a great help in the dark.

"How nice to see you, Rebecca."

Rebecca slid into the seat opposite her, longing for a nice well-lit Tim Hortons with its double-doubles — to go. "Likewise. Why is it so dark in here?"

"Dark?" Vanessa looked around with surprise. "I hadn't noticed. Though it's the perfect ambiance when you want to have some privacy with someone you hope will become a close friend. Oh, before I forget." She opened her purse and drew out a small brown envelope. "Here's your locket. All fixed."

"Thanks." She accepted the small package from the outstretched hand, their fingers touching, then Vanessa grabbed her hand. She gave the woman a look of inquiry. *What is her deal?* Maybe Vanessa was bi, considering the intense looks she'd been blessing her with since they'd met. Perhaps she should be feeling flattered.

"I just wanted to say how sorry I am that I broke it. It's a lovely piece. But good as new now. And as the Bard wrote, '*All's Well That Ends Well.*'"

"Thanks." She tugged her hand away, then slipped the locket from the envelope. It looked the same, thank goodness. She opened the side of the heart-shaped section, exposing the strands of hair braided in a tight circle that she figured must have belonged to either her father or mother. Still intact.

She put it around her neck, doing up the clasp from long practice. She'd felt odd without the talisman, almost naked, having worn it all her life.

"Looks good on you," Vanessa said, bestowing another smile.

"Yes, thank you. Shall we order? I don't have too much time."

"That's a shame. I had hoped to pick your brain for at least a couple of hours. Adoption is such an important subject in my family right now. Surely they give you time off from work?" Vanessa looked crest-fallen.

"Yes, of course, I can stay as long as you need," Rebecca relented.

"Thank you. Say, are you free next Friday? I'm having a party for some close friends. You can meet some of our neighbors. The rest of the family's invited, including Ash. Please, say yes. We can talk more then if you're rushed today."

"Not sure of my schedule. Can I get back to you?" She pushed a wayward strand of hair behind her ear. She bit her bottom lip, feeling a bit ungrateful. The woman was trying very hard to be nice, to include her. It wasn't like her not to give people the benefit of the doubt. And she had fixed her locket right away.

"Ash hasn't gotten your ring sized yet?" Vanessa glanced at her hand.

"Ah—no. No hurry." She shrugged. She could only hope it took weeks and everything had been resolved about the sham of an engagement before it turned up again.

"Most women don't like to even take off their newly received engagement rings, flashing them at everyone they meet."

"Guess I'm not most women. So, what can I help you with?"

"Please, if you could just share what it's been like for you growing up. Like when did you find out you were adopted? Things like that. I would just like to hear first-hand."

Rebecca let out a deep cleansing breath, digging inside for the right way to express her experiences. "Well, I think I must have been told quite young. Seemed like I always knew. They—my adopted parents — told me I was chosen by them, more special than even if I had been born into the family."

"Nice." Vanessa nodded.

"Yes, I think that helped. Problems often happen when people keep secrets." Rebecca bit her lip, realizing what she had just said. If only things could have been different from the get-go with the Piers family, maybe she and Ash wouldn't be at such loggerheads and she wouldn't feel like such an ingrate for keeping her true purpose hidden. She thrust the idea away. They would be getting plenty of payment from her for housing her for the summer. Why, the Teddy Bears' Picnic alone would raise a nice lot of funds, even with a percentage going to charity. She'd work her heart out to see to it.

"So true. My brother, Ian, and his wife Susan — you'll meet them Friday — are considering an open adoption. One where the birth parent continues to have contact with the child. Personally, I think it would be confusing." Vanessa shrugged, seeming to have forgotten that Rebecca had not accepted her party invite. "And it sounds messy and complicated. What if something goes wrong? Like the birth parent is a psychopath and steals the child back?"

"That sounds a bit extreme. I think most people care about children — want to do right by them."

"You're living with rose-tinted sunglasses on, sweetheart," Vanessa charged, shaking her head.

A large man joined them, bending low to whisper in the professor's ear. Rebecca stared at him, feeling slighted by the 'rose-tinted sunglasses' comment. A second later she recognized the figure. *The man in black lurking on the street! Bigger and more imposing close up.*

And not too hard on the eyes, either. In fact, rather handsome in a sensual sort of way.

Vanessa nodded at whatever the man had informed her of. "Thank you, I'll see to it." The man left, but not before reaching over and tweaking the professor's left breast, saying, "Anything for you, Mistress." He didn't bother saying anything to Rebecca. *Did I just see that?*

"Who was that?" she asked, taken aback by the turn of events.

"Ajax? He's my bodyguard. Quite useful to have around, if you know what I mean." Vanessa smiled wickedly, wiggling her eyebrows for emphasis.

"Bodyguard. Really?" *And apparently, quite a bit more too. Does Ash know about him?*

"Threats at the university, believe it or not. Not everyone thinks imparting knowledge about the occult is a worthwhile endeavor."

"In this day and age?" Rebecca was flummoxed. She'd had no idea. A wave of sympathy for the professor overcame her. "Wasn't the last law against witchcraft repealed in Britain in 1951?"

"Yes." Vanessa gave her an appreciative look. "It's supposed to be a free world now. Not bloody likely, if some oddballs get their way. By the way, if you're wondering about Ajax taking liberties just now, my personal philosophy is one of indulging your senses. Take the time to taste fine wine, enjoy each bite of food, affirm your life. Aren't you in England as part of a growth experience?"

"Yes. I do hope to gain fodder for my writing. Though of course my chief concern is helping the family any way I can."

"Of course. But stick with me, sweetheart, and I'll give you all the fodder you can handle. My credentials are impeccable, due to my intensive years of study at Cambridge, and my research skills are second to none." Her smug look did not ingratiate her further. She gave the impression that no one from Canada could possibly come close to rivalling her abilities.

Ha, right, if she only knew. Sure, Rebecca might wish she had Casey's Masters of Archeology qualification, but she would put in the hard work to hold her own. And she had picked up a lot from her fellow Ringer over the years of their friendship.

"If you only knew what I am close to discovering, you'd be blown away. A find beyond the imagination. Beyond your pay grade to even know about," Vanessa said.

"Really? Something that will help raise your status with your boss?" It was always good to remind an egotist that there was someone above them.

Vanessa narrowed her eyes. "You have no idea what I'm capable of, do you? For your information, I am hot on the trail of an artifact that will be the discovery of the millennium."

A discovery that makes up for that cliché, I can only hope. "What is this elusive artifact? The Holy Grail, the Ark of the Covenant, the Philosopher's Stone? You ready to turn metal into gold? Not many things would make the fuss you're talking about." She shook her head, pursing her lips.

"How about the Seal of Solomon? That do it?"

Shocked, she stilled. "Wow, very impressive, Professor."

"Are you ladies ready to order?" The waiter finally appeared, interrupting at the perfect moment.

"Yes, I am. Rebecca?" Vanessa raised an eyebrow.

"Please, I'm starving." And intrigued beyond measure to realize she had a rival for the same artifact.

"I'd recommend the salmon. It's always fresh."

"Sounds good. And coffee, thank you."

"No wine?" Vanessa asked, looking scandalized.

"No, I'm driving."

"Ajax could drive you home, if you like."

"Thanks, but I'd rather not. I brought my motorcycle and I don't want to leave it on the street."

"Motorbike. Very cool. You're an intriguing woman," Vanessa complimented her.

Rebecca warmed a bit, accepting the praise. There was more to the woman than met the eye. She was a free thinker, something Rebecca reluctantly admired, even if she didn't want to be part of such a 'handsy' group. And her assertions about the Ring of Solomon. Ha, priceless, when she, Rebecca Fairfax — of a lesser pedigree, apparently — had found the ring first. *Bring it on, professor. Careful, Rebecca, don't tempt fate*, a voice warned. Okay. But did the woman even know about the connections to the Piers family? She couldn't, or she'd be at the castle day and night, snooping around.

"You remind me of a character I write about in a series. Xaviera St. Clair, a strong superheroine who's always getting in and out of international trouble."

"Hmm, that does sound intriguing. What's her superpower?"

"Telepathy. Reading minds."

"Nice." She didn't do what most people did at that point in any conversation that she'd had in the past discussing the fictional character — say what they wished their superpower choice would be.

"You never wished for a superpower of your own?" She couldn't resist asking.

"Oh, I got that covered." Vanessa gave her a wink, accepting a glass of wine from the waiter and taking a sip. "What would you want yours to be?"

"I always wanted the gift of healing."

"Very commendable. What do you think of Ash?" The question came out of left field.

"He's all right. Bit of a womanizer, I've been told."

The waiter dropped off their food, waiting to see if it met their expectations.

"Great, thanks."

"Yes, he loves the ladies. Bet you've been having to fend off his advances. Though he is one sweet specimen, all that curly dark hair and smoldering eyes, not to mention a spectacular physique." Vanessa said, her dark eyes glittering with emotion.

"Ah—"

"It's fine." The woman shrugged. "We're not exclusive. But, sweet young thing like you, best guard your heart. He'll just break it to smithereens, given the chance. Bet you didn't know he was once engaged? Didn't make it to the altar though. Broke Samantha's heart the day of the wedding. Stood her up."

"My God. Really? That's awful." And just when she was starting to think he was a decent guy, caring about his family like he did. She firmed her resolve. No way was she letting him get to her again. Not ever.

Chapter Twelve

The best laid schemes o' Mice an' Men,
Gang aft agley. — *Robert Burns*

The morning of the Teddy Bears' Picnic began with cloudy, dreary skies, threatening to put the kybosh on proceedings. However, the weather man promised the rain clouds would disperse by noon, and Rebecca was keeping her fingers and toes crossed he'd made the correct assumption.

She'd gotten up before dawn to make certain everything was primed to go, checking with suppliers and vendors and staying in constant touch with performers. Running around with the ubiquitous clipboard, checking lists against lists, she barely had time to acknowledge Ash when he asked what he could do to help.

"I've got this covered, thanks. You are free to do whatever it is you do," she assured him, not wanting him to hang around and remind her of things she had no time for today.

"Okay. Call me if you need me."

In your dreams, buddy. Unfortunately, he was still featuring prominently in her dreams, but what he didn't know couldn't come back to bite her in the ass. The guy had to have an ego as big as the castle to think she should be falling at his feet, like all the women he'd bedded in the past year, leaving a trail of broken hearts. Not to mention the jilted Samantha and her pain.

Gracie ran up, nearly out of breath, her pink and brown teddy bear T-shirt making her look all kinds of adorable. "The musicians canceled. Grandmother just took the call. Something about possible rain affecting their electric instruments. What are we going to do about the Teddy Bears' Lullaby for story time? The whole picnic will be ruined without it!"

Her big blue eyes filled with tears, the end of existence as she knew it suddenly falling on her birdlike shoulders. The guy heading the small band must have been a coward, not wanting to tell her but calling the dowager instead. *Wait till he gets a piece of my mind.*

"Gracie, there are lots of other things going on. My goodness, the courtyard is filled with things for our guests to do," Ash intervened with a wide wave of his hand to indicate the colorful booths and displays set up, trying to get his sister to see reason.

But the little girl was not convinced, the tears spilling over and breaking Rebecca's heart.

Before she gave herself time to think about how intimidating it would be to perform in front of a crowd, Rebecca stepped forward. "Ash, can you go to town and get a guitar? Right now. Not an electric, just a folk style one will do. You know — acoustic. Then we don't have to worry about the rain."

"Why? What good will that do? Or do you know someone else that plays one?"

"I do." She swallowed hard, wicked fairies dancing in her stomach, zapping her with their wands. "Me."

"Wow! You can do that! Thanks, Rebecca." Gracie threw her arms around her, hugging her so tightly she nearly dropped the clipboard. As it was she stumbled back a step from the enthusiasm.

"No worries." Her heart thudding wildly, she made herself smile reassuringly at the beaming child clinging to her. The young girl finally untangled her limbs, leaving the warmth of acceptance and approval in her wake. *Stage fright begone.* She'd do whatever she could to make this sweet child's life happier. She'd been through so much at such a tender age.

"Okay, I'll be back soon. Thanks for doing this. As you can tell, it means the world to my sister." Ash bestowed a smile, then hurried away, leaving her to get on with things.

Hours passed while she ran around, making sure everything was on track, the courtyard filling with enthusiastic teddy bear lovers and their families as soon as the event venue was declared open. The rain stayed away during the teddy bears parade of festive wagons and occupants, during the games of chance, and for the boo-boo bandage station attending to the wounded warriors, the clouds finally parting and letting the sun shine through just in time for the Teddy Bears' Lullaby.

A large group of spectators were already gathered at the picnic area, seated on lawn chairs for the three o'clock event, when Ash came rushing up and thrust an acoustic guitar into her hands. "Will this work for you? Sorry, I had to go a lot farther than I imagined. Then I ended up borrowing one from a friend. Funny that, eh."

"O — kay." She gave him a look. *Friend, yeah, of course. Code for lover, right?* "And sure, this will be fine. Is it tuned up?"

"No idea. Not my forte." He shrugged, pushing back his hair with a hand. It had fallen over his forehead from all the running around. He looked boyish, even giving a grin, as if he'd enjoyed his errand. *Of course he had. And the green-eyed monster strikes again.*

"Do you sing?" she asked, to take her mind off it.

"Not much. Just along to the radio once in a while. And I've got a horror of speaking in public."

"I confess. I'm terrified," she admitted, chewing on her bottom lip as she placed the guitar strap over her head.

"And yet you're going to do this. To make Gracie happy." He shook his head in total disbelief.

She shrugged, tamping down her nervousness. "Seems the thing to do. She was so disappointed. Can't have that. Look at what she'd been doing for the past hour." She pointed at Gracie helping a toddler navigate a set of stairs to the small slide that had proved popular with the wee tykes.

"No, we can't disappoint others." He looked directly into her eyes as he spoke.

"Okay, then. I think this crew is about ready for story time, and my lullaby is supposed to announce it."

She sat quickly on the stool provided in front of the microphone, afraid her shaking knees in her beige capris would be noticed by the waiting crowd.

"I want to thank everyone for coming today. I'm hoping you will all join in with me. The words will be flashed up on the screen behind me." She pointed at the large white screen. She'd set up the projector while waiting for Ash to bring the guitar, making sure everything was ready. "This song is a personal favorite of mine. My mother often sang it for me as a child. The *Teddy Bears' Lullaby.*"

She strummed a few chords, making sure the instrument was in tune. It was, and she launched into the first verse.

"*'Tuff, the magic baby bear, lived with Mommy and me. He never ate his berries, but drank cups of tea. We shared a lot of sleepy hugs, saved a jar of lightning bugs, dancing round the Christmas tree.'* Please, join me for the chorus. *'Tuff, the magic baby bear, lived with Mommy and me...'*"

* * * *

So unfair. Ash signed with frustration. Starstruck about summed it up. She had the voice of an angel and a body built for sin. He looked upward at the heavens where the sun had broken through the clouds, and down at the light reflecting off her golden hair. He'd thought she was spectacular in the tunnels, chasing a thief, but here, looking so pure and vulnerable, this was something entirely different. Something amazing. Thank goodness Arthur had lent him the guitar. He took in the rapt faces of the crowd listening to her, some rocking their children to the slow beat of the lullaby. *God, give me the strength.*

Chapter Thirteen

Though no one can go back and make a brand-new start, anyone can start from now and make a brand-new ending.
— Carl Bard

Finally. Enough of planning a wedding that's not going to happen. Rebecca slipped into her rooms at the castle, exhausted from discussing guest lists and upcoming events with the dowager. She'd had to work hard to keep the conversation steered toward the concert in the park she was planning next, rather than the engagement party. And she was tired from avoiding Ash for days on end. Though that was easy enough to do with Edward — he always seemed to be busy elsewhere. Afraid his fake fiancée might do a runner if pressed too hard? Or maybe he was going to pull what his son had done to his bride, leave her at the altar. Now that would be perfect. *But today, I'm going to quit thinking of that.* She would begin by perusing the underground tunnel system. Jeans, boots, a hoodie and a backpack would suit.

Luck was on her side in avoiding contact with anyone, and she soon found herself at the top of the stairs leading downward to the catacombs. The very spot she'd nearly tumbled from. But she was prepared this time, carefully descending the stone steps one by one, flashlight lighting the way.

She discovered the tunnel floor less flooded, the distant sound of a motor humming being the likely culprit. *Pumps run by a generator. Good idea.*

She strode forward with purpose, enthusiasm rising with each step, making her blood sing with excitement. *What's behind door number three? Either the biggest find in the history of the Ringers – or nada.*

It was important to focus on results and not the eternal press of the tunnel walls, knowing what lay above them, the lake. Her eyes involuntarily followed her thoughts though, looking upward at the rough-hewn roof. *Don't go there. It's held for centuries, it'll hold a few minutes more, right? Tell that to an erupting volcano, a tsunami, a hurricane force wind...*

Focus.

Now, where were those amazing carved artifacts? Her heartbeat increased, awestruck by the history and grandeur of such an experience. *Worth its weight in gold.* Something to tell her grandchildren, Mrs. Johnson's health class be damned. She would strive for the life she wanted.

She rounded a bend in the tunnel, her flashlight glinting on the carved imprint in the rockface. *Yes.* There they were, the two distinctive impressions, the first representing the Freemasons — an eye within the compass and the square, forming a partial pentagram — and the second, King Solomon. That had a pentagram within a double ring with an Egyptian ankh housed inside.

She ran a reverent hand over the ancient images. Logically, there should be some indication of where to look next. *At least that's what I would do if I didn't know how much time I had left and wanted future generations to find what I had hidden.*

She began a minute inspection, working her way around the images, clockwise. She searched for a long time, not finding what she needed and about ready to call it a day.

"You'd think they could have left an arrow or some indication," she grumbled out loud. She pulled a water bottle from her backpack and took a swig, then splashed the water on the wall, looking for any manmade sign, no matter how small.

There.

Her eyes then her fingers located a tiny symbol, easily missed, carved below the images, about six inches up from the stone floor. *Okay, now we're talking.* The symbol was of The Hermetic Order of the Golden Dawn legacy, obviously passed through the hands of the Rising Sun group. It represented the bottom of the Tree of Life, before even getting purchase on the first step. The Neophyte Grade. *Very, very clever.*

Am I onto it? The hiding spot of the Knights Templar treasure, including the part protected by them for King Solomon, then given over to the Freemasons to follow through to the present day with the help of the Golden Dawn? The treasure hoard with the greatest artifact she could ever imagine locating? It might not be at the level of the Ark of the Covenant or the Holy Grail, but the king's seal would still be an amazing discovery. There was one way to know for certain. She got down on her hands and knees, prepared to follow the yellow brick road. Only this time, she wanted to find the end of it.

It was a hard slog, occasionally with having to stop to wipe streaming sweat from her burning eyes, but she managed to find one, 1°=10°, the Zelator Grade, about five feet from the first, the same distance from the floor. The first number meant the steps up from the bottom of the Tree of Life, the second number the number of steps down from the top of the tree. *Perfect.*

She found six other indicators more quickly this time, then she was into the Portal Grade with 5°=6° for Adeptus Minor, 6°=5° for Adeptus Major, and 7°=4° for Adeptus Excemptus, the end of the Portal Grade, before approaching one of the spots where the tunnel branched off. So down the side tunnel she went. Of course, it wasn't lit at all, but dank and dismal, with cobwebs hanging from the ceiling. *Yuck.* Maybe not ventured into in decades or even centuries. Just one more abandoned shaft, like in an Old West gold mine she'd sometimes read about in her favorite sleuthing stories as a kid.

She tamped down her growing excitement, remembering what those stories suggested an adventurer could find hidden inside an abandoned shaft. *If* they had the courage to continue. She found the next symbol, the beginning of the Third Order, the highest level, thought to have only been achieved by unearthly beings. That left only two outstanding – 9° =2° for Magnus and 10°=1°, the top of the Tree of Life.

The now claustrophobic and eerily dark tunnel, lit only by her flashlight bouncing circles of light off the rough-hewn walls, led through an opening to another space with an old metal door standing guard at the entrance. She pulled the heavy barred door open, its ancient hinges squeaking nosily in protest, bracing it with a rock to keep it from swinging shut.

Still wincing at the banshee pitch ringing in her ears, she stepped through into an even smaller space, so tight she now had to bend over slightly at the waist. It continued another fifty feet before coming to an abrupt end. About twenty-five feet in, she found the $9°=2°$. But the final symbol at the end of the road was the one that made her heart thud. The Holy Grail of symbols, if one belonged to and believed in the splinter group the Order of the Rising Sun, of Piers family linage. Samuel. W. Piers, the man who'd run the Osiris-Sun Temple, was responsible, she was certain, for this trail of golden crumbs. His voice had called to her across time.

She kicked at the lower wall with her booted foot, making the crumbling rock give way. A small avalanche of stones soon followed the more she kicked at it, leaving a shallow impression. *Should have brought a shovel,* she mused, crouching and realizing the spot, about two feet round, traveled deep under the stone wall. Was this it? The final hiding spot of King Solomon's treasures? She pulled work gloves out of her pocket. *Only one way to find out.*

Okay. Here goes nothing.

She shrugged out of her backpack, an awkward action in the confined space. Noises in the distance alerted her to possible company. *Shoot.* Just when she was about to get at it. *What to do?*

Another banshee screech of the iron door slamming shut made her heart skip a full beat. Had the rock she'd used to brace it open slipped? Or…was it something more sinister?

Moving quicker, cold sweat slithering down her sides, she swallowed over the hard lump of fear rising in her throat. She ran the last ten feet to the iron door and pushed against it with all her might. Solid and ominous, it would not budge, its rusted bars still capable of great strength. The built-in lock must have engaged, tying together the iron clasp of the door and the frame driven into the stone wall, effectively keeping her in and the world out. The damn stone had rolled away, or maybe been pushed away — she shuddered at the idea — letting the door clank shut.

She pulled out her phone, dismayed to find no service. *Well, this sucks.*

"Help, help, I'm stuck in here," she screamed at the top of her lungs, hoping to alert a passerby to her predicament. She kept at it until she was hoarse, alternating it with checking her phone, but no service magically appeared and no one came to her rescue. Hours passed. Slumped behind the corroded bars, looking at freedom just mere inches away, she had no choice but to bide her time. When would she be missed? At dinner? Surely there would be a search party sent out? But no one knew she was down the tunnels. How long until they figured it out? And she was a long way off the beaten path. *God, what if I become like one of the Oak Island men that perished in pursuit of treasure?*

No. Think positive.

She took a sip of her water, conserving it, her stomach rumbling to remind her of its urgent wants. Her breakfast had been a very, very long ten hours ago. And she had not packed any food in her backpack. *Dumb move.* But she hadn't expected by any stretch of the imagination to be down here so long, and it was nearly six o'clock.

She took out her phone for the umpteenth time. *Finally.* One weak bar! She quickly sent a text. Then began actively praying it got through.

Time passed. She shouted out every few minutes as loudly as her sore throat allowed, hoping against hope someone would hear.

Then footsteps echoed in the distance. *Thank you, God.*

"Help! I'm in here!" she continued screaming, all thoughts of a sore throat forgotten. She turned on her flashlight that she had been conserving, sending its rays down the tunnel.

Another light. Coming towards me.

Rescue was at hand. At least if it wasn't the dastardly asshole who might or might not have locked her down here in the first place. She was finding it hard to believe that so large a rock couldn't have done its job. She gave it another death-ray glance. Then held her breath, waiting to see who would appear.

A familiar face.

Ash. The person she had been avoiding for days. But boy, did he look fine now. All prowling maleness with tousled dark curls. A rush of suppressed emotions overcame her. She was just so darn happy to see him. To be rescued.

"Rebecca! Thank God!"

He set his flashlight down and wrestled with the door, stern and worried. "How did this happen? Did someone lock you in?"

"I don't know. I braced the door with a rock, but when I came back down the tunnel, the door had swung shut. I did hear some noises earlier, but I never saw anyone." She swallowed hard, chewing on her bottom lip. She was antsy now, her body feeling like a caged animal planning its impending escape.

"The rock must have slipped. I can't imagine anyone would do such a terrible thing, unless maybe they didn't know you were in here?" His looked at her, his deep brown eyes glittering in the torchlight. "I'll need to go get a tool to cut through the lock. It won't budge."

"I'll wait here."

He caught the humor after a split-second, giving her a rueful glance.

"See that you do. I'll be right back."

"Promise."

"Pinky-finger swear."

Over a huge lump in her throat, she stuck her hand through the bars, seeking out his hand on the other side. They locked little fingers, his hand so warm and her fingers cool from the damp and fear.

"Okay then." His voice sounded a bit rough. He turned and left at a fast clip, hopefully to retrieve a sturdy set of metal bolt cutters.

She bided her time, taking deep breaths to steady herself. So many unanswered questions, and the biggest of all one that struck a chord of pure fear and loathing she could no longer deny—had someone locked her in? The rock she'd rolled against the door had been so damn heavy. And she had heard those sounds earlier. But to think someone might been prepared to leave her for—how long? Forever maybe? *The evil bastard. Hmm. Evil equals depraved, damnable, loathsome, heinous, repugnant, repulsive, nefarious, vile, villainous...or whatever, but I will not let some seriously demented reprobate ruin my first overseas adventure.*

An hour, or maybe ten minutes later, Ash reappeared. He bore a pair of heavy red-handled bolt cutters, and quickly went about setting her free.

"I noticed the water levels are better." Breezy, everyday subjects suited the occasion. Anything to keep from stewing on her situation any longer.

"Yes, the pumps are doing their job splendidly." He stopped for a moment and ran a hand through his hair, pushing it back from his face, taking her up on keeping the conversation at an even keel. *Yeah, remember what that handsome mug is hiding. A rascal of a womanizer.* She would just be one more notch on his bedpost.

"Say, what are you up to now? I would love to take you to dinner. Talk over the current predicament. See what we can come up with to get you clear of the old man."

"That old man is your father and he's been nothing but nice to me, like the dowager, and even your sister Gracie has come around." She and Gracie had even enjoyed a couple of evenings playing chess of late — ever since they'd been co-hosts at the Teddy Bears' Picnic, she'd been hanging around Rebecca a lot more. The girl was darn good too, practicing on an app that allowed her to play against her computer. "And don't we have that party at Vanessa's tonight?" She hadn't planned on going, but it beat the alternative, dinner with a man she could barely resist. She freely admitted her weakness for all things Ash. Every night this past week he had featured prominently in her dreams and daytime fantasies. *Damn annoying.*

"Are you saying I haven't been nice to you?" Ash's brows knitted, the expression in his eyes clearly one of deep hurt.

"No, I didn't mean it that way."

"Then what did you mean? You've been avoiding me for days on end. That's blatantly clear. Ah, here we go, you're free, m'lady. Come forth." He stepped back, making a courtly bow that dissolved all her defenses. Or maybe it was just she was so happy to be free.

She slipped through the small opening, giving the iron door a hard kick for good measure, then looked at Ash, just coming up from his deep bow, and walked right into his waiting arms.

She held on to his solid frame for dear life, tears prickling behind her eyes. He felt so unbelievably good that no words could possibly capture the experience, the overwhelming emotion.

"Hey, beautiful, we'd best get you out of here. You need a hot shower and a good meal. ASAP."

She allowed him to take her by the hand, leading her like a small child back through the tunnels and up the steep stone steps to the main floor. With her feet back on terra firma, she wanted to dance. To fly. To celebrate new beginnings. Unable to stop herself, she tuned to him, giving him a big kiss on the mouth.

"Thank you for finding me and setting me free."

"Any time, beautiful, for a reward like that." He held on to her, tucking a curl behind her ear. He let his fingers linger on her face, drifting down to rub lightly over her lips.

"You have such a beautiful mouth and such a beautiful face and spirit." His words made her heart pitter-patter. The good kind this time.

She tried to pull away. This had gone far enough. But he held on, his arms grasping her gently but firmly to his rock-solid body that was doing all kinds of delicious things to her.

"Why have you been avoiding me?"

He took a chance with the asking, opening himself to being vulnerable, a state worse than death. But this past week, her avoiding him at every turn, had cost him. Especially after seeing her at the picnic, and watching her shine in her own element. It turned out nothing could divert his thinking about and wanting to spend time with this little Canadian spitfire. Not trying to connect with any of the women in his black book, nor following any of his old pursuits of partying and drinking. Not even the scenarios that Vanessa was so good at creating in her devilish mind that had begun to bore him, make him feel less of a man and more like a damn robot. Sex was overrated when it was only done for the mere rubbing together of body parts. He longed for more. A connection that he was beginning to feel with this incredible woman. If only he could trust her.

"Well, since I'm supposed to marry your dad in a couple of months, it seemed prudent."

"Well, that can end now. I'll have a talk with him tonight — catch him after the party. Make him see how insane this all is."

"But his heart?"

He sighed. "I'll be very careful and tackle the subject with finesse. That's if you want to stop it?"

She froze, spitting out the words. "Why wouldn't it?"

He gave her an assessing look. "You've been very amenable to date. Let this all happen of its own accord. Makes me wonder."

"I told you I'm not a gold-digger!" she snapped back, crossing her arms over her chest. "And good luck with that talk. It seems eccentrics abound in the Piers family tree and this apple didn't fall far."

Obviously, she meant him. He snarled in spite of his best intentions, "I'm not the one who's gone along with it. You don't even *know* my father. At least I have the excuse of loving him."

She skewered him with a look. But he had her there and she knew it. "Don't bother upsetting your father on my behalf."

He knew it. She was in it for the money or she'd pull out now. He watched her walk away, his heart raw, his stomach churning with emotion.

Chapter Fourteen

The truth is the safest lie. — *Anonymous*

Rebecca hurried to take a hot shower, wanting to put the last few hours out of her mind. *The man's insufferable.* But she needed to stay at the castle a while longer, and pulling the plug on the engagement was premature. And she cared too much for this family to just abandon them, if she were being honest.

She was grateful she had managed to go clothes shopping earlier in the week. She now had a few good choices of dresses for the party, along with her new favorite purse — a black Lulu Guinness evening bag resplendent with silver stylized initials and matching chain. Her fellow Ringers were going to be so jealous. On second thought, she'd better take them all one home as a gift, or she'd never hear the end of it. Though it would chew up her funds, it would be worth it to see the expression on their faces when she presented them with one each.

She washed away the toxic mix of perspiration created by fear and hard labor, enjoying the plenitude of warm water after the hours spent sweating it out in the freezing dungeon. The calming smell of lavender from her shampoo helped clear her mind, and soon she was toweling her hair, applying make-up, then blow-drying her thick mane to a going-to-a-party finish.

A knock at the door alerted her to the possibility of imminent food. Her stomach rumbling at the suggestion, she hurried to invite Sloan in, tying the sash on her bathrobe.

"Thanks. I'm near starved."

"We wondered what happened to you at lunch."

"I made other arrangements." *Yeah, not to eat apparently.*

At least her secret was safe for the moment. Sloan obviously did not know anything of what had happened. She shook her head. It seemed so unreal now that she was safe. But it had happened and it needed to be gotten to the bottom of. What if someone else had the bright idea to scamper into places in the deepest, darkest part of Castle Piers? Perhaps the entire catacombs would be blocked off now? That would be bad news.

She itched to go back and make her way those final few feet, see what was there. She'd have to do it soon too or maybe lose her chance forever. Her thoughts turned to her current predicament. There was no hope of fixing things any time soon. She'd have to play the hand she'd been given. She sighed, doubting Ash would let her stay if the engagement ended.

She thanked Sloan for the food and went to work, demolishing the stack of pancakes, sausages and eggs in record time. The tray set aside, she scampered to the closet, looking for just the right dress to knock someone's proverbial socks off.

Dressed a few minutes later in a midnight blue lace dress that skimmed her knees, she checked her reflection in the mirror and twirled around on her matching high heels just for the pure pleasure. *Yes. Perfect choice.* She was certain she could hold her own and not embarrass fellow Canadians or the Piers family.

She descended the stairs to the Great Hall where Sloan had informed her everyone would be gathering, noting she was the first to arrive. She walked over to admire the impressive display of portraits she assumed must be family lining one wall. To know one's ancestry, to live where they had all lived — such an awesome experience. She envied them, finding it hard to imagine what that must be like. Sometimes she felt rootless, not knowing her birth family. Her life held no history linked to her DNA, other than a locket and a short note.

"Quite the collection of reprobates, I'm afraid. I always found this room rather overbearing as a child. Didn't spend much time in it." She spun around at the sound of Ash's voice, taking in his changed appearance. *My oh my*, did he clean up nice. From his impeccable tux, snowy white shirt, onyx cufflinks set in heavy gold, the mirror-like surface on his expensive leather shoes, hair pushed back off his handsome face, he might have just stepped right out of a *GQ* fashion shoot. And of course there was that intense charisma rolling off him in waves that lit her body up, like fireworks were set to go off any second.

"Hmm. At least you have a family tree."

"Yes, though it's vastly overrated." He came closer, the expression in his eyes suggesting he more than approved of her changed appearance as well. "You look stunning."

"Thanks." Shyness overcame her, something she'd thought she was over. But it was different now. Soon she would be free, once she found the treasure for the family. And what would she do with that freedom? It was getting harder and harder not to admit that there was something going on between them. Something that scared her, though not enough to keep her from wishing it were different. That they could see where it would all lead, even if it was just a summer fling. It just might be worth it. Not that he would be interested now. It rankled that he still thought her a gold-digger.

His expression drew more serious. "How are you doing? Such a terrible thing, what happened today. I'm so sorry. I'm going to have that door removed and other tunnels checked for booby traps. I'll see that it's safe or I'll fill it all in, make sure no one can go down there ever again. If anything had happened to you — if I hadn't found you — "

Guilt struck for the information she was hiding from him and his family. "I'm fine now. Don't worry." She realized she could not live with the guilt a moment longer. "There is something I should tell you about — "

"Ah, my son and my fiancée. I'm delighted to see you two are getting along so splendidly. Soon we'll all be one big happy family." Edward, dressed similarly to Ash, came into the room, just as she was about to admit to Ash what she had been looking for in the tunnels, what she suspected was still there. Rebecca wasn't sure if she should be relieved by the interruption or not. She didn't want secrets between them. But the timely interruption suggested something else. Perhaps the hand of fate. That she should keep the trump card next to her chest, at least a little while longer. Then she could come clean.

Ash gave her a look and a tight nod. What was he thinking? Maybe she didn't want to know.

"You look beautiful." Edward gave her a beaming smile. "Doesn't Rebecca look beautiful, Ash?"

"Yes, very."

"And tonight will be the perfect opportunity to make our engagement official. We can announce it at the party. I rang Vanessa, and she's on board, offering Harlequin Manor for the occasion. I've already taken the liberty of sending over a crate of champagne for the toast."

Oh God. She gave Ash a look. *Do something.*

"Father, about that, Rebecca and I were talking and we've decided you need to know something—"

Edward gave a great sigh, a frown appearing between his eyebrows. "Yes, I need to share something with the two of you as well—quickly—before your grandmother and Gracie come down."

"Sounds serious. What is it?" Ash asked.

"We need to move the wedding date forward, I'm afraid." Edward clamped a hand to his chest, his breathing labored.

"Forward?" Ash looked as stunned as she felt.

"Yes, best if it's done quietly and very soon. A couple of weeks, I should think." The breathing turned to panting, scaring the bejesus out of her. Is he going to collapse?

"Why? What's happened?"

"Now, don't get upset. Your grandmother and sister will be here in a moment and they don't know about it."

"Maybe we need to tell them."

"No. I forbid it. I need time to prepare them."

"But you just said time is running out." Rebecca was certain the room tilted sideways as a huge tsunami of emotion washed over her, leaving her beached.

"Ah, mother, how lovely you look this evening." The dowager came into the room, Gracie in tow.

She forced a smile, taking Edward's cue to remain silent. He had even managed to right his breathing, making it less obvious that he was in distress. Not that it was her place to tell the family what they would inevitably have to know. That the patriarch was dying. She swallowed hard, stepping forward.

"Good to see you. You look gorgeous." She took the dowager's hand and gave Gracie a nod of approval. "I love your dress."

"We missed you at lunch." The older woman's sharp eyes seemed to miss nothing, yet what she didn't know was going to tear her world apart. Rebecca sucked it up with great difficulty, emotion almost overcoming her best intentions.

"Yes, I had something to take care of."

"You didn't take your motorbike?"

"No." She shook her head, trying to keep a bright smile pinned in place. "Sometimes it's good to take a long walk." *On my way to Crazy Town, the train about to leave the station and I've got lots of company. Oh, I got a better one. You can't fix crazy, but you can watch it in action.* Things had taken a drastic and unexpected turn and were headed so far south they must now be entering the seventh ring of hell. It was getting a tad too comfortable, being in Cloud-Cuckoo-Land. She'd better start thinking of heading back to Canada before she became one of them and didn't know the difference. Then she caught sight of Ash watching her over the dowager's shoulder, and she knew that wasn't going to happen. She could never leave him mired in this mess. He would need support now more than ever, no matter his failings as a romantic hero. Though that wasn't entirely fair. He had stepped up at the last moment, trying to do the right thing. *Or maybe just trying to get rid of me?*

"I would love to hitch a ride on your motorbike, if you can find the time."

"Really?"

"Me too," Gracie spoke up.

"Ah, sure, anytime. Tomorrow?"

"Perfect. Right after morning tea. It's on my bucket list, you know. Right up there with having a tryst with the movie star, George Clooney."

Rebecca sputtered. "You do know he's married now?"

"Yes, that does put the kibosh on it, I'm afraid. Must rewrite my list. Perhaps a good substitute would be George Hamilton. Such a lovely tan and all. And he was so hot in that movie, *Love at First Bite*. Always had a hankering to meet a vampire. But then again, he might be a bit old for me."

"Oh, grandmother!" Gracie gave her a look, rolling her eyes at the matriarch, but not nearly as embarrassed as Rebecca expected her to be. Of course, she'd had more practice. By the end of the summer, maybe Rebecca might not be noticing the shenanigans at Castle Piers. She couldn't say whether that was a good thing or a bad thing.

"Do you have a bucket list, Rebecca?" Ash's deep voice interjected. She looked up and into his eyes. The connection was so intense she swore everyone must be noticing, if they weren't blind. Steam had to be rising from her lady parts, right?

"Not an actual bucket list, per se. But I do have some places I want to visit in my lifetime." She bit her lip, considering their next move. But what was there left to do, other than breaking a dying man's heart?

"Where would you like to go on our honeymoon?" the wrong voice asked.

"Dawson City. The land of the midnight sun. My sorority sister, Casey, once found a cache of nuggets there—Soapy's Gold—stolen by a con man who frequented the town in the 1897-99 Klondike Gold Rush." No way would Edward want to go there, having told her days ago he was an Englishman born and bred and had no patience for travel. She was safe.

"Not sure I'm up to that sort of adventure." Right on cue, he bowed out. "But Ash, didn't you once say how much you wanted to spend time in Canada?"

Ash cleared his throat. "Yes, visiting Canada has always interested me. Now more than ever."

"That so?" Rebecca gave him a quick glance, her interest piqued. "I'd be happy to show you around. Lots of great tourist spots in Canada. Might take a long time though, even if you're just hitting the highlights." Was she flirting with him? *Get a grip, before everyone knows what's going on.* But a quick glance around the room showed no suspicious looks at all.

"Shall we?" Edward asked, giving the dowager his arm and leading her from the hall. "There is something I wish to discuss with you, Mother, something I think you'll approve of." Gracie moved to follow, dancing her thumbs over her phone.

Their voices dimmed as Ash moved to her side, taking her hand in his.

"I'm sorry about this." His face smoldered with repressed emotions. She placed a hand on his cheek, the smooth planes of his jawline and his well-formed lips making her want so much more. Too much more. She wanted to run her hands all over his body, discover what gave him the most pleasure...

"No worries. There's still time to figure a way out," she said in a breezy tone, not at all certain of her assurances. "I think you should spend as much time with your dad as you can." She swallowed against the lump growing in her throat. At such a drastic time, their needs could and should be repressed at all costs. She didn't want to think ahead, what this would all mean to the family she deeply cared about.

"Yes, of course. You're quite right." He ran a hand over his hair in an effort to control his wayward curls that were already springing loose of whatever product he'd applied earlier. Why bother? They made him so charmingly approachable. She wanted to run her hands through his hair, grab hold of those thick locks and never let go.

"I think we need to plan strictly family events for the next weeks."

"Of course. I'll bow out of the family affairs. You need to send as much time with your father now as possible." The thought hurt, not being included, but it would be for the best.

"No. You misunderstand me. Rebecca, you must know you're a vital part of this family. You must join us on all the events. From taking the dowager for a motorbike ride to helping us arrange a picnic. And I'm certain I'll think of others. Nothing too strenuous of course. We don't want to tire him out."

"I'll help you. I'm good at planning. We can make sure it's a special time the family will always remember."

"Thank you."

She didn't know how to respond. The whole thing was too surreal.

"Shall we?" he asked, her hand still in his, and at her nod he walked her forward to the foyer and the waiting car.

They discovered Edward, the dowager and Gracie had already driven off and a second car had been called, waiting for them near the castle entrance. Ash held the door, and she climbed in ahead of him, careful to keep her skirt from exposing too much thigh. He stepped in behind her, reaching over and closing the car door, confining them in the intimate space behind and separated by darkened glass from the driver. Immediately Ash's closeness was an impediment to clear thinking.

"Does Vanessa have a lot of parties?" *Think small talk, Rebecca.* Anything to get her mind off the hot man emitting a cloud of magical pheromones threatening to derail her. And as angry as she was that he considered her a gold-digger, something else was going on to that she didn't have complete control over. It frightened her, knowing his history, and attracted her when he was in her vicinity. There was no getting away from it or fighting it.

"From time to time. She enjoys entertaining." He drummed his fingernails on the metal shelf created by the door handle, the tension obvious in the tightness around his mouth and his furrowed brow.

"It's okay, Ash." She laid a hand over his.

"Is it?" he said with a huge sigh. "I only see trouble ahead."

"No, you mustn't think of it like that. Enjoy the now. Isn't that what we're advised to do? That this moment, living in it, savoring it, is what life is all about?" The words tipped from her lips, buoying her up. She hoped to do the same for him.

"That's what I want more than anything." And with that he pulled her into his arms, kissing her like this was *that* moment. The only perfect moment. His lips slid over hers and he took complete possession of her, enticing in gentle nips, devouring her as if she tasted of something so delicious, he could never get enough. She moaned, her panties flooding with heat. She had never known it could be like this. That she would want a man so much she was willing to take chances. *Who cares if someone is watching? Who cares who finds out? I want this. And I want this now.*

Somehow, he managed to have his hand brush against a nipple, and she moaned louder, the nub tightening and turning super sensitive to his touch in a split second. A throbbing began at the apex of her thighs and her legs drifted apart. Her mind shut down while her body sought what it wanted. What it had to have at any cost. He grasped at a bare thigh where her lace dress had risen up from her squirming under his searing touch, then ran his hand up her trembling leg. She waited for him to touch her, to discover how much her body wanted his. Needed his.

"Rebecca, God, I want you, more than anything. Please, say yes." His voice roughened and he nearly pulled her out of the seat to get closer, to have her body entwined with his. His hot breath followed every movement as he caressed her, stroking her through her panties. Her skin felt too tight, too sensitive. She longed to join her body with his with every fiber of her being. She wanted the barriers to come down between them. She wanted him. Inside her.

Then his fingers pulled aside her underwear, exposing her sensitive flesh to the cool air. She gasped as he ran a finger across her bare skin, then shuddered as he dipped his fingers inside.

"So *good*. Don't stop," she murmured. He obliged her, his mouth closing over hers, swallowing her moans. She bucked against his hand, a throbbing need building and coiling tightly in her groin.

The throbbing grew more intense, the primitive desire for release taking over, entirely. It pressed against her, making her aware of her femaleness, her need for him.

At the height of pleasure, when she could focus on nothing else but achieving an essential, life-affirming orgasm, her internal muscles tightened one last time. Then sweet bliss softened her body, giving it over to the final throes of euphoria.

Aftershocks rippled through her, her breathing slowing in small increments. He held her while her head cleared. Then some semblance of reality took hold and she sat up, pulling her skirt down.

My God, what have I done?

She swallowed. Surreal. She had never, never, *never* in her wild dreams thought a man could make *her*, book nerd and all-around-sensible Rebecca Fairfax, lose control like that. But that was exactly what had happened. Just now. And there was proof. Proof in Ash's eyes as they bored into her, proof in the spicy-scented air that flowed around them. Proof in her need for more.

"I—I don't know what got into me."

"I know exactly what got into you," he teased, his smoldering eyes setting her libido right back to high simmer.

"This is wrong, Ash. I didn't mean for this to happen. *My God*, it can't ever happen again!" Anxiety overtook her, making her voice rise awkwardly mid-sentence.

"Relax, beautiful, you didn't steal the family jewels. You have needs. We all have needs. No shame in that. Weren't you the one just saying we should live in the now?"

"I didn't mean this! Acting like, like a—"

"Normal human being with needs," he filled in the sentence with a cocky smile.

"No. Like a harlot, a floozy, a vamp…"

"I like the word *woman* better. Because you're all woman, and it's good to discover how receptive you can be. And that you can't resist me."

She punched him on the arm, none too lightly. "Careful, I might hit you in a more delicate region if you're not careful."

"Ouch." Like all men, he instinctively barricaded his personal jewels by crossing his legs, grimacing at the phantom pain. She glanced down. Yup, he did indeed have a lot to protect.

He caught her looking at his ample package. A wide smile wreathed his face, making him even more heartbreakingly handsome.

"Like what you see, beautiful?" he teased, reaching one hand out to tuck a stray curl behind her ear.

She cleared her throat. "Too damn much." She turned her head to stare out of the window, not at all certain she could manage the next few hours pretending to be someone she wasn't. This time in England was meant to be fun, a lark, not difficult to navigate.

"I'm sorry about how things unfolded." He looked uncomfortable, pensive.

"Not your fault. I should have spoken up sooner. Made Edward understand it wasn't meant to be taken seriously. Does insanity run in your family?"

"What? No. Well, not usually." He rubbed the back of his neck. "Though this does have the hallmarks of some serious mental issues, looking at it from the outside."

"Do you think he's playing us?" A sudden inspiration, or perhaps just a ray of hope, made her ask.

"No! My father's incapable of such a thing." He turned even more pensive, obviously thinking about it. "I think he's just fallen for you at first sight. Makes perfect sense."

What does he mean by that? "But he hasn't been spending time with me. I hardly see him."

"He's been going to visit his doctor a lot."

"Oh." Deflated, she slumped back in the seat. Here she had been enjoying herself too much, and Ash's father was facing the end times. It was hard to compute, and damn confusing. She'd always thought of herself as a good person.

"Ah, we're here. You ready to face the fray, beautiful?"

"I have to be, right?" If Edward could face death with such aplomb, surely she could manage to be an actress for a few short weeks? Pretend she wasn't falling for His Hotness while looking like she was pleased to be engaged to Edward.

Was this some kind of payback karma? Here he'd spent years footloose, flying above the field, enjoying the company of women, and now? Hell, he didn't understand now at all. He fairly itched to take the gorgeous, talented, fascinating Rebecca to his bed. He wanted this woman. He wanted her for more than just one night. He wanted to discover everything he could about her. And he could not. *Damn it all to hell.*

Frustrated beyond belief, he helped her from the back seat of the Rolls, wanting nothing more than a stiff brandy. Or the whole fucking bottle.

As she exited the vehicle, he caught a whiff of her perfume and his knees weakened. *Good Lord, this is insane.* He took her arm, leading her to the reception line, planning his exit to the bar.

"Ash, Rebecca, how lovely to see you both. Welcome to Harlequin Manor." Vanessa greeted them with a cool smile. "You just missed your fiancé. He arrived with the dowager and Grace." She turned to the two people standing to her right. "Rebecca Fairfax, I would like you to meet my brother Ian and his wife Susan. The couple I was telling you about."

"Nice to meet you both."

Ash hovered by her side while she gracefully answered the couple's rather personal questions about her adoption, admiring her all the more. A servant came by and he signaled him, requesting a brandy. It was promptly delivered and he downed it in a couple of gulps. Setting the glass back on another passing tray, he waited for the potent alcohol to commence calming his jangled nerves. Another couple arrived to greet Vanessa and her entourage and he stepped up, directing Rebecca away.

"Would you like to see the conservatory?" he asked, keeping an eye out for his family. More people were milling about the foyer now, making him antsy to just find a quiet space for reflection. Or maybe more intimate pursuits. It was against his better judgment, but he couldn't seem to help himself. *How do you know if you're out of control?*

"Sure. I love flowers."

"What are your favorites?"

"You're going to laugh. But I found one little purple pansy last summer growing near a sidewalk with no room to flourish and I carefully dug it up and planted it in a pot. Did you know that it now has over a hundred blooms on it? Here, I've got proof." She dug in her purse and pulled out her iPhone, calling up the camera roll.

"Amazing. I didn't know they would do that. You have a gift. Rescuing strays."

"Thanks. Do you have a favorite?"

"No, not really. I just love beautiful things." He turned and smiled directly into her eyes, letting her know what he meant.

"You're far too good at that."

"What? Telling the truth?"

"No. Being charming. Vanessa warned me about you. She told me about Samantha."

"Did she also tell you that the night before our wedding Samantha got it on with the best man? My best friend? I came upon them quite by accident." Startled, he blurted out the truth. The memory of the pair locked in an embrace dug up a host of bad feelings, making his stomach roil in sympathy. He had never shared this with anyone, stunned that he was doing so now. *Guess I now have proof of my out of control state.*

"No. I'm so sorry, Ash."

Rebecca looked floored by the information, her face filled with sympathy.

"It was a few years ago. I've more than recovered." It felt good to get it off his chest. It had been such a sharp thorn in his soul for too long, being blamed for something not of his making. Or maybe he had to accept some blame? She had felt the need to cheat on him. A part of him he'd buried worried it was a lack in himself that had caused the infidelity. Perhaps that was what made him move from woman to woman more than anyone in their right mind would consider wise. A blurry series of mostly one-night stands that for the first time he felt ashamed of. His only saving grace was that he'd always used protection and made certain his partners knew he had nothing to offer them beyond the physical.

"Rather explains things."

"My family doesn't know about it and I'd prefer them never to know. Rather a point of honor. I guess you've noticed how good my family is at keeping secrets."

"I understand. And yes, your family is one of a kind." She gave a half-chuckle and snort, a funny combination that made him smile. She made life simpler and richer all at the same time.

He put his arm protectively around her waist. "Let's slip into the conservatory and 'smell the roses'. Or maybe a pansy or two."

"Okay."

The conservatory had a high cathedral ceiling, but even so the space was a bit warm and moist from the fragrant earth and flora that had been recently watered. Dewdrops lay shimmering on botanicals. It was as though he hadn't noticed before how beautiful such an indoor garden could be. Something that he hadn't even realized was missing was coming back to life in him.

They strolled arm-in-arm down the patio-stoned path, admiring the offerings.

"Ash, Rebecca, so this is where you got off to. I want to borrow Rebecca if I can pry her away from you." Vanessa came into view, her expression smug and self-serving. He inwardly groaned. What else would she share with Rebecca that would put him in a bad light? She had a few stories he was not proud of. She was one of the few women he'd seen more than once. If he could go back in time, he'd do things differently, no doubt about it. *Too late for that. But not too late for the future.*

"You up for this?" Ash leaned down and whispered in Rebecca's ear. "She tends to get a hold of an idea and not let go until you agree with her. We could just make a run for it."

"No worries. I can always text you. One frowny face for hurry and two for 'get the hell in here'." The accompanying whimsical look endeared her to him further.

Vanessa approached, blocking any further conversation.

"Come, I have a proposition for you."

Rebecca released his arm, giving him a reassuring smile before heading off with their hostess. A moment of disquiet at seeing them together. But Rebecca already knew the worst of it, the broken engagement. What else could Vanessa share without incriminating herself? They were two consenting adults, after all. But an uneasy sense he couldn't explain invaded his mind, making him worry afresh, as though they didn't have enough strikes against them with his father's illness.

Chapter Fifteen

Tough times never last, but tough people do.
— Robert H. Schuller

"For a woman engaged to one man, you do seem to be spending a lot of time with another. People will begin to talk if you're not careful." Vanessa nabbed two flutes of champagne from a tray. She handed one to Rebecca and waved off the server.

"Really? I think being seen getting along with the whole family would shed a good light on things. I spend far more time with Gracie and the dowager than Ash, anyway. I've hardly seen him this past week." Rebecca took a sip of the bubbly liquid.

The surrounding displays of orchids in the vast space were beautiful but cloying, their scent making her screw up her nose. She took another mouthful of the sparkling alcohol, scrutinizing Vanessa with narrowed eyes. She had been all too happy to share that little gem about Ash and his broken engagement. Of course, she didn't know the real deal. The fact that Ash trusted Rebecca enough to share it with only her did say something quite positive about them, though how she could have been so reckless on the drive over still rattled her mind.

"Relax. I was just making conversation. Come, we can talk in here. I have something rather important to share. Something that affects your future."

Intrigued, Rebecca followed the woman inside the doorway to a room that turned out to contain a massive library, filled to the rafters with books. And not just any tomes, but hundreds upon hundreds of what appeared to be first editions.

"Very impressive." She couldn't help herself, walking right up to the first section of neatly stacked leather-bound books and checking out the titles on the spines. She ran her hand reverently down the row, reading aloud.

"The occult, grimoires, Satanism, black magic, Egyptian histories, *The Book of Revelations*, Horus, even translations of the Hermetica and the lost wisdom of the Pharaohs. All the demons listed in alphabetical order. And with enough books on witchcraft and spells to keep a person busy for decades. Some display, professor."

"I need the research for my work." Vanessa sipped her champagne. She moved to a desk and set her flute on the desktop, taking up another book. "This is one I think you'll be interested in. It mentions William G. Allman and the Order of the Black Sphinx."

Rebecca took the book from her hands after setting down her glass. "William G. Allman. The man whose wife, Roseanne, swore that the Egyptian god Horus was trying to contact him through her? Then did so directly for a number of days, that became the basis for his writings, the *Book of the Law*. Some connection in the story to the number of the beast too, I believe."

"*And his number is six hundred threescore and six*. Yes, you are well read. I admire that in you. It was the connection to ancient knowledge through an Egyptian god that most intrigues me. *Do what thou wilt shall be the whole of the law*," Vanessa quoted with authority, her expression animated. The heightened color made her even more beautiful. "Imagine finding and experiencing such an event. Perhaps even locating the missing *Book of Thoth*."

Vanessa took up her champagne and downed it. Her eyes were glazed with an almost mystical reverence for achieving such knowledge.

"What has all this have to do with me?"

"Ah, now we get to the crux of the matter. I think you're William G. Allman's great-great-granddaughter. You, sweet Rebecca, might have a closer connection to Horus that you could ever have imagined. A direct link to the ancient gods through your very DNA. Maybe you're even a summoner."

Floored, Rebecca dropped the book back onto the desk, knocking over her drink. Horrified, she watched helplessly as Vanessa sprung into action, quickly sopping up the spill with a roll of paper towels she pulled from a desk drawer.

"No damage." She threw the sodden towels into the wastebasket.

"I'm so sorry." Right off her game, she pressed her lips together, considering sending out a frowny face. Or maybe two. Which was worse? The near destruction of a valuable manuscript or Vanessa thinking she knew the name of Rebecca's great-great-grandfather? "If you think that, then you must know the name of the man you think is my father, right?"

"It's just speculation at the moment. I need a blood sample to test your DNA, of course, but I think I may know your bloodline."

"Blood sample? Isn't a cheek swab enough these days?"

"Blood's always best. If you like, I could take a sample right now and we'll have the results back in a week. I have friends that can speed up the process for you, if you like."

"What's brought this about? I mean, I don't understand. Do I look like somebody you know? Please, I need an explanation." 'Flummoxed' barely covered the reeling sense of her world breaking into pieces.

"Exactly. You do look like them. At least the female line with the rare eye color you share. Here, I have a photo of a woman who would be your great-grandmother on your father's side."

Vanessa pulled out a black and white photograph from her top desk drawer, handing it to her. She stared down at an image that bore a distinct resemblance to her. Fair hair, same large eyes. Were they green and with a bright gold starburst? The picture suggested the oddity, though it was impossible to be certain without color. And the face shape was similar under the old-fashioned hairstyle.

"This isn't enough proof, I mean, we do look alike, but surely there must be more to your assertions?"

"Yes, of course. Your birthdate is August twenty-first. Born in nineteen ninety-three, right? And put up for adoption a few days after being born?"

Rebecca nodded, not trusting herself to speak.

"And your mother was a nanny? Spent time in England in 1992 and '93? Which was where she came into contact with your father, Henry Morgan Allman."

She stared at the woman, who seemed so sure of her facts. *Henry Morgan Allman.* The name seared instantly into her brain.

"That means my father's alive?"

"Unfortunately, no—car crash. I'm sorry to say you are the last of your line, if indeed, you are who I think you are."

"I don't know what to think—to say." She shook her head with dismay. She might have met her biological family. And now all hopes were dashed before she could even get her mind around the concept. It was too much.

"But I can find out for certain for you. Just a small blood sample is all that's required."

"Why bother? If I have no one left." A dismal sense of bitterness and defeat flowed through her, chilling her to the bone. Why share this if it didn't make any difference to her life? It just churned things up.

"I think it's always better to find out these things. You can at least know about yourself, like whether you would be prone to certain health conditions. That's important, right?"

Vanessa rummaged through another drawer on her desk, pulling out the tools for blood retrieval. "Here, let's at least take the time to find out. It won't cost you anything, but it might save your life or your children's one day. Give you a heads up on any possible inherited health issues."

"Sure, why not." She slumped down on a chair, her world spinning too much for her to grasp anything else. She let the woman tie the rubber tourniquet around her upper arm. Vanessa swabbed her inner elbow with an antiseptic swab, then placed the needle into a plumped-up vein, removing a full vial of the dark-red essence.

"I thought a few drops were enough."

"More will make the test go quicker and easier."

She frowned, not convinced but too discombobulated to object. She needed time to figure this out, to make sense of the mind-boggling news.

Her hostess pulled off the tourniquet and placed an alcohol-soaked cotton ball over the small puncture wound. "There, all done. Just hold this and I'll get a small bandage."

Great, now she would have to go back to the party with something everyone would ask about.

But the covering turned out to be nearly transparent.

"There. Good as new."

Definitely past time to send a few dozen frowny faces. She stared at the vial of red, then thought better of it, grabbing it off the desk and storing it in her small evening bag dangling from her shoulder. The room reeled a bit, then righted itself. *I need food. And I need Ash.*

"What are you doing?" Vanessa's angry tone broke into her thoughts.

She gave her a look meant to quell all objections. It was her life and her blood, hers to do with as she saw fit. *Enough of the crazy.* "Just taking back what's mine. I'm sorry, I'm not ready for this. Maybe another time. I need to think about it before I do anything so drastic." Just having the vial in her purse made her feel better. More in control.

"I thank you for your interest in me, Vanessa. Now, I need to get back to the party. The family will be wondering where I am."

"I was just trying to help." The polite words did not line up with the daggers she was shooting her way from eyes that had gone cold and hard like shiny reflective marbles. The reaction was extreme and made Rebecca even more uncomfortable. She wanted to shout, *it's my life, stay the hell out of it*, but she restrained herself, nodding only once and exiting the library.

She ran into the dowager speaking with a group of women. She joined them. Maybe she'd be in her usual fine form, keep her mind busy and away from the train wreck.

"Ah, Rebecca, your ears must be burning." The older woman playfully tugged on one of her ears, making them both smile, although Rebecca's felt wobbly. "I was just telling Delores all about you. How you are adding so much vigor to our Edward. He hasn't looked this virile in years. You are good for him, child. Best gird your loins, I think you're going to be in for it."

Rebecca glanced over at Edward, noting that he was talking with his son. They both looked strained. Were they still at odds? She didn't want to be the one creating any difficulties for their relationship, not with time running out for both of them. They all had to get their act together if they were going to make these last weeks count.

"I shared that you have a motorbike with my friends, and a few more want to take advantage of your generous offer to go for a ride. Sharon and Elsie are both wanting very much to join our group tomorrow, if you're up for it?" The two older women nodded.

"Sure. Why not." She pasted on a smile. "Would you excuse me, I need the ladies'."

She hurried away, eyes seeming to bore in to her from a number of directions. She slipped into the powder room and hurried into a stall, hanging her newly purchased black evening purse from the top hook on the back of the closed door by its silver chain strap. *Finally. Some breathing space.*

A slight noise made her look upward, just in time to catch a hand sneaking over the door to grab at her purse.

"Not my Lulu Guinness, you don't!" Rebecca slapped at the hand, struggling to pull up her underwear. A muffled curse sounded, followed by the click of heels running away. *A woman, eh?* By the time Rebecca was decently covered and able to exit the stall, the room was deserted.

After washing her hands, she exited the bathroom. She gave a quick look around for anyone looking guilty just in case they hadn't strayed too far. Nary a one fit the description though she squinted her eyes to show she was a woman to be reckoned with. The altercation had refueled her confidence and she rejoined the party with satisfaction. No one took advantage of Rebecca Fairfax. No one.

"You're looking decidedly stoked," Ash remarked.

"Yes. Just stopped a thief."

"What! Again?" His expression made a total one-eighty.

"Someone just tried to steal my purse over the bathroom door. I grabbed for it just in time. You didn't happen to notice anyone exiting the ladies just now?"

Their conversation was overheard by the dowager, who turned around to face them, chiming in, "I saw a couple of women leave the bathroom. Vanessa, our hostess, and another woman I don't know personally. Say, I had my purse stolen once. I was visiting the King's Arms, having requested a private room for myself and my male friend, when a thief tried to make away with my handbag. We were both in a state of déshabillé at the time and couldn't give chase, if you catch my drift. I was quite the looker in my younger days, you know."

She waggled her eyebrows in case anyone missed her meaning. But would Vanessa have gone so far as to steal Rebecca's blood back for testing? It sounded crazy, even with everything else that had gone on since she'd arrived in England. More likely the woman the dowager didn't know had tried to steal a designer bag. It had cost a fair amount and was a lovely piece.

"Well, you're safe now, beautiful." Ash caressed her shoulder, reviving the stunning memory of their recent interactions in the car. Her breath hitched. His grandmother raised her eyebrows but didn't comment.

"If I can have all your attention, please, Edward, the Duke of Piers, has an important announcement to make." Vanessa was striking the side of a heavy crystal glass, sending a tinkling sound reverberating throughout the room. She looked composed, not like she'd just tried to steal a Lulu Guinness bag. *She can't be the culprit, right?* It made no sense. A woman who could afford all those first editions would hardly need to steal a purse. Unless she was a kleptomaniac? But that would be chancy as well. *It has to have been the other woman.* Forcing her mind away from the dilemma, Rebecca waited, pretty sure of what was going to happen next. She mentally girded her loins. Now was not the time to embarrass the Piers family. Now was the time to be a grown-up and accept responsibility for her part in the charade.

Ash leaned down. "I'm sorry, Rebecca. I will make this all up to you, I promise."

She gave him a smile, waiting her cue.

"Rebecca, if you will join Edward?" Vanessa called out.

She moved to the front of the room where the pair were standing in front of a glorious old stone fireplace. The cedar log fastened over the hearth had a carved garland of roses trailing along the length of the huge beam. Perfect, if she had been there with the right man...

Edward came closer and held up a glass of champagne.

"I must say I never thought to be standing here tonight, having you all share in my happiness of announcing that this beautiful woman has consented to be my wife. Would you all please share in my blessing by drinking a toast to my soon-to-be wife, Rebecca Fairfax?"

"To Rebecca," a chorus of cheers broke out as the crowd toasted, sipped their champagne. She swallowed, a sudden lump in her throat taking her by surprise.

She managed to keep the smile pasted to her face and avoid looking anyone in the eyes. Thank goodness the moment in the spotlight quickly faded, with people going back to their conversations and partaking of the light supper just now appearing on tables set up to one side of the room. She wasn't hungry, but she was damned thirsty.

"Here, try this." Ash shoved a drink into her hand. Even Edward had deserted her, off somewhere. She caught a glimpse of the family lined up at the buffet tables.

"What is it?"

"Moonshine."

"What?" She gave him a look, catching a glimpse of a twinkle in his brown eyes.

"Brandy. You look like you need it."

"I do." She took a sip, appreciating the mellowness of the potent drink, and downed the rest of it with relish. "Thanks. It was good. Maybe not as good as moonshine, but it will do."

"Ever had real moonshine?"

"Hardly. I don't live in the southern states."

"I'm thinking of buying a stake in a business. A brewery. Perhaps you'd like to take a drive with me tomorrow and check it out? It's not far."

"I thought money was an issue for your family? That the castle required great sums just for upkeep alone?"

"It's a money pit, all right." He sighed. "But I need to come up with a new way to add more revenue. And distilleries are all the rage right now. Especially popular with the hipster crowd who enjoy a family-owned brewery creating specialty lines. We could have the tasting rooms right here at the castle, and they could purchase what they liked." His voice became more enthusiastic as he warmed to the subject.

"You know, that's a great idea! With the ambience the place has, adding a tour of brandy tasting or whatever it is you want to produce would add quite a lot of extra luster. I see a private label incorporating an image of the castle in its logo."

And what if she found the treasure to finance such a venture outright? She made up her mind to head back down to the dungeons. Go those final few feet and see if her theory was correct. Excitement filled her. It was having to stand around and wait that sucked. Xaviera St. Clair would not have wasted a second. A new thought popped into her head. Xaviera would have also enjoyed the tryst on the way over, perhaps adding something for Ash to make certain his needs were met. She forced her mind away from *that* image. *So not helping.*

"How soon until we can leave?" she asked.

"For the road trip? I'm thinking tomorrow after the motorbike rides."

"Good. But I meant tonight—this party?"

"Another half-hour or so. Would you like another brandy?"

"Please." She watched him stroll to the bar. She could watch him move about all day. He walked with a panther's grace, his long legs eating up the distance. She shook her head. It was good to be on the same wavelength, but oh boy, it was dangerous too.

"Still spending more time with the son than the father, I see." Vanessa moved like a damn phantom, suddenly at her side. It grated.

"Did you try to steal my purse?" Rebecca accused, facing the woman down. What did she have to lose? Being thrown out of the party did not seem half bad.

"Excuse me? Are you accusing me of being a damn thief?" Then the woman broke into peals of laughter. "I can buy and sell stock in the Lulu Guinness company anytime I want, sweetheart. I don't need to steal *anything.*"

"Well, someone tried to steal my bag not twenty minutes ago. In the bathroom. You don't happen to have cameras in there?"

"As it happens, I do. We can get to the bottom of this right now if you like?"

"Eww. Do you photograph women using the toilet?"

"Of course not. Just in the common areas. We rent out the main floor for events, which is why I had security cameras installed ages ago. Come. We'll check out the footage together."

"Okay. I should tell Ash where we're headed. He was getting me a drink."

"He can join us, if he wishes." Her dark eyes glittered under the thick bangs.

Ash was working his way through the crowd, carrying two brandy glasses.

"What's up?" he asked, glancing at the two of them.

"Rebecca accused me of trying to steal her handbag and I want to set the record straight."

"You did?" He gave her an odd look.

"Well, it was her or the other woman." She pressed her lips together.

"Come. I have footage we can check." Obviously, it hadn't been Vanessa or she wouldn't be so quick to prove it. She suddenly felt ashamed. The woman had only been nice to her. So why did she mistrust her the way she did? Gut instinct was the best she could come up with.

"That's okay. I see now that I was way off base. Please, accept my apologies, Vanessa. I was out of line. And no real harm done. I still have my purse." She patted it for emphasis.

"Thanks, I appreciate that. But I still want to see what happened. Who's to blame."

"Fine. Let's go take a look then."

They trooped off together, away from the milling crowd that had grown noisier in the past half hour. A jazz trio had begun to play near the fireplace, adding to the level of sound with everyone trying to talk over the music.

Vanessa escorted them to a room at the end of a long hallway and invited them inside.

"Here we are," she said with satisfaction. "The security room. I wished you had shared the attempted robbery with me sooner, Rebecca. I could have checked immediately, maybe caught the culprit right away. I don't like to think of someone like that in our midst. In my home."

Guilt dampened Rebecca's earlier enthusiasm. She wanted to get this over with and get back to the castle. She hated having stepped wrong. Calling her hostess a thief was right up there near the top of the list of things she'd regret for the rest of her natural-born life.

She couldn't even look at Ash, avoiding his inquiring looks that bored right into her, feeling an utter fool for her accusations.

"Hey." He leaned in close, making sure Vanessa couldn't overhear. "Don't feel bad. I'd suspect her too."

She choked on a snort of hysterical laughter she covered with a cough. But she did feel better.

"Ah, here we go." The professor moved to a bank of cameras and computers, using the touch screen to call up the information she wanted. "This is the footage from that ladies' powder room from an hour ago. Can't be more than that amount of time since it happened, right?"

Rebecca nodded. She viewed the screen's footage, watching the women come and go. A surprising number didn't wash their hands, making her queasy. Then she had the strange experience of watching an image of herself come into the facilities, open one of the stall doors and close it.

A couple of seconds later Vanessa popped in, washed her hands, then left. *Good to know.* Another woman came in, quite tall, who leaned over a sink, looking a bit dizzy and pale. Rebecca didn't recognize the woman.

The woman then pushed herself back from the sink and leaned up against the bathroom door that Rebecca was still behind, reaching over and holding onto the top of the door. She couldn't say one hundred percent for certain that the woman was involved in stealing her purse or just trying to hold herself upright. Then came the sound of her own voice shouting, "Not my Lulu Guinness, you don't!" The woman looked startled, then rushed out of the bathroom, with Rebecca taking the time to wash her hands before hustling after her.

"Well, that was interesting. That was Mary Chambers, a friend of the family. It's kind of hard to say for certain *what* she was doing. Could you have misconstrued her actions? She might have been trying to hold herself upright, by the look of things."

"It's possible." But something just didn't set right. She'd seen the hand creep over the top of the stall, making her dead certain the person was up to no good.

"Well, thank goodness that's cleared up." Vanessa looked pleased. She casually touched another spot on the screen and the same bathroom appeared on screen, only this time the image was from another angle. And two people were making out on the top of a sink. In fact, more than making out, the man's hips thrusting back and forth in a powerful action between the women's long legs, her face thrown back and visibly charged by sexual throes.

And the two people? Ash and Vanessa.

Chapter Sixteen

The future is much like the present, only longer.
— Don Quisenberry

Face burning from a rush of emotion, Rebecca swallowed hard, unable to tear her eyes away from the train wreck.

"My God, Vanessa, turn that fucking thing off!" Ash's mortified tone sounded a long way off, smothered by the roaring filling her head. A thousand insects buzzed, making her hold her hands up to her ears to dislodge them. But no amount of shaking her head could dislodge the annoying sound or the devasting image. Right there, right where she had just been, Ash and Vanessa had gone at it like a pair of damn rabbits.

She pushed past Ash, who reached out a hand as if to stop her, exiting the room in a whirlwind. Finding herself in the hallway, she could not face anyone. She raced toward the Entrance Hall that led outside. Hurrying past the uniformed guard, she rushed down the stone steps and stood at the bottom, surveying the manicured grounds. *Which way to go?* A path that led to an orchard looked inviting and she jogged along it, wanting nothing more than to disappear into the trees. If she were back in Canada, she'd head for her cottage at Delta Beach, curl up in front of the fireplace, drink wine and read a good mystery. Anything to blur the godawful image burning behind her retinas.

Why now? She swiped at the tears unexpectedly filling her eyes. *Just when things couldn't get any more hectic and weird, this had to be added.* She felt overloaded. Swamped by just too darn much information. The air turned cooler as the path led into the canopy of trees. She slowed her step, finding solace being alone in nature. She needed time. Time to sort things through. Time to know what to do next.

Coming across a bench, she sat, tucking her skirt around her legs and her hands under her thighs as she'd often sat as a child. The fragrance of blossoms scented the air, filling her with nostalgia. Her adopted grandparents had a farm in the Marquette area of Manitoba's Interlake. She'd spent summers there, helping with chores like those damn annoying chickens. She smiled lopsidedly at the memory, but her mind was unable to give up the ghost of what she had just witnessed, try as she might. The image was too stubborn, but now that the shock was receding, she found it one thing to know in theory that Ash and Vanessa had been together, but quite another to see the pair blatantly going at it like that. Why had that happened? Was Vanessa that angry at her for accusing her of being a thief? Jealousy seemed the additional culprit. She sighed. *A woman spurned and all that.* She hadn't accepted her help about finding out her birth father either. *Payback's a bitch, eh.* But partially deserved. After all, everyone had warned her that Ash was a playboy.

The sound of twigs snapping underfoot alerted her to company. She glanced in the direction of the noise, watching for movement among the fruit trees.

"Ah, there you are." Edward came from the opposite direction of the sounds she'd just heard. *Odd. Who or what caused the other noises?* "The family is about to leave and my son suggested you might be out here. Mind if I join you?"

"Sure." She scooted over to make room, happy to see him. At least helping this wonderful, caring man made sense, while his son could go to hades. She gave a final scan in the direction of the earlier sounds, then let it go. No movements were visible between the tree trunks.

"Lovely evening," he said, pressing a hand to his chest over his heart. His breath was a bit quick as well, making her look more carefully at him to see if he was in any distress.

"Are you all right?" She felt closer to him now, experiencing a deep urge to make his final days good ones. The engagement was the right thing to do. She had no doubt of it now.

"Fine, just need a moment to compose myself." He sat quietly, looking off into the trees. "I know my son can be quite an ass at times. Did he say something to upset you?"

She snorted, then realized how that sounded. "No. I just witnessed something from his past that startled me."

"Well, his past is rather checkered. You know about his breaking his engagement?" He shook his head, his lips pressed together disagreeably. His silver hair shone like a halo against the greenness of the trees and grass, making him look otherworldly in the gathering twilight.

"Yes, seems the thing to do, though. If one isn't certain of marriage," she added. She found that even under the circumstances, she wanted to defend Ash for something he wasn't guilty of. The broken engagement had not been his fault and likely the main cause of all this grief with his family over the years. He certainly had enough things that were his fault. Another flash of pain at the memory of what she had just witnessed cut to the bone.

"Well then, it's a good thing I'm so certain." He reached into his pocket, pulling out a small pill box. He popped the lid and placed one in his mouth, under his tongue. "Just for reassurance."

She swallowed hard, his words a grim reminder of death's door not being too far from opening for this man. Ash and Gracie's father, the dowager's son. It stirred something inside her, made her want to do something, anything to help.

"Ash is trying to turn over a new leaf, you know, not going out so much. He's quite taken with his new step-mum, I think."

She sputtered and near choked when she swallowed incorrectly. The thought of being Ash's step-mum was so far beyond the pale, it had been invisible to her eyes. *Till now.*

Edward began pounding on her back to relief the coughing fit. "There, there. You'll be all right, my dear. Just breathe."

"Thanks," she gasped, finally getting a full breath.

"I have had a good life. My children may not get this, but once you have them, take them into your arms, they become everything to you. I love my children, no matter what they do. I want to see them to be happy in this world. You'll understand once you have children of your own. If you ever decide to, that is."

"I imagine I will one day."

"My son was a rascal, always getting into things," he said the words with a half-smile, enjoying the memories. "Always had to know the why of things. How things worked. Quite a good mind." He took a deep breath. "He and Gracie were terribly affected by losing their mother so young. Especially Gracie. I think it's very hard to reassure a child that they're not to blame when their mother dies at birth, though Lord knows I've tried."

She shivered. "I can only imagine."

"Shall we head back?" he asked.

She took Edward's proffered arm. She found comfort walking through the orchard with him. One thing was abundantly clear in the muddle her life had become. She cared for this family, cared deeply about what happened — to most of them.

"My son's a good man, you know. Still looking for the right woman, but when he finds her, my money's on it being a forever kind of thing. That he'll give up his wandering eye and settle down for good. At least, that's what gets me through the bad days." Edward gave a half-laugh, patting her hand atop his arm.

"Well, for the sake of his future wife, I hope you're right."

"Ah, I see the dowager and Gracie about to leave. Care to join us?"

"Please." The last thing she was prepared to do was step into a car with Ash.

Speaking of the devil, she suddenly spotted his shining crop of rich brown curls above the crowd. Before he could get any closer, she dropped Edward's arm, hurried to the Rolls pulling up for the family and stepped inside soon as the driver drew the vehicle to a stop. She leaned back against the seat, grateful for the reprieve. No way was she going anywhere alone with Ash. *Never. Ever. Again.*

Edward followed her in, while the dowager and Gracie got in across from them. The seats faced each other, allowing for easy conversation.

"Lovely party, don't you think, Rebecca?"

She nodded. "Yes, quite enlightening."

"We must send Vanessa a thank-you note. Will you take care of it?"

"No worries." *Thanks for meddling in my life and turning it upside down.* That had a ring to it. She sighed.

"Tired, dear?" the dowager asked.

"It was kind of boring, grandmother. Rebecca would rather be doing other things, right? Like riding her motorbike. I can hardly wait for tomorrow. I call dibs on first ride." Gracie's eyes lit up with excitement.

"Sure, get up early and I'll take you into town," Rebecca promised. "Make all the villagers jealous."

"Oh, that's a fab idea!" Gracie squealed, making everyone else cringe.

"I prefer my zees. I'll catch you after you get back. Susan and Elsie can't come until after tea, anyway. An emergency church meeting's been called. Something about some vandalism at the rectory and a pair of valuable silver candlesticks that date back hundreds of years stolen. I hope it's not those demon-loving Satanists again."

Remembering whom Vanessa suspected could be her great-grandfather made Rebecca's heart thud. If she were indeed related to William G. Allman, it was close enough to the dark side to make her uncomfortable. *It can't be true, right?*

"What kind of vandalism?" she asked.

"Same old, I think. People having those awful ceremonies trying to call up demons. Such craziness. Did you take notice of the lovely flower arrangements, Rebecca? I think something of the like for your wedding."

"No, absolutely not." She didn't realize how that sounded until it was out of her mouth. But no way were her flowers going to reflect Vanessa's taste. *Calm down.* "I'm thinking something simpler. Fresher, like lilacs fresh-cut from the garden. Nothing too fancy."

"Yes, that does sound nice. Orchids are rather cloying when you get too many of them together. Stifling."

Rebecca looked out of the passenger window, catching a glimpse of Castle Piers' battlements. A lopsided moon hung above one corner. Another week and the moon would be full. An eeriness gave her pause once more when a finger of cloud slipped dark and ominous over the shining orb. A sensation overcame her similar to the one she'd had her first day riding over the jut of land. A prescient feeling that all was not what it seemed. She shook it off. It had been a far too eventful day, and it was not over yet.

After disembarking from the Rolls, she followed the family. In no time, the castle had become like a second home and the family a naturally extended adopted group. When the inevitable occurred, as unfortunately it must, she would be there for them. To help them with grieving the loss of the patriarch. It was the least she could do, considering their kindness to her, a stranger.

"Want a game of chess?" Gracie asked.

Worried that Gracie's brother might be home any second, and yet not wanting to turn down the young girl's request, Rebecca paused, giving a quick look around for the second car. *Just give me time to slip inside.*

"If you're too tired, that's okay." The young girl gave her a wide-eyed look that captured her heart all over again.

"No, sure, I'd love a game. It's early yet." She laid an arm over Gracie's frail shoulders and hugged her.

"Great. I'll set up the board." Gracie took off at a gallop, hurrying inside and in the direction of the library, where they'd played the last few nights.

"That child has taken a shine to you, Rebecca," the dowager remarked, standing on the steps leading into the castle. She was right. Gracie's hundred and eighty-degree shift in her attitude was one of the best things that had happened of late. "But I'm headed to bed. Quite exhausted from the day. It was a lovely party, Edward. Congratulations to you both. Thanks for making my family so happy, my dear." She kissed Rebecca on the cheek. The sweet words and gesture tugged at Rebecca's heart, the soft fragrance of face powder filling her lungs. She pressed her lips together to avoid spoiling the moment by saying something untoward.

No Ash yet, thank goodness.

"I'll see you in the morning, dear." Edward gave her a quick kiss on the cheek. She barely noticed, watching the driveway from the perimeter of her vision. She detected distinct sounds of a motor. *Is that him?*

Her heart jumped and she chewed on her bottom lip. She needed to get inside, not be discovered standing around. But she was reluctant to move, hating how it now stood between them. If nothing else, they needed to establish a truce. They could hardly avoid seeing each other these next few days, not if they were going to make sure the family was okay. And that should be their number one goal.

The sounds were not Ash's car arriving home, however, but one driven by Sloan. Rebecca sighed, catching a glimpse of the woman driving into the courtyard. *Well, so be it.* They would just have to carry on the way everyone else seemed to manage quite well in this place—pretend that nothing untoward had happened.

She hurried inside and made for the library with a determined stride. She had a game of chess to play. And possibly lose. Gracie had a clever mind.

"You still don't have your engagement ring back?" Gracie asked casually, though she was staring at the chess board intently, waiting for Rebecca to make her next move.

She clasped her hands together, looking at her bare fingers. *At least one thing to be grateful for.* "Yeah, I guess the jewelers were busy."

"You know he likes you, right?" Gracie raised one eyebrow, then made a move that instantly put her on the defensive, closing in on Rebecca's queen.

"Who, Edward? I should hope so. We're getting married soon." She stared at the board. Gracie had her on the ropes. Again.

A big sigh made Rebecca look up and she caught a look of derision. "*Duh*, Ash, my brother, remember him? He's also got a crush on you. And I think you like him. But don't worry. I won't tell Daddy."

Her stomach roiled. *Since when did twelve-year-olds get so smart?*

"It's not like that." But it was exactly like that. How could she forget the infamous car ride? Before she was faced with the brutal evidence of his liaison with Vanessa. Well, it had to have been lust. Nothing else could explain it. And it was time to steer this conversation in a different direction.

"So, you want to stand up with me, Gracie? Be my maid-of-honor?" The words spilled out before she had time to think better of them. *Please let me be doing the right thing.* The situation felt so volatile.

The young girl's eyes widened. "Really? How about your friends? The Ringers you're always talking about?"

The very ones she had not been entirely truthful with, not letting them know exactly how far this whole thing had gone. If she had, they'd all be on the castle's doorstep, clamoring for an intervention, because there was no way in hell they'd approve of her actions since she'd arrived at the castle. There was so much she hadn't told them, couldn't tell them. And soon, she would be a widow. The horrid idea popped up from the dark recesses of her mind. *Oh my God.* That didn't seem possible. She thrust the idea aside as nausea threatened to overtake her.

"They'll understand," she said, calming Gracie's worries while opening a big chasm of it at her own feet. Just how much longer could she continue to keep this from them? But it served Ash right she was marrying his father — he had made it abundantly clear that his interests lay elsewhere. Or at least until quite recently. But no comfort to be had there.

Ash stood and watched his sister and Rebecca play chess, not wanting to interrupt the sweet scene. He'd caught the tail end of the conversation, his breath stilling in his lungs, aware of how incredible Rebecca was being for his family. She could have run for the hills by now. *Should have.* Left them in her dust. Instead, here she sat, playing chess with his sister who badly needed a female to look up to. When looking back at the entire line of women who had warmed his bed, there was not one he'd want to spend time with Gracie. No one but Rebecca. His mind filled with the look on her beautiful face when she'd caught the image of him and Vanessa on the stored video feed. Horrified and disappointed summed it up. It hurt like hell to think he was responsible for that. She deserved so much better. And he only had himself to blame.

At that moment, Rebecca turned and glanced his way. Their eyes locked and hers widened with intensity before narrowing, accusing him of vile deeds. He deserved that. He'd take his lumps to get back into her good books. And he had time to do it. At all the promised family events for these next few days, he would be on his best behavior. Show her that he could be trusted. That he wanted to change and be a better man. *For her.*

"Ash," Gracie called out.

"Hey, Gracie," he said, clearing his throat and advancing a few steps into the room.

Rebecca remained silent, staring down at the chess board.

"Guess what?" Gracie asked, her eyes alight with suppressed excitement.

"You're going to play the lead role in the next ballet recital? As a flying unicorn?"

"Yeah, and I eat rainbows for dessert. No, silly, I'm going to be the maid of honor for Daddy and Rebecca's wedding." Gracie clapped her hands together like she'd done as a small child, making his heart squeeze painfully. He rubbed at his chest with one hand, trying not to let his smile falter. His father had let this happen, not sharing details of his illness with his own daughter. Now her happiness would all too soon be followed by grief and there was nothing he could do about it. He swallowed past the lump in his throat and made himself stay in the moment. Gracie would need him now more than ever.

"That's great, sweetheart. How's the chess game going?" He advanced farther into the room, moving up to stand behind Gracie's chair. He peered down at the board.

"I've got her on the ropes," Gracie crowed, her face filled with delight.

He watched Rebecca make a cautious move, that Gracie immediately trounced, shouting, "Checkmate!"

"You got me fair and square. Good game, sweet pea." Rebecca avoided looking his way, endowing his sister with a spectacular smile. A smile that lit up her whole face like a chorus of angels were singing in the distance, anointing her. He wanted that smile to be directed his way, but knew he had not earned the right. *Maybe one day…*

"You want some hot chocolate, Gracie?" Rebecca asked.

"Yes. Do you want some, Ash?"

"Who in their right mind ever turns down hot chocolate, especially if it's got mini marshmallows melting into it? Am I right or am I right? That is, if I'm not intruding? And I get to make it."

Rebecca gave him the evil stink-eye, not backing down an inch.

"Duh, of course you're invited!" Gracie got up and hugged him, leading him toward the kitchen. He glanced back and caught Rebecca reluctantly following them. *Good. It's a start.*

Chapter Seventeen

The more he talked of his honor, the faster we counted our spoons. — Ralph Waldo Emerson

Damn him. Acting like butter wouldn't melt in his mouth. Happy as a tick on a fat dog. Awful clichés, but so darn apt.

She'd never been caught between a rock and a harder place. No instruction manual existed that she knew of on how to handle such a flaunting of...of... She couldn't even come up with the right zinger of a word for it. All she could do was take a deep breath, gird her loins and head into the fray. *Nothing else for it.* Ash had hurt her. Badly. Seeing him and Vanessa — there was no coming back from that.

She couldn't imagine facing her. *What is that woman thinking? Showing me that?* She narrowed her eyes, considering. That could not have been an accident. It was a set-up, pure and simple. Done to make her feel bad. It had worked, all too well. Colored everything that had just begun between her and Ash in a horrid shade of *yuck*.

Well, she'd just focus on the getting through the next few weeks, helping the family cope with all the changes happening and about to happen in their lives. It was the best thing she could do. And, as soon as possible, slip down to the tunnels and find out what lay beneath Castle Piers. The excitement of sleuthing out the treasure and getting the artifact before Professor Masters might be the only things helping keep a lid on this situation, by giving her something to look forward to. She reluctantly followed the pair, shaking her head all the way, thinking of the unbelievable path she'd placed herself on since arriving at the castle.

"You want to get us three mugs from the cupboard, Rebecca?" Ash asked, looking up from his self-appointed role of making hot chocolate at the gas stove. The very one she'd nearly set the castle on fire with. The mess had been entirely cleared away, as if nothing had happened. There was no real damage done, it appeared, though a new pair of oven mitts lay on the counter and fresh curtains hung at the window. She was about to say she didn't need any of the hot drink when she caught sight of Gracie. All smiles, seated at the island in the kitchen, waiting for her cup of chocolate. She looked twelve going on five. Adorable, swinging her long colt-like legs out from the stool she perched on.

"Uh, sure." She rummaged around in the cupboard that Gracie pointed at, finding three huge mugs that bore the family crest.

She set the mugs on the counter near Ash, careful not to get too close. She went and sat next to Gracie. *Note to self: only spend time with Ash when others are present.*

"I had no idea you could cook." She admired the deft way he heated the cocoa and cream with the sugar to avoid scorching or lumps, stirring the mixture constantly at a lower heat. Most men used too much heat in the kitchen, thinking high heat equated to the best setting. *Bad idea.*

"There's lot of things you don't know about me, beautiful," he said with that annoying smugness surfacing again.

"It's the only thing he makes. That's why he's good at it," Gracie interjected. She made a *gotcha* face at him.

"Now don't be giving away all my secrets, young lady, or I might need to mention a couple of yours. People in glass houses shouldn't throw stones is a real thing. In fact, I can think of —"

"It's not a stone if it's true." Gracie trumped his card with her spot-on logic.

"You got me there, sweetheart." Ash poured the sweet nectar of the gods into the three mugs, adding marshmallows to top them up. He set a cup in front of each of them and waited for them to taste it.

"Delicious. Thanks." Rebecca reluctantly gave her review as it became apparent he was waiting for it, not even trying his own share. The man was too darn good at what he chose to do. That was one of his faults.

"Thanks. I've made it a lot over the years for us."

"It's good." Gracie's white and chocolate mustache made her smile. She looked up to catch Ash staring down at her.

His mouth twisted in a grin.

"What?"

"You got marshmallow on your lip."

She pulled a paper napkin from the dispenser and dabbed at her mouth.

"Better?"

He came closer and used his finger to swipe at her lip before she could duck, his eyes meeting hers once more. An unfathomable look deep inside his irises made it hard to look away.

"There, all gone."

"Thanks." She swallowed. The soft touch, his warm finger, all reminded her of earlier in the evening. Her body buzzed with too many sensations. *Hold on to the anger. That'll help.*

They sipped their chocolate in silence. Rebecca drank hers quickly, then hurried to rinse the mug in the sink before adding it to the dishwasher.

"I'm off to bed. Don't forget about our plans for tomorrow, Gracie."

"I won't."

"I'll take you to see the brewery right after. When do you figure that will be?" Ash asked.

"Sorry. I don't think that's possible. My whole day's booked up." *Thank God.* "After Gracie, I promised the dowager and her friends rides."

She glanced at him. Was that a trace of sadness in his eyes?

"Fine. Maybe another time."

"Yeah, maybe. Pretty busy getting ready for the wedding. Don't let me hold you up from doing *whatever* it is you need to do. I've got my own plans." She gave a fake smile, then left the room without checking the result of her zingers.

She made her way back to the library to retrieve her purse holding the blood sample, then headed upstairs to her bedroom. Once inside, she tucked the vial of blood into a dresser drawer, covering it with a T-shirt. *Maybe I should just throw it away?* Then she decided it could wait until later. She resolutely walked to the bathroom to shower and wash away the sins of the day. *Just keep moving.* Feeling refreshed ten minutes later, she donned her comfy old robe and sat cross-legged on the bed, laptop computer open. *Time to go to work.*

Her fingers raced across the computer keys, looking for everything she could find on William G. Allman and his ancestors. Two hours later, blurry-eyed, she sat back, staring into space. It had been pretty much already what she knew from her extensive reading. There didn't seem to be anything more to connect her to his bloodline. Maybe the professor had been off-base? Everything Rebecca had found was circumstantial, nothing that would hold up in court. She thought about the blood sample hidden in the drawer. *No.* That was taking things way too far. She didn't want to know that badly. At least, not yet.

She was far more interested in the Piers' family connections anyway. She brought up the e-files she'd collected pertaining to their ancestry and scanned the information for the tenth time. *Yes.* All of it pointed to what she was now almost certain of. Solomon's treasure lay beneath them, a long line of protectors having guarded it over the centuries.

She checked the time. One in the morning. Too late to go down there now. But tomorrow, after she'd finished with the dowager's crew, she'd find the time.

After shutting the lid of her laptop, she snuggled under the bedcovers, asleep almost before her head hit the pillow.

What are they chanting? Words came at her, but nothing made sense. She strained harder. She understood other languages. French from her bilingual classes at high school,

Spanish from university, but this sounded ancient. Very formal. Latin?

The repetition of sounds drilled into her mind, filling her body with an icy dread.

Sanguis in virtute. Sanguis in virtute. Sanguis in virtute.

What did it mean? It sounded ominous, like a chorus for an exorcism. Her stomach roiled, filling with writhing knots. Nausea threatened. She moaned aloud, trying to escape the gauzy spider's web of the dream. Wake up.

She sank deeper into the dream instead. The scene became more detailed. Undeniably real.

Black-robed figures appeared through the hazy mist, surrounding her and keeping up the horrid chanting. One held a chalice high overhead, their white bony forearms catching the shadows and light from flickering candles.

She realized she was lying down, that the bed beneath her had changed. It was now hard, like stone. The odor of damp and mildew assaulted her nostrils. Where am I? Have I been kidnapped? This was too real. She needed to wake up.

Sanguis in virtute. Sanguis in virtute. Sanguis in virtute.

A flash of light glinted off a dagger held by another black-robed figure. She followed the knife with her eyes, unable to move, struggling against whatever held her in its grasp. She found she couldn't move even the tiniest bit, try as she might. Paralyzed. The weapon moved over her head. She wanted to scream. To get away.

The knife descended in a terrifying arc.

Down.

Down.

Down it came in slow surreal motion.

The sensation of sharpness slicing into her flesh, into an artery. Hot blood spurting out, soaking her.

She awoke in a panic and turned on the lamp on the night table. She checked around the room. Yes, she was still in her bedroom in the castle. *Thank you, God.* She took a few deep breaths to steady herself. The dream had been too real, the words from the chant still branded in her mind. They came rushing back with a vengeance. *Sanguis in virtute.* What did it mean?

The time on the bedside clock registered. Three a.m. She'd only been asleep a short time, but now she was too wired to fall back to sleep right away. She stared at the ceiling, willing her heart rate to slow down. It didn't take a dream therapist to explain what had caused the dream. The last couple of weeks had been off-the-charts crazy. But there was something she could check on. She sat up and grabbed her laptop.

Sanguis in virtute. Blood is the power. *Yuck. Not nice. But perhaps understandable after the day I've had. Ha. All those ominous figures represented all Ash's ex-girlfriends.*

Calmer now, she checked her email for new messages. *What?* There was one from Vanessa. *The nerve of that woman after the stunt she pulled.*

Please accept my apologies for the way I acted tonight. No way to excuse myself, except to say that I guess I fell for Ash. Thought we had more going on between us than we did. Please, can you find it in your heart to forgive me? I don't deserve it, but I want to make this up to you. You were so kind to help Susan and my brother Ian. They feel so much better now about adoption after talking with you. Some lucky young person will have a great future home, thanks to you. I would love to take you to lunch sometime –

Okay, Vanessa, that's pushing things a bit –

perhaps next week before your wedding? Anyway, think about it. Regards, Vanessa.

Hmm. She had a cheek. But a part of Rebecca understood. Ash was one major distraction. When he looked at her, she thought she was the only woman on the planet. It stood to reason others would feel the same way, caught in the charming net he was so adept at throwing. And he did have that reputation. He'd truly reaped what he sowed. *So why did I have to get dropped in the middle of it?*

She powered down her laptop without answering the message. *Best to sleep on it.*

* * * *

"Is everything ready for the ceremony, your highness?"

The sorceress looked up from reading the ancient grimoire to give her assistant a stern stare through her falcon's head mask representing the Egyptian god Horus. She did not appreciate the interruption, even though it had been asked with proper reverence for her exalted position. Lately she felt driven by an unseen power, most likely the golden angel, pushing everything along in an elaborate filial dance which ended with herself. She had been warned by the entity to be content with the one vision, though she had many unanswered questions. But time was drifting through her hands like grains of sand through the hourglass, and her final push to achieve earthly glory had to be now, or she would lose her chance, and the opportunity for her followers, the promise of immortality. Forever. That thought was beyond horrifying.

"Of course."

"Excellent."

"Is there anything more I can do for you, your highness?"

"Just see that all is ready and prepared. Time's running out. The moon is gibbous right now, growing larger, the best time to cast a spell. And summer solstice is almost upon us."

"I'll take care of it." The woman pressed her lips tightly together. "What do you think of the candlesticks I brought you?" She made a nod toward her gift. The woman was becoming too needy. And too familiar. She needed to keep her distance from earthly annoyances if she was to bring everything to its zenith at the proper moment. She made a difficult decision at that second. After they carried their current plans to fruition, she would think of a way to let her assistant down easily. She wasn't to be one of the chosen ones.

"Stealing them from the church was bad form. What if it's traced back to us?"

The young woman shook her head adamantly. "No way they can be. I took precautions. They'll think it's the usual hooligans. I'll keep the items out of sight. They're perfect for the ceremony, right?"

"Yes. They'll do."

"Do! They're ancient. And they were once used by the sorcerer himself. Surely they will increase the power during the ceremony?"

"They're important, yes." She didn't bother to say that their use by the exalted man was just a rumor, never confirmed. "But not as important as the knowledge. I need to finish reading this." She pointed at the ancient text.

A pout pushed her assistant's plush bottom lip out. She inwardly sighed. She needed her full cooperation for the upcoming week. There was too much to manage all on her own.

"Come here." She beckoned the younger woman with a curling forefinger, slipping easily into seduction mode.

Her assistant came forward, and she held out her arms to embrace her. Kissed her on the cheek.

"Okay then, I'll leave you to your reading." Mollified, the woman left her alone.

Am I losing my touch? The thought floored her — she'd always found it easy to enlist cooperation from her crew.

The sorceress went back to rereading the passage she had been perusing when she was rudely interrupted, but her mind wouldn't cooperate. She opened the top desk drawer, took out her prescription bottle half-filled with lithium, then changed her mind and put it back. It would only dim the growing excitement. She needed to keep her mind clear, now more than ever. Besides, she hadn't taken it for weeks and she felt fine, had even been blessed with the amazing vision that directed her very existence. The doctors were likely far too cautious, insisting she needed to stay vigilant, take her meds every day. What did they know anyway? The damn drugs just took the edge off her creativity. Kept her from tapping into her unconscious where the golden answers lay.

Ah. The time of the Prophet of the New Aeon lay directly ahead. Speaker of the truth of Horus. The proof of Satanism being linked to ancient Egyptian roots. If she could become the new Seeress, she could tap into the most ancient supernatural presence on earth. Have access to ancient knowledge. And, best of all, channel the power of demons, control them to do her bidding.

She was on the cusp of discovering the secrets of immortality. *Then I will be unstoppable.*

She took a satisfying deep breath, imagining the upcoming ceremony. She needed to get every detail correct. Nothing could be allowed to go wrong this time. She refocused on the passage in the grimoire — it was time to channel all her energies to the task. The clock was ticking. Loudly.

Chapter Eighteen

No one can make you feel inferior without your consent.
— Eleanor Roosevelt

"Oh, did you see that?" Gracie asked, brown hair flying out from under her helmet, her voice nearly blown away by the wind turbulence created by the motorcycle. "Those guys are mega jealous!"

Rebecca smiled, loving the exuberance. The young girl had stopped wearing such heavy eyeliner these past days, making her look closer to her age, and making Rebecca hope she'd managed to improve something at the castle. Even if Vanessa wasn't one of Rebecca's favorite people, she'd been right about one thing—Gracie did need someone female in her life to offset the zaniness of others who would remain unmentioned.

Rebecca had shared a confidence with Gracie that she had one of those faces, one so classically pretty with fabulous bone structure, that she didn't need heavy make-up. All perfectly true of course. She hated to see a young girl feel she needed to hide herself, no matter what nature had endowed her with. As far as she was concerned, all women were beautiful, naturally. Of course, that didn't mean she was giving up her favorite lip gloss anytime soon. *A gal has to have some standards.*

They were travelling down the main drag of the small village, watching for a place to stop at for lunch.

"There!" Gracie poked her in the back. "Serendipity's open. I love their hamburgers and French fries."

Rebecca pulled into a slot right in front and cut the motor.

"A girl after my own heart. Though maybe I should be eating a salad. I ate too much last night. Sloan's Rocky Road Brownies are going to be the death of me." Rebecca gave a pretend moan, rubbing her stomach.

"I had three. You only managed two. Don't worry, you'll still fit into your wedding dress."

The thought sobered her. *Only six days until the wedding.* It had been moved up by the duke's request, and it loomed over her, a dark cloud that refused to dissipate.

A sudden hug and a kiss on the cheek took her by complete surprise. "Thanks for being my new step-mum."

The young girl skipped away, swinging her shiny red helmet by the chin strap. The world soft-focused. Rebecca blinked back tears, a lump forming in her throat. Oh boy, that had caught her off-guard.

She followed Gracie into the café, feeling like the biggest fraud ever. She had no intention of sticking around once her contract expired. But the whole funny side of Edward being so taken by her that he'd planned their wedding based on a single kiss did not seem funny anymore—if it ever had. The pair of them were setting up false premises and it wasn't right. She had to either step up and set this straight, or pull the plug now, before anyone got hurt. *No, too late for that.* Gracie would be hurt. They had just begun to bond, really bond, ever since the Teddy Bears' Picnic. Looking at the beautiful young girl standing at the counter preparing to order their food made her heart squeeze, and a second time even more painfully when Gracie turned her head, gifting her with a wide, innocent smile.

She caught movement out of the corner of her eye, just before she was knocked into by a large flailing body. She fell against a counter. Hard.

"Beggin' your pardon, missy." The words were slurred. The older man who'd fallen against her was either drunk or having a health crisis.

She righted herself, knowing she'd have some bruising on her side later where she had hit the counter top.

"Are you all right?" she asked, running a hand through her hair to smooth it back from her face. *Is he having a stroke?*

"So sorry, fine." The odor of alcohol permeated the air, relieving her concern, the cause for the altercation now obvious.

"Earl, get the hell out of here! I told you not to come back in here today." An employee came around the end of the counter, confronting the man. Rebecca moved away, wanting nothing more than to sit and gather herself. *Earl.* The name was familiar. Yeah, the drunk on the street the day she'd met Vanessa for lunch. The memory further soured her stomach.

"Are you okay, miss?" the employee asked after shooing the man back out the door. "I apologize for that. Do you need any medical help?"

"I'm fine. I just need to sit."

"Of course. I'll get you some water."

She joined Gracie, who stood staring in horror at her, not having moved away from the counter.

"I'm okay. Let's just sit."

They found a table near the windows and Rebecca slumped into it, wincing at the sudden pain in her side.

"Are you sure you're okay?" Gracie looked worried, her mouth set in a grim line. She pulled out her phone and sent a quick text.

The employee brought Rebecca a glass of water and she downed half of in one large gulp. It helped steady her, and she gave the young girl a smile.

"Really, I'll be fine. More surprised than anything."

"Yeah, that sucks. That Earl guy's a menace."

"He's just sick, sweetheart. Addiction makes people their puppet. In his right mind, I'm sure he'd be horrified at what happened."

"Maybe." Gracie didn't look convinced, her pretty face strained. She was a sensitive young girl. The knowledge drove the guilt pangs deeper.

Their food arrived, but Rebecca's appetite had vanished, and she just picked at the plate of food. Grace barely touched hers either.

A few minutes later, the door banged open and Ash raced in, gave a quick look around, then hurried over to their table. His look of concern was sincere and touching. And unwanted.

"Rebecca! Are you okay?"

"I'm fine. Don't worry. I can take a little tumble and keep on ticking."

He slipped into the booth beside her, giving her his thorough attention. "Are you sure you aren't hurt? What were they thinking—letting drunks in here? A family restaurant?"

"Shush, it's not their fault who shows up at the door. No one meant it to happen."

He raked a hand through his hair. "Well, it's still not right."

"I need to use the washroom." Gracie got up, still looking pale, and walked away.

"I should check on her." Rebecca moved to get up, but Ash was in her way, blocking the entrance to the booth.

"She's fine. It's you I'm worried about. We're going to call this whole thing off. Today. This crazy thing has gone far enough."

A sense of déjà vu hit hard. And something else, far more important. Did she want to call the whole thing off? She cared very much for Gracie—heck—for the whole Piers clan, including Ash with all his foibles. Maybe especially for Ash. Not good. But for some reason fate had set her up here in England and she needed to see it through. The biggest question of all, the one she had only skirted briefly in her mind, was would she be staying after the fallout? *But how can I not stay? That's when they will need me the most. Ash included.*

"No. I'm going to see this through." She nodded her head vigorously. "It's important."

"You don't have to do that, unless that's been your plan all along."

She ignored the dig. "Yes, I do. You know what Gracie said to me today?"

"No, I have no idea."

"She thanked me for becoming her step-mum." She choked on the words, her throat tightening at the memory.

Ash's face paled. "My God, I had no idea what all of this was going to cause. It's a bloody minefield. But you can't just marry a man you don't love, Rebecca."

"Lots of women marry men they don't love. And it's not as if it's forever." She wanted to take the words back as soon as she said them. The thought registered, straining Ash's expression further.

"But what about after? Will you stay then? Gracie's only twelve. Are you willing to help her through her teenage years? Immigrate to England and all that will take? It will change your entire life, beautiful. I don't think you realize what you're letting yourself in for." He shook his head, his expression grim.

"Yes. I get it. I can do this. It's the right thing to do and I want to do it." Even as she spoke, doubts remained. But she would overcome them. *Anything is possible if you just believe.* The words of her grandma soothed her, gave her the courage.

Silence.

Then Gracie bounced into view, looking much better.

"Now, if you'll excuse me, I'm going to take Gracie home."

"No, I'll drive you. You may still be unsteady and no way will I let you take a chance like that."

"Fine."

Her phone chimed, announcing an incoming text. She groaned when she glanced at it. *Not again. Vanessa.* That woman could not leave well enough alone.

Please let me throw you a hen party before your wedding. There are women in the district you should meet and I would be pleased to do this for you. Please don't say no. It will be fun, I promise. V.

"By the look on your face, I'd hazard a guess that's not good news."

"Vanessa wants to throw me a hen party before the wedding." She'd never talked to Ash about the videotape evidence that Vanessa had so thoughtfully provided, knowing in hindsight it was a vindictive action on the woman's part. And it wasn't as if she didn't know about his legendary pursuits. Just having it pushed in her face was a whole other thing.

Ash had the grace to wince. He chewed on his bottom lip, capturing her full attention. It sent her spiraling backward in time to the memory of how wonderful they tasted. How warm and enticing the entire package was. Well, that was all over now. The thought hurt more than she cared to admit, but she pushed it away. She had an important course to take. A path that meant no straying away from the straight and narrow for the foreseeable future. Live a life bigger than just herself and her beloved Ringers. Oh boy, telling them would be the hardest part of all. But they would understand. A woman does what she must when called upon. And surely as God created the rain, she had been called upon this time, to do the right thing. And Brass Ringers always tried to do the right thing, no matter the cost.

"Well, you can always refuse. I'm certain she'd understand, considering her actions. I'm so sorry about that." He gave her a look of anguish, his brown eyes dark with the pain. "I'm equally at fault. But if it helps, what little there was between Vanessa and me, it's all over now. She was a diversion, nothing more."

213

"No, I think rising above is the answer." She ignored the intel, none of it being her business anyway. What Ash did with his spare time was his problem. She ignored the sense of relief the news gave her. "It's the ideal opportunity to meet more women my age in the neighborhood. And it just might be fun." *Okay, the last part might be pushing it.*

"I don't think I've ever met anyone quite like you." He looked conflicted, as though he was entirely uncertain of his next step. So much left unsaid hung between them, almost too much to bear.

"Well, I get to stay in this country and live in a magical castle. Hardly a sacrifice." *Just not with the right prince.*

"Hey, hurry up, guys!" Gracie called out, waiting by the side of the Rolls.

Ash fished out the key fob from his pants pocket, pushing the unlock symbol to let his sister inside.

"Well, I think you're very special, like no one I've met before." He rubbed the back of his neck, his eyes somber.

"Thanks. So are you."

"Me? Hardly. Somehow I've managed to keep you entangled in this mess."

She reached up and touched his cheek. A smoldering passion flared deep in his eyes, and she swallowed hard. She had to look away, the flames threatening to consume her, make her do the wrong thing. "Don't be so hard on yourself. You did all you could. No one could have seen this coming."

"If there's anything I can do, anything you need, just ask, okay?"

It sounded so final. Certain her heart had just cracked wide open and her life's blood was pouring out of the mortal wound, she gave a perfunctory smile and climbed into the passenger side of the vehicle. It was best to just get on with things. There was nothing else for it. Too bad doing the right thing had to hurt so damn much. She pressed her hand to her chest, trying to ease the phantom pain.

"Am I invited to the hen party?"

Rebecca gave Ash a quick glance. He shrugged.

"I don't know, sweetheart. Not sure what Vanessa has planned. It might be an adults only night."

"I have to be there! The step-daughter has to be at the all female party to celebrate a wedding. It's written in the constitution, I think."

Rebecca couldn't hold back a chuckle. "It is, is it?"

"And Daddy has to have a party too. Ash, as his best man, you should be putting it on, right?"

"I don't know, Gracie. There's so little time left."

"I hope I never get so old I can't manage a party."

Rebecca didn't need to turn around to know a pout was forming on Gracie's pretty face.

"I'll think about it." Ash's crisp tone effectively ended the conversation.

Silence descended. Rebecca spent the time sending a text to Vanessa, asking about Gracie. Better to have a non-drinking party anyway. Right now, given the chance, she might tie one on and that would be a complete total disaster.

Pleased you are taking me up on my offer to make amends. I won't let you down. Unfortunately, its not for Gracie. All adult fun. V.

"Vanessa says the party is adults only. Don't worry, I'll make it up to you," she said to take the sting out of it.

"Yeah, how?" The pout was still obvious through the interest.

"Don't know yet, but I promise to come up with something fun."

"There's probably a male stripper or two, if it's adults only." Ash's tone was part teasing, part serious and a touch annoyed.

"I should be allowed to go," Gracie cajoled. "I can look eighteen and borrow a fake ID."

"No way, young lady." Her brother put his foot down.

Rebecca sighed. It so did not sound like fun. More like an endurance contest. *How am I going to get through this week?*

"You okay?" Ash asked, turning the Rolls onto the road leading to the castle.

She shrugged, muttering, "Sure. It's going to be interesting, if nothing else."

Ash sat too close. Every breath she took brought the intoxicating fragrance of him deep into her lungs, an outdoorsy fresh scent with undernotes of pure male essence that spoke to her on such an elemental level her body was in a constant state of arousal. It made her feel as though she was cheating on Edward, even though she had no intention of acting on it.

The castle came into view, its high stone walls a reminder of how it could be a sanctuary or a prison, depending on perspective. And right now, it was beginning to feel like the latter. *Not a good sign.*

He had never before experienced such a life-sucking quagmire. He'd always gotten pretty much what he wanted, been indulged even as the only male heir. And now, when the outcome mattered to him, he was at a loss for what to do. The realization was sinking in that his father and the woman he was falling in love with were getting married. This coming week was going to be excruciating torture, of the absolute worst kind. And he had to participate, whether he wanted to or not. Rebecca needed him. His family needed him. He couldn't just pull a vanishing act and find some female to shack up with. He had to suck it up. Well, if Rebecca could put a good face on it, so could he. But if only there was some way to stop it, he'd do it in a heartbeat.

He parked the car, cutting the motor.

"Grandmother's going to be disappointed," Gracie said. "The bike's still in town and she was *so* looking forward to a ride today. Bragging to all her friends this morning."

"I'll make it up to her." Rebecca promised, giving his sister a look of reassurance before opening the passenger door and getting out.

He watched the pair stroll off together, arm-in-arm, the sunlight glinting off Rebecca's fair hair and his sister's rich brown locks until both women vanished from sight. He swallowed hard. He was the bigger loser in this unfair situation and it ate at his soul.

Chapter Nineteen

Good things happen to those who hustle. — *Anaïs Nin*

Rebecca escaped to her bedroom. She needed some time to reflect. To gather herself.

The first thing she noticed was a dresser drawer pulled open, all the items removed. The one that had held the vial of blood.

What the hell?

She rushed over to the dresser and peered inside. The bottom was wet, obviously freshly scrubbed. *What had happened?*

A knock at the door and she hurried to answer it. Sloan, carrying a bundle of clothing.

"Do you know anything about this? I had a vial inside this dresser drawer and it's gone now."

"Yes, it leaked all over the place. Disgusting mess. I just washed and dried all the items it bled into."

Stymied, Rebecca rocked back on her heels. Sloan dropped her load on the bed.

"Oh, I'm sorry about all the extra work."

"No matter. But what on earth were you doing with a vial of blood?"

"It's a long story." She sighed. *Figures the blood would continue to contaminate my life.*

"I would imagine. Not many people keep such a thing around."

"It's not what you think. It was for DNA testing."

"I thought just a cheek swab was enough." Sloan shook her head, her dark eyebrows knitted.

"Yeah, me too. Someone had other ideas."

"Well, it's cleaned up now."

"Yes, thank you." *Odd that it leaked. It looked perfectly sealed.*

"Anything else you need?"

"No, in fact, I'd like to be alone. I have a headache." Not far off, she had a heartache. "Maybe skip dinner too. Please give my regrets to the family."

"Okay, can I bring you anything? Pain medication?"

"Thanks, I have some pills. I want to nip it before it turns into a migraine." A forgivable white lie. What she had planned was going to benefit the family far more than they could ever imagine if her treasure hunt proved lucrative.

Sloan left and Rebecca hurried to change, wincing slightly when the skin over her ribs stretched from her exertions. Checking her side in the vanity mirror, she noticed some bruising from falling against the counter. Nothing too bad. Certainly not enough to keep her from achieving her aims. *A Fairfax just gets on with it.* The words of her mother came back, the older woman's voice firm when it needed to be, soft when it was warranted. Because no matter what any DNA tests revealed, she had been raised a Fairfax and a Fairfax she would stay.

She pulled a few items off the bed and dressed in one of the freshly washed T-shirts and jeans, happy to see they had emerged from the wash stain-free. *Good job, Sloan.* After pulling on a hoodie, she found the tools she had gathered earlier in the week. A sharp trowel and a compact folding shovel. She shoved them into her backpack along with a flashlight and extra batteries. Her fully charged phone went into her pocket. Too many heroines in stories had alerted her to that foolish oversite by the protagonist. *There. All set.*

She slipped out of her room, hoping to remain unnoticed, and stealthily made her way toward the stairs that led to the underground passages. She may have missed the royal wedding by a few weeks, arriving in England in June, but darned if she was going to miss out on recovering some possible royal treasure.

* * * *

"Sanguis in virtute. Sanguis in virtute. Sanguis in virtute," the sorceress chanted. She stood inside the freshly chalked pentagram, naked, arms raised, hair spilling ink-black down her back, the hawk mask of Horus obscuring her identity. She faced the ancient altar with the tall black candles lit, their flames caressing the rock walls of the cave. Starlight shone down through the natural opening overhead, the moon at the proper angle to add its blessing of glow and promise.

She threw a handful of incense on the flames, making them spark and sizzle. Strange shapes danced along the walls from the ever-changing firelight. Twelve black-robed witnesses stood outside the five-pointed star, repeating her words, hands locked together in prayer and tribute.

"I call on the power of King Solomon." She plucked up a single strand of hair from the silver tray held at the ready by one of her coven and burned it as an offering over the candle. "Accept this gift from the sorcerer you chose to spread your words of law. That you endowed with the words of Horus, words we are humbly grateful for."

The slight odor of burning hair tainted the air. With a gesture of supplication, she picked up the vial of blood. Pulled out the stopper. Anointed her body with the red fluid, drawing the third eye on her chest. Poured the rest on the altar as an offering.

"Sanguis in virtute. Sanguis in virtute. Sanguis in virtute."

The coven spoke the words, the singsong chant repeated in perfect unison until their sorceress dropped her arms, head bowed.

"Give us your blessing to undertake the true path. We call upon one of the seventy-two messengers of Solomon to come to us, to speak with us, to show us the way. Use us as you have done before. In the name of King Solomon, we share these gifts, and I thereby command you to give us a sign of your great power. Speak to us. Endow us with your continued blessing. Show us to the light."

She threw more incense on the flames, making it flare and dance. She so did love the power. But under the cover of coolness she had a huge frisson of hope that just maybe, this time, she would cast the spell perfectly and they would reap the rewards of long-forgotten knowledge of raising a demon to enlist in their search for immortality, without having found the final artifact — the ring of King Solomon. It would change the world. Forever.

* * * *

The floor of the tunnel remained dry as Rebecca made her way back to the location of the side passage with its iron gate now removed. *Thank goodness for that small mercy.* Now at least it couldn't clank shut on her again. Down the narrow, backbreaking tunnel she duckwalked to the spot where the rocks had crumbled from age, revealing the location of the possible secret hiding spot. It looked like no one had bothered to venture down this far since she'd been there. *Good.*

It was hard going, occasionally having to stop to wipe sweat from her burning eyes, but she managed to clear away a couple of larger stones with the help of the shovel, ignoring the trepidation bordering on fear about the irrational image of the walls collapsing around her. She had to keep reminding herself the original builders on the site, the Templars, not only loved a good mystery but were heralded as excellent builders. Then an odd sound stopped her in mid-action. A stone sounded like it had fallen a great distance behind the wall. Odd. *How deep a mystery do we have here?*

Well, under Temple Mount in Jerusalem the tunnels went astonishingly far into the earth, not wanting to give up their ancient mysteries. And speculation was that it was the final resting place of the Holy Grail and Ark of the Covenant. So, maybe it was true to course.

She gave a final push and the area caved inward on itself, away from her and down into a pit running under the wall. She sat back on her haunches. *Can I do this? Crawl under the damn wall?*

She shone the flashlight into the hole, trying to see all along the edges of the shaft. The tunnel travelled inward, about eight or ten feet past the narrow breach in the rock that was no more than eight or ten inches wide. Most of the rocks and stones had fallen into this chasm and the way lay open to the other end. Someone had built this hidey hole, most likely to hide something of great value. What lay just a few tantalizing feet beyond? The treasure? A body? She shuddered at the idea. Or had everything been removed already? Though that seemed unlikely or the whole world would know that King Solomon's ring had been found. But the biggest question of all was could she, Rebecca Fairfax, with her fear of confined spaces, slide through this final small space into the unseen beyond?

What if it was booby trapped, like the treasure so many had sought on Oak Island, in Nova Scotia, Canada? The very island where her sorority sister Casey had spent time with her now-husband Truman, searching for and finding his family's heritage? Now, that was the best part. Would she be the new heroine and find the treasure? Well, at very least, she'd have a heck of a story to write about. There was nothing like real-life experience to give an author the edge.

Okay. Time to pull on my big-girl panties. She took a deep breath, then wiggled through the opening, reaching over the narrow chasm and pulling herself across by grasping the sides of the rock. She slid over the scariest spot with the sense of her heart being lodged in her throat. Rebecca tried not to think of how deep the vein ran down into the earth when more pebbles fell in and splashed a few seconds later. A hell of a long way down, apparently, to take that amount of time for the sounds to echo. *At least my ass is way too big to possibly fall through that opening, right?*

She fought her way forward, grunting with the effort, her ribs over the sore area not overly excited by the twisted exertions necessary. She held the small penlight in her teeth. It bobbed around mercilessly as she exerted herself. *Just a little bit farther.* She pulled and dragged her body through the narrow pathway, trying not to think of the tons of rock pressing down from overhead. She began to sing an almost unrecognizable lyric of *Brave* by Sara Bareilles in an effort to quell the obnoxious butterflies in her stomach.

"*Say what you wanna say, And let the words fall out, Honestly I want to see you be brave.*"

"If there is treasure in here," she muttered, "it's going to take a month of Sundays to get it all out. And that's going to be someone else's damn job. This is a one-time deal, I can promise you that."

Like a baby coming forth from the womb, she finally tugged free of the rock, dropping a couple of feet into what she hoped would be the last chamber.

"Damn Templars and their insane building skills. Who creates a vault in middle-earth that's not fictional? And all this effort better not be for naught or someone's going to hear about it." Though that begged the question of who she'd hold accountable, since everyone even remotely connected to this case was dead. *A sobering thought.*

She stood, took the flashlight from between her teeth and shone it around the space, kicking at the inches of debris surrounding her to find sounder footing.

Clanking, odd crunching sounds alerted her to the fact that it was no ordinary debris in the way.

"Holy shit!" she whistled through her teeth. *Mesmerized, enthrall, hypnotize, ensorcell, spellbound, stupefy.* No earthly synonym could possibly come close to capturing the excitement bubbling and spilling into a full-on grin. Her face felt split in two with the rush of intense emotion, like a leprechaun in heat. *Yeah, well if one of the wee folk are female and sexual.*

She surveyed her domain, taking in an expansive breath. *Are my feet even touching the ground?*

Stacked from floor to ceiling were all manner of chests and containers. Some had fallen to ruin, releasing their precious cargo onto the hewn rock floor. A cargo of glittering gold from these waterfalls littered the yellow brick road leading right up to her. She had been kicking away at gold coinage, for heaven's sake!

She leaned down and picked up a handful of the riches. The first one she inspected was an ecu produced by King Louis IX of France in 1266, his stamped-on fleshy profile attesting to his love of rich foods. She checked another, laying it on the palm of her hand. A gold florin coin from Florence, demonstrating the value of its coinage for international trade. The third was a ducat coin from Venice. Would she find some Roman bezant coins as well in the hoard? The priceless relic she was near certain it contained? In truth, all the coins were priceless, a lost history of the world.

She slipped the heavy coins into her pocket as proof, then leaned over and picked up another handful, tucking them into another pocket. She pulled out her iPhone and took a series of photos. Hardly able to contain her excitement, she tried calling Ash just in case the lousy reception gods were cooperating today.

Please. Let it go through. *All I need is a few seconds.* But the lack of bars reminded her of the humble place in the world humans held. She sighed. She'd have to contain her secret a while longer. At least until she crawled back through the tunnel from hell.

She was about to leave when something glittered oddly, catching her attention. A small jeweled box, different from the surrounding gold, lay atop the hoard a few feet away. *Hmm.* What was in it? The hoped-for King Solomon's ring? Was it going to be this easy, just lying there for her to scoop up? Her heart skipped a beat, then thudded madly against her ribcage. Obviously, it wasn't the Ark of the Covenant or the Holy Grail. Not near big enough. She waded over to it and picked it up. She tried to open it but the lid was stuck fast. She stuffed it into the back pocket of her jeans for safe keeping.

The return trip was endless, her brain seared with the glorious images of gold of the realm beyond the counting. The snapshots locked forever in the charged-up image bank of her mind had sparked something in her she had never experienced before. She, Rebecca Fairfax, had found the Piers family's Holy Grail. Enough money to last and repair the castle in perpetuity for all the generations to come. She had single-handedly guaranteed it. But waiting to share it was hard.

"If I can't tell someone soon I'm going to bloody explode!" she muttered, worming her way back through the tight passage, sweat dripping in her eyes, the coins jingling in her pockets. And yet, she found herself reluctant to share it with the film crew who had promised her a deal for an exclusive. In fact, she hadn't communicated with them in weeks. Maybe she just

January Bain

didn't want to be a screenwriter enough to make the trade? The thought sobered her, of how much she wanted to protect the family more than anything, enough to keep her focused on getting through the cramped tunnel without having a full-blown panic attack.

Finally.

She struggled to her feet, wincing at the throbbing pain in her side. Taking a moment to catch her breath, she pressed her hand hard against her ribs. *Careful. Don't want to give yourself a heart attack before the find is reported. It could end up being left down here for another millennium.*

She straightened up, took a deep breath and began the run back through the tunnels to the biggest reveal in her life. Nothing would ever compare to this moment. It was like finding the keys to the universe, or discovering how the pyramids were created or how the Bermuda Triangle worked or what had happened to DB Cooper or... She entertained herself as she ran, trying to hold on to whatever marbles she had left, not certain it could even be done or was worth the effort.

* * * *

Ash sat, drinking from an amber glass half-filled with whatever liquor his hand had grabbed first. He didn't care. He needed something to dull the ache. *Anything.* The pain of seeing the first woman he had ever truly cared about other than his mother, grandmother and Gracie, marrying someone she was not in love with hurt more than he could ever have imagined. When had it happened? His falling in love with her? Yes, the very first time he had set eyes on her, all indignant about his calling her a thief. Funny — now it didn't seem that important, the why of her being in England. Or maybe it was singing about teddy bears just to please his sister at the picnic that had made his heart capitulate? He would never forget how beautiful she'd looked with the sun bouncing off her face and hair.

But why had his father taken her so seriously when she'd kissed him? He shook his head and took a gulp of the liquid, feeling the burn, *needing* the burn. She was a generous spirit. Way out of his league. The thought that all he might have of her was that one sweet moment in the Rolls on the way to the party cut him like a knife. She had been so receptive to him, so pliant under his touch until she had caught fire, dazzling him with her beauty and passion.

But the situation with his father plagued him, sending his mind around in circles. Maybe it was time to talk with his father's doctor, plan what needed to be done? His stomach roiled. *Time.* It was going to be in too short supply. Hardly any time until the wedding day, and hardly any opportunity to plan for what was coming on its heels. The wedding day loomed at the end of the week. A woman he wanted more than anything now marrying another. It didn't compute. His mind refused to accept it. No way could this happen. And round again it went in an incessant loop to *what choice is there?* A last bit of happiness for his father. But the cost. The cost was brutal. To think of anyone else's hands on her was beyond painful, filling him with a seething rage with no outlet.

He gulped the rest of the liquor, pulled the stopper from the bottle and splashed another few ounces into the glass. What did it matter if he got soused? The situation was already past saving, anyway. He looked up, catching sight of himself in the mirror. He looked right off his game, his eyes burning with an intensity that made him stop in his tracks.

No. God damn it.

He set his glass down too hard, whiskey sloshing over onto the side table and puddling around the bottom of the glass. *I refuse to play the victim.*

He stood. At least he could act his part with dignity. It was only for a few more days. Especially since she was doing all she could for his family in their time of urgent need. He would be the head of their clan now, for better or for worse, and he had to own it. Make peace with whatever came. A part of him knew he was lying, that he had no idea if he could pull it off, but the part that admired people like Rebecca, who did the right thing whatever the cost, won. He had to do the same.

Loud footfalls echoing in the hallway alerted him to company. *Now what?*

"Anybody home?"

Rebecca.

"I'm in the library."

A flash of movement streaked through the doorway. Fair hair flying, sweat dripping down a face alight with a strange emotion, Rebecca raced right up to him and threw her arms around him.

Her body pressed tight against his, hot and sweaty and oh so curvy. His cock thickened with lust and desire in an instant, out of sync with all his good intentions. He wanted to push her to the floor, tear off all her clothes, have her right then and there. Her fragrance, heightened by the heat of whatever she had been up to, filled his nostrils with an intoxicating aroma that undid him in a single heartbeat. Undid all the

229

centuries of proper protocols. He was back in the ancient woodlands, back before civilization began in Britain, back to a time when man and woman were unrestrained by conventions. For one sweet moment he was an uncivilized man. And he wanted his woman. To claim her as his own.

She tried to pull back from his iron grip, half-laughing. "Give me space to breathe, handsome. I have something to tell you! Something so incredible that you won't know what to say or do!"

He held on, ignoring her pleas, burying his face in her hair, pushing his cock against her loins. He wanted her, and so fucking badly.

"The only thing I want is you," he growled.

She went limp in his arms and he took it for consent. As he leaned down and ravished her mouth, seeking entry, she kissed him right back, whispering into his mouth as her tongue danced around the edges of his lips. "I found a fortune in treasure and gold down in the tunnels."

At first the words did not register. All he wanted was to hold her in his arms, to share in the passion she had fired in him. All the blood drawing away from his brain made clear thinking impossible.

"Did you hear me?" she asked.

He shook his head. "What?"

"I found a hoard of gold buried in the dungeons—you know—the damp and dismal crawlspace under your castle you're so fond of accusing a certain woman of being a thief and a gold-digger in."

"What!"

"Yeah, you heard me right." She gave him a speculative look, wiggling her eyebrows.

His look of horror caught her by complete surprise. "Is this why you're here? To use my family in some nefarious scheme? Did you plan this from the beginning? Got my father enamored with you to pull off this stunt?"

"What?" Now it was her turn to look horrified. "I'm not here to steal your treasure! It wasn't like that at all."

"Then what is it like? How did you find it?" He crossed his arms over his chest and glared at her, obviously full of hurt and indignation.

"Well, I...researched and followed the breadcrumbs. From historical records over the centuries to the last person known to take an interest in the subject." She stood her ground. But dread crept up her spine. This reaction had not been what she had expected. At all. She'd hoped that the discovery would push aside the why of how she had come to find it. She chewed on her bottom lip. What she could say to smooth the waters? Being on the outside and looking in — that hurt like hell.

"And this last person. Was it Samuel W. Piers?"

"Ah...yeah." She nodded, the dread settling further into her stomach.

His eyes narrowed, his posture stiffening. "This is just great. The nemesis of our family dragged up all over again from beyond the grave. That damn leader of the Rising Sun cult."

"But...he left you a fortune. Surely that makes up for whatever it is he did to your family. And that was so long ago — ancient history. What does it matter in today's world?"

He shook his head, his expression annoyed. "The press will have a field day with this. If one word of this find leaks out."

Guilt struck. Hard.

"What did you do, Rebecca?"

"I…I was supposed to alert my publisher if and when I found it, but, if you don't want that to happen, I can pull back. Not notify them."

"So, I was right. You are a gold-digger. You planned this from the beginning. Everything you've done here has been a fraud. Did you ever care about my family?"

"Of course I care! Very much. I care about all of you." She shook her head, pleading her case. "I swear, I won't tell a soul about this find. Now, or ever, if it matters this much to you. I had no idea that you would feel this way. I thought you'd be happy about it."

"I'm not happy about any of this." He spat out the words. "Having my family exposed to such things at this time…" He shook his head, as if he couldn't say it.

"I'm so sorry. I had no idea. I just wanted to come to England and live in a castle and do my thing. The research was just a part of it. I never expected the engagement when I kissed your father. That was just in response to a silly bet."

"*A bet!*" His look of anger intensified and she stepped back, alarmed. "This whole mess is over a damn bet!"

Oh boy, she'd blown it now.

"Please, let me explain. I never meant it to go this far. At first, it seemed like a good idea. My ticket in. I'm not proud of that. But that was before I got to know all of you, and I started to care. And now I want nothing but good things for you. To be here for this family and help you all get through whatever comes."

She hesitated. How to make him see it, to understand. Her mind raced, trying to put the words together in a way that would show she was sincere. How very much she cared.

"Go on. I can't wait to hear the rest of this tale. I imagine that's why you're such an accomplished writer."

"What's the use! You won't believe me anyway! That I've fallen in love—" She went on the attack, to cover her insane slip of the tongue. "What did *you* just say? Have you read one of my books before?"

He had the grace to look a little shamefaced. "Okay, I've read a few pages, enough to know that you know what you're up to."

"I'm no mastermind, Ash. I'm just a woman who came all the way from Canada to work at a castle, do a little research on the side and hope to have an adventure. Is that so bad?"

"What did you mean just now?"

"What are you talking about?"

"When you said you'd fallen in love? Are you talking about my father?"

"No, not him." She clammed up, looked away from his commanding stance. "I gotta go. We can't have this conversation. Not now. Not ever."

But before she could exit the room, he pulled her back tightly into his arms and traced a line with his lips to the collar of her T-shirt, nipping at the damp flesh, enjoying the taste of saltiness on his tongue. His fingers grasped an erect nipple. A low moan escaped her lips. Who cared about anything else with her in his arms?

"I'd rather have ten precious minutes with you right now than a lifetime of riches."

"Ten minutes? That all you need?"

"I can go all night, beautiful, given half a chance."

"Really?" The thought made him forget everything else, imagining them in bed. His arms around her, their flesh pressed together. *Has the room just gotten warmer?*

"Anytime. Just say the word." He pressed himself against her even tighter, wishing they were both naked. Heaven. He was certain this was how it would feel to be there with her. He was never more alive than when they were together, ignoring everything else. And there was so much to hold at bay — he needed this, like a man in the desert needs a drink of cool water.

Someone cleared their throat noisily nearby, demanding his attention.

Sloan stood in the doorway, her face screwed up in complete disapproval.

"Miss Fairfax is wanted on the telephone. Professor Masters wishes to speak with her. *Now.*" The last word was said with a sharp edge. Rebecca startled in his arms, pulling away. He reluctantly let her go. Empty arms. A painful condition, he quickly discovered, though his mind was full of confusion. Too much information in the past few minutes had left him with a sense of discombobulation.

"Tell her I'll call her back."

Sloan continued staring at them, still frowning.

"Okay, okay. Can you transfer it to the library at least?"

"I can do that." Thank God the woman left, her footfalls going away.

"Okay. What else were you trying to tell me just now about the treasure?" He collected what was left of his wits, running a hand through his hair in agitation. Sloan had the worst fucking timing. Always had. Like she had some kind of radar for catching him at even the slightest provocation for years now. No wonder he'd never felt comfortable in his own home.

Instead of answering, Rebecca reached into her pocket and pulled out some gold coins.

He laid them out on the palm of his hand. He looked first into her beautiful starburst eyes which were dancing with excitement, then down at what he was holding.

"Okay, wow." He turned the coins in his hands, inspecting them. "You say there's a lot of these down there?"

"Yes!" She held up her phone and showed him photo after photo of piles of gold coin and treasure beyond imagining, even in his wildest dreams.

"I can't believe what I'm looking at." Even knowing the source of the treasure, the pain it could yet bring, it was something to see.

The phone rang in the library.

"I've got to take this." She crossed the room and picked up the desk phone.

"Hello, Vanessa."

"Tomorrow? Okay, I guess."

A brief pause.

"Eight. I'll be ready."

She hung up and rejoined him.

"Hen party?" he asked, not at all liking the reminder. The last thing he wanted to think about was what was happening on Sunday. *Too damn close.*

She nodded, her ponytail bobbing from the gesture. She looked so adorable, her lips bee-stung from his kisses, her hair a charming mess from being so obviously ignored today during her treasure hunt. His hands in it had not helped.

"Well, this is unbelievable."

"I know! It's something, isn't it? I can't wait for everyone else to know. To have all that gold brought up from the tunnels and locked in a safe place for your family." He had never seen her more beautiful, her eyes shining, her face flushed with happiness. If only things were different. Instead, he was being kept in constant state of purgatory. He couldn't reconcile all the facts she'd given him. Not yet. He needed time to sort it all through.

"My family's going to be quite impressed with this. If it doesn't blow up in their faces."

"I promise, it won't. I will not share this information with anyone. No one person. Not if you don't want me to."

"What about your publisher?"

"I can't say enough how sorry I am about all that. But, no, not even them. I will pretend it never happened. That I never found it. I'll even sign a waiver if you like. You can sue my ass off if I let one word slip." She gave him a look that said she meant it.

"Okay. You swear to keep this discovery secret for all time?"

"I do. Pinky-swear." She looked so lost when she made the gesture and he didn't immediately respond. He stepped up and did the deed with her, earning a small smile of relief.

Footfalls in the hallway and his father came in, looking pale and drawn. He hurried over to him, worried.

"Are you okay, father?"

"Hmm." The older man gave him a strange look. *What now?* "I'm fine. Just a bit tired. I heard voices."

"Yes. Rebecca has something to share with all of us." Would his heart be strong enough to withstand the shock? *Maybe best to keep it quiet.* The last thing he wanted was good fortune to upset his father. Guilt at what he had been doing in this very room just a short while ago struck home. Hard. If he thought purgatory painful, hell was worse.

Rebecca looked at Ash, chewing on her bottom lip, asking what she should do or say with her expressive face.

There was nothing for it but to quietly lay it out. Not make too big a deal of it. "Rebecca has been treasure-hunting in the passageways."

"Really? Did you find something of value then? Just let me sit first." The older man sought out a sofa and slumped onto it. Rebecca poured a glass of water from a decanter and handed it to his father, then sat beside him. She gave him a small, reassuring smile, downplaying what had happened. He admired her restraint. But a part of him still worried he'd been played. How could he ever trust her again?

"Yes, I found a lot of gold coins."

"Good. This castle needs a lot of upkeep. I knew Rebecca was going to bring us good luck." A wan smile accompanied his words.

"Thanks."

"Well, we'll have to see it taken care of. Brought up and stored in the bank and some in the safe."

"It will take some time. There is an awful lot of it. And we might need to purchase a larger safe." Ash informed him.

"A lot? How much exactly?"

She looked at Ash. He nodded and she pulled out her phone, sharing her photos again.

"My goodness. You weren't kidding." His father's eyes opened wider. *Please, please don't let him get too excited.* But all appeared well. His father's color was improving. He took the phone from Rebecca to get a second look.

"You'll see to it, Ash?"

"Of course."

"We need to share this with the dowager and Gracie. Celebrate."

"Great idea. I'm cooking."

"What? You just saved the family castle. You're *not* cooking. I'm taking us all out to eat. Put on your best party dress. I'll get Grandmother and Gracie. Meet you back here in thirty minutes."

"You're on!" Her face wreathed in happy smiles, her dimples caressing her cheeks where he had just been kissing her, he felt all the air leave his lungs. She literally took his breath away. *What am I going to do?* Kidnapping and hauling her away to his own private high-walled castle was his best idea yet. Like in the better olden days, when it had been common practice. But unfortunately it was frowned on in this modern age. *Damn it all to hell.* She was meant to be his—he'd never been more certain of anything in his life. Everything else could be worked out or negotiated.

.

Chapter Twenty

Everything I know now – the pitfalls, the highs and lows, everything – it taught me and made me stronger.
– Ray Allen

I'm too damn excited, that's the problem. Her whole body felt as if it was full of tremors. The clash between the high of finding the treasure and her buried worries about the wedding only days away had pushed her into an agitated state, in which she was unable to make a whole lot of sense of the day.

Just keep moving, kid.

The words came at her from some place deep inside – and the big surprise was that they worked. Got her through her shower, grooming and dressing in short order. She was about to tuck the jeweled box she'd forgotten to hand over earlier in the library into her purse when she decided to pry it open. She grabbed a tool from her kit and sat on the edge of the bed, getting right to the job.

Never had she so much to celebrate or so much to despair. She shook her head as she worked on the stuck lid of the small box. Riches without true love, they meant zip. She knew that for a fact now. Nothing like real life to drive the point home.

But, just a darn minute, now that they were so going to be inundated with riches beyond their imagination, maybe this was a game changer? A brilliant idea came to her at that second. *If Edward wants a prenup to protect the wealth, then I can duck and dive this wedding!*

She went back to working with a vengeance on the lid of the pretty jeweled box covered with gemstones, impatient to try out her new plan on the family but not wanting to damage something so priceless. Finally she got the artifact open.

Yes! An unusual engraved sigil attached to a thick gold ring greeted her eyes. She peered at it, turning it around and admiring it from every angle. A faint image of a star with the eye of Horus from Egyptian mythology dead center made up the simple pattern. She plucked it out of the box and held it. A heavy ring made of pure gold, it covered the central portion of the palm of her hand. It was far too big to wear for any period of time. Ceremonial in nature, just as expected. It felt warm in her hand, mesmerizing, and she hesitated.

She stared at it for ages, losing track of time before she shook her head and tucked it in her purse. Archeologists would have a field day with it, no doubt, but they weren't going to have the chance, even though it was the real McCoy, having sat undisturbed in the vault for centuries. To think it had once graced the hand of King Solomon blew her mind. But she would honor her word and keep the find secret.

Hope filling her to the bursting point at her new plan, she made a dash from the room and landed in the library a few minutes later all aflutter, her heart beating rapidly. Ash had beaten her to it and he turned at her rushed entry, his eyebrows raised in surprise.

"I've got it!" she stage-whispered, hurrying to join him.

"What have you got?"

"I know what's going to break up this crazy thing with your father."

"Go ahead," he said, his face giving away more emotion than she expected. She stared at him, wanting to know more, then pushed the thought away. *First things first.*

"I'm thinking all this wealth is the answer."

"How so?"

"Well, with so much of it, wouldn't a man want to protect his family? Not give it away to the new wife who will only be married to him for such a short time?" She looked away when she said the last words, feeling the pain of what they entailed and not wanting to see it reflected in Ash's eyes.

"You mean make you sign a prenup that you refuse?"

"Exactly."

"That's good thinking—even if the prenup isn't legally binding yet in England, it would hold some sway, especially if certain conditions were met." His eyes brightened. "I'll start that ball rolling right now. I'll call his lawyer and get him to contact father and pressure him—carefully of course—into doing something."

Ash pulled out his phone and went to work. Antsy, she headed over to the bar, poured herself a small brandy and drank it while watching Ash talk to the man. He kept nodding and went he finally rang off, he looked encouraged.

"We got someone else on our side." His voice filled with satisfaction, he joined her and poured them both another brandy.

"A toast to you, beautiful, for all you have done for this family." He clinked his glass softly against hers. They locked eyes and she froze. The raw desire in his chocolate-brown eyes had been replaced by an expression that made her spellbound. Her knees weakened. His eyes were filled with an intensity that plainly said he cared for her. She wanted to know more. Needed to know more.

"Thanks." Being a heroine in her own time was sweet beyond measure. "Ash, about —"

"Ah, the incomparable Rebecca. I say, well done." The dowager entered the room on her son's arm like the figurehead of a ship, her cheeks colored with large round red spots from either passion or rouge.

Please, no more wide hip references. Fair trade for a fortune in gold, right?

"I think we should schedule the motorbike rides for Sharon and Elsie for after the wedding. Time's in short supply. I should warn you about Sharon, though, she speaks ten words a second with gusts up to fifty." A twinkle lit up the grandmother's eyes. *Good, a different target.* Rebecca returned the grin.

"Father, Tomas Bradshaw wants you to call him right away. He said it was urgent."

"My lawyer? What on earth does he want? I just spoke with him a few hours ago."

"You did? Don't let him be charging you overtime for calling during the supper hour," Ash's grandmother warned, her eyes on the prize.

"Billable hours by lawyers are not going to break the bank, Mother. We have more than enough for many lifetimes, thanks to our Rebecca."

"Hmm, though that may very well be true, no point in wasting it."

"I'll excuse myself." Edward make a courtly bow and left the room.

"Would you care for an aperitif, grandmother?"

"A dry sherry will do very nicely, thank you."

She turned her gaze on Rebecca. "Tell me how you came to discover the treasure. I'm fascinated by treasure hunting myself. You think it was the Templars and Freemasons, correct?"

"I do." She took a moment to gather her thoughts. The treasure seemed the least of the prizes now. She wanted nothing more than to be a fly on the wall during Edward's conversation with his lawyer. That was what most mattered to her. Being free to be with Ash. To find out what this thing was growing between them. Maybe it was just because they couldn't have each other due to strange circumstances? No. Her heart said it was much, much more than that. Her mind might lie to her, but her heart never would.

"How did you know there was any treasure to be had at Castle Piers, Rebecca?"

"Mostly due diligence and research. Your home has an ancient history that includes original Templar knights and Freemasons. And since it's been barely changed from the twelfth century, it stands to reason there might have been treasure buried beneath it when the order came to such a brutal conclusion. And that first day here, I found symbols in the tunnels and followed the clues to the hidden hoard. A series of markings representing the tree of life was added by the

Order of the Golden Dawn, carved near the floor and down the side tunnel where it was hidden all those centuries ago."

"Order of the Golden Dawn. Hmm, so there's the connection to the family's black sheep. One Samuel W. Piers. Well, cheers. He's finally paid us back for all his follies." The older woman nodded her head sagely, looking pleased.

Rebecca took a deep breath, happy that part had slid by easily enough. She deliberately avoided looking at Ash, not needing to be reminded of how he felt about it. "My sorority back in Canada, the Brass Ring, all have a vested interest in treasure hunting. We use the proceeds to finance each other's dearest wish."

"I say, that's brilliant. Will you be wanting to use some of the new-found treasure to help one of these Brass Ringers have a wish?" The dowager gave her a direct look, her sharp eyes missing nothing.

Could she have asked a more perfect question? "Of course. It's payback for the money they fronted me to come on this summer's adventure to visit all of you."

"I suppose that's more than fair. I will speak to my son about it."

Damn, wrong answer.

"I've noticed those carvings on the wall, of course. Never put two and two together to find treasure," Ash added, his face inscrutable. She sighed. This moment was bittersweet. Though he now knew the truth, giving her some relief, she still found she was holding her breath, waiting for the other shoe to drop. Had they finally planted the right seed to end this charade?

"And I never venture down there. Too dreary and damp." The dowager gave a shudder of revulsion.

Edward came back into the room, his expression calm. *Please, please, let the lawyer have talked some sense into him.*

He gave a quick perusal of the room, not giving away the game. "Where's Gracie?"

"Don't get your knickers in a twist. She'll be here soon. Ah, speak of the angels." The dowager gave her granddaughter a fond smile. Her son frowned, not pleased with her slur on his masculinity. *Great. An annoyed mood would help.*

"Hello, darling. You look very pretty."

Gracie walked over and gave her grandmother a kiss before bestowing one on Rebecca.

Tears came instantly to Rebecca's eyes. This family had a way of unnerving her, undermining any and all intentions.

"Shall we go?" Edward offered his arm to Rebecca instead of his mother. She took note before accepting it, not used to this sequence of events.

They wound their way through the castle to the car park. Edward gave her a solicitous glance, speaking quietly not be overheard. "I want you to know, sweetheart, I trust you implicitly. No prenup for us. You've more than earned your fair share. And, by the look of those photos, there's more than plenty to go around."

Rebecca bit the inside of her cheek to avoid screaming expletives and throwing an all-out temper tantrum like little kids were famous for right then and there. As it was she stumbled, needing Edward's help to keep her steady in her high heels. Gritting her teeth, her mouth filled with the horrid taste of iron, she managed a reply. "That's nice of you."

Why does this family have to be so darn inexplicable? They made her head spin. Nothing she had done or said had made an ounce of difference. *Still at the junction of Crazy and Insane.*

"Why, if you hadn't come to visit this summer, I have no idea what a muddle we'd have made of it. I don't know if you've noticed, but our family can be a tad eccentric."

"No, can't say I've noticed." *Liar, liar, pants on fire.*

* * * *

"It's not working. Damn it! We need something more." The sorceress pursed her lips, narrowing her eyes in thought. "A bigger sacrifice to the gods."

"Perhaps the real thing?" her assistant asked, arching an eyebrow.

"Precisely. And I happen to know the perfect opportunity."

Chapter Twenty-One

I have not failed. I have successfully discovered ten thousand things that do not work. — Thomas Edison

Ash paced the floor of the library the morning after the celebratory dinner. Not even a thorough workout with Arthur had taken the edge off his agitation. How had it come to this point? They'd tried everything. Rebecca had been brilliant thinking that a prenup would end it. But no, his father had driven right on by that road block. When had he gotten so generous? Maybe because of what he was facing, he'd had a complete change of heart? Not that he had ever been a stingy man. But before he'd gotten the medical diagnosis, he had been much more protective of the family assets.

And blast it. Tonight, the hen party. And tomorrow the wedding loomed hard and heavy. How could he possibly be asked to bear what was coming? The woman he loved — wanted to be with — marrying another? It was so wrong, so cruel, it ate into his very soul with an ache so intense it threatened to push him some place he had never been before. Could never have imagined being.

Oh God, what should I do?

Then a spark of an idea flared from the deep recesses of his brain. The thought began to grow, emerging from the quagmire. He needed help, and he knew who just might be called upon to do that, remembering how important they were to her. He pulled out his cell phone and got down to work, sleuthing out the numbers.

* * * *

Rebecca sat on her bed, hefting the ring. Did she truly hold in her hands the legendary ring thought to be able to call on the aid of seventy-two demons? Intriguing idea, but who believed it could do such a thing in the twenty-first century? Certainly not her. Fellow Brass Ringer and expert archeologist Casey would be the perfect choice for more answers, but she was on a dig, ironically, in Egypt for the summer, and unreachable except for emergencies. And of course, she had to keep the discovery top secret or incur the wrath of one Ash Piers, Earl of Craigmere.

She held the ring in the palm of her hand, enjoying the substantial feel of it. There was something about it that called to her, some kind of vibration that was disquieting. She sighed. Her itching curiosity needed scratching in the worst way, and to confirm it with someone like Casey would have been awesome.

Now what? A few hours until the hen party. She groaned. That sounded like about the last thing she wanted to be corralled into doing. If only her favorite goddesses were here. A sudden case of homesickness descended with a vengeance and tears flooded her eyes. She swallowed a sob, swiping the evidence off her cheeks. *No. I won't give into self-pity.*

Escape. The last resort. She longed for it and dreaded it. How could she leave this wonderful, crazy, sweet family to swim in a pool of grief? It seemed all she'd been doing these past weeks was oscillating between acceptance of her fate and wanting to run for the hills.

A knock at the door made her start. The door flew open just as she slipped the artifact into her purse.

Sloan stood there, struggling with a gimongous black and gold box. She was barely visible behind it.

"Present for you."

"Present?" *Right, the wedding.*

Sloan crossed to the bed, setting it down with a groan. "It's your goody bag for tonight's hen party."

"Really?" Intrigued despite her mood, or maybe to get herself thinking about something else, she eagerly went to work on opening it. "Who sent it?"

"Vanessa Masters, the woman in charge of your party. She throws the best themed parties of anyone in the UK. I wonder what yours is going to be?"

Excited in spite of her recent meltdown, she popped the lid off the box and pushed back the thin layers of white tissue paper to reveal a great deal of black leather and lace goods. *Is that a whip? A corset? Thigh-high black boots with killer heels? A riding crop?*

"What's all this?"

"Wow, I know what it is! *A Dominatrix hen party.* Never been to one of them before, but I hear they're unbelievably sexy and raunchy. Nearly naked slave men at your beck and call. Everyone's going to have a fantastic time."

Rebecca had never seen Sloan in such a state of excitement and looking so pretty, her cheeks stained red and her dark eyes glowing. "What if I don't want sexy or raunchy?" Rebecca gingerly picked up a pair of see-through sheer black bikini bottoms between her thumb and index finger, shaking her head in disbelief.

"Nonsense! You can't refuse now that she's gone to all this trouble. There might even be a lesson on the art of being a dominatrix. I've heard that's the new gold standard. And what female worth her salt isn't interested in all that?"

Ah, this one. About the last thing on her mind was learning how to use a whip to keep a man in line. *Just a minute, on second thought, maybe the idea does hold some merit.* She'd been trying to be so accommodating to the males of this family of late, maybe it was time to gain a new perspective. At least for them. She squinted her eyes, imagining a whip in one hand and Ash's face as she lovingly ran the whip around his sculptured body. *Hmmm.*

"Oh, nice mask." Sloan pursed her lips, waking her from her erotic daydream, plucking the item out of the box and prancing over to the mirror to check it out.

When Sloan turned from the mirror wearing the black mask that bore glittery sparkles and was shaped like cats' eyes, she had upped her wow-factor by a thousand percent.

"Looks good on you. You should keep it."

The woman tugged it off and laid it beside the box. "No, I'll get my own. Surprise! I'll going to be at the party too."

"Nice." At least she would know a couple of the women. She sighed. But not having the Ringers attend sucked big time. They'd relish this outrageous theme, trying to outdo each other like they'd done at university for the sorority parties. She about giggled, thinking of some of their antics. Like the time they had all dressed as mermaids and Will had stepped on Lacey's tail, turning her costume into a mini-skirt. It had worked for them. Best friends to lovers. Now they were married, after enough twists and turns to have their own novel. Hmm, maybe she should consider writing biographies about her friends?

"What's this?" Sloan asked, picking up the open jeweled box she'd abandoned on the bed.

Shoot. I should have tucked that away too.

"Something I was researching." That part was true. The family was right to be keeping such a momentous fortune secret. Such an event didn't usually bring out the best in others, often leading to all kinds of problems, greed for one.

"Looks ancient. I adore any kind of artifact. May I look more closely?"

"Sure, but it's just a replica box. I thought it real at first too. But it's not. Great fake, though." She made her tone upbeat, wanting to deflect the woman's curiosity.

Sloan picked it up, rubbing her thumb over the surface of the jeweled box. "It's a nice piece, must have held something of value—a ring perhaps? Even as a replica, it must be worth a lot. It's as heavy as real gold with its embedded gemstones. Where did you get it, if you don't mind my asking?"

"Ah, a friend asked me to check it out. He was in the village on his way up north on a bus tour and caught up with me. No idea where he got it from. Probably an online website." Not her finest excuse, but she'd been caught off-guard by the question and needed to fend off any more.

"Hmm." Sloan appeared fascinated by the piece, turning it over and inspecting it from every angle. The only thing missing from the picture was a jeweler's loupe. "May I take a quick photo? I'd love to share this with a friend who's a real aficionado of ancient relics."

Before she could object, the woman whipped out her cellphone and snapped a quick shot of it.

Rebecca held out her hand palm upwards, her mouth set in a grim line. *Damn it.* What if it came back to haunt the family? Sloan handed it to her reluctantly, her expression filled with longing as she laid it lovingly on Rebecca's outstretched palm. If it had been a fake, she would have been tempted to just give the object to her. But it wasn't hers to give. And she wasn't prepared to court more trouble. It was bad enough the woman had seen the box that held the supposed magic ring.

"Please, please don't share that with anyone else. My friend gave it to me in strictest confidence. It might embarrass them, as they paid more than it's worth."

"Okay, I promise. I'll leave you to prepare. The limo will be here to pick us up in an hour."

"That soon?"

"Yes, it's going to be a long day and night. Prepare yourself. I can promise it's going to be a party you will never forget and someday can share with your grandbabies."

"Okay." *Grandbabies.* That was beyond weird to think about. She wasn't even ready for *babies* yet.

The door closed behind Sloan and she turned her attention back to the box of goodies laid out on the bed. *Oh, boy. Now what?*

In less than an hour, she was inspecting herself in front of the mirror while shaking her head in complete denial and disbelief. Her reflection might not be recognizable, but damn it, the woman in the mirror was *hot*.

Thank goodness a cape had been provided. Prancing around the castle in this get-up might incite a riot. Or at least get one guy's blood up. She smiled at her reflection, a part of her wishing she could see Ash's reaction. Her red-painted lips curved upward like a fancy Cheshire cat — yup — even a tube of *Siren Red* had been included. That professor woman left nothing to chance. A human dynamo.

She checked the time. Okay. Take a deep breath. Well, if only she could. The corset came with certain restrictions. At the last second, she tucked the ring in its jeweled case into her carryall rather than put it in a dresser drawer, remembering the vial of blood discovered by Sloan. She added a change of clothing and her small canister of mace. Then, pulling the black cape with the red silk lining, like Dracula, around herself, she ventured out of her bedroom and into what felt like either a spotlight or a bounty on her head. She shrugged the odd thought away. *Writers are too darn fanciful at the best of times, eh.*

Scurrying across the flooring on her insanely high heels, she wobbled a bit trying to keep her footing. *Slow down.*

"Where are you off to in such a hurry?" She turned at the sound of Ash's voice, then found herself scrambling for purchase, dropping her bag, her arms wind-milling about and catching in her long cape. It exposed her outfit in slipping off her shoulders and rustling to the ground in a heap of black and red silk cloth.

"Fancy running into you here," she deadpanned.

"Yeah, quite unexpected since I only live here."

"The limo's on its way for the hen party. And this weird get-up is what I'm supposed to wear." Her face flooded with heat. Her cheeks had to be blood-red. She had an urge to wipe the red lipstick from her lips and look less like a siren and more like herself. And pull the darn corset whole lot higher to cover some of her ample cleavage. What would Xaviera do in this situation? Darned if she knew. But most likely pretend it was all on purpose — the woman had so much confidence. *If only I had a tenth of hers, I'd be a strutting cock of the walk.* No, wait. That referred to the male species. *Whatever. It fits.*

She looked up to catch Ash's eyes locking onto hers. *Oh boy.* Heat flooded her entire body. The expression in his deep brown eyes had shifted to out-and-out smoldering.

"You look amazing," he growled. The low vibrations of his voice caused an immediate response in her lower belly. *Aflutter is a thing then.*

She bit down on her lower lip. *Get a grip, Rebecca. Or get a hotel room. Oh boy, if only we could just scratch this distracting itch, maybe it would be a whole lot easier to get on with things.* And if only he was disappointing in the sack, she'd get over it. *Maybe.* But instead, here she stood. Dressed like a slut about to get into, no doubt, deep shenanigans with a crew of women who had taken a shine to the event. She could only imagine what a character the professor could be in her off-time. She had the look of a dominatrix down pat in real life.

"I don't know if amazing is quite the right word. More like kind of slutty. Not sure it's me."

"I have to say I prefer the real Rebecca without the artifice. She's beautiful without even trying. Not that I've ever gotten the chance to wake up with her in the morning to check if she's an expert at the 'natural face', I think the experts call it. Maybe you look a whole lot different without it?"

She shook her head. Ash seemed more relaxed, more himself, like maybe he was in the process of forgiving her. "No, never been an expert at make-up. Now, if you want to know something about how to put on a dinner party that can set the place afire, I'm your woman."

"I wish." The words electrified the air between them. Ash came closer, too close, leaning down to whisper in her ear, his warmth breath trailing along her neck. *Yup, definitely one of my extra-sensitive top-five erogenous zones.* "If you were mine, I'd be after you twenty-four-seven, never let you out of my sight. You're going to put the other women to shame at the party, beautiful, looking like you do."

She gulped. "Thanks, I think."

"Great, you're ready. Pick up that cape and bag and let's get at it, girlfriend!" Sloan appeared like a genie in a puff of smoke. She joined them before they could back apart, a smile plastered all over her face. She was ignoring the situation between her and Ash or had just given up worrying about it.

"I'm giving you fair warning. Vanessa has a lot of treats planned. Don't expect her until tomorrow morning, Ash. Good thing the wedding's scheduled for one in the afternoon. She's going to be busier than a Canadian beaver!" The last statement was accompanied with the smuggest grin imaginable. This party was already proving annoying and it hadn't even begun yet.

"Don't be slandering our national animal," Rebecca muttered.

"Did you remember to bring the special items of punishment sent with your outfit?"

Ash's eyebrows shot up. *Priceless.* "Where are you holding this event, if I may inquire?"

"At Hill House aka the Red Dungeon, up in the wilds of the north country." Sloan smirked, giving him a sly wink. "The owner has an affection for Shirley Jackson's gothic novel, *The Haunting of Hill House.* No regular men allowed unless they have no objection against being turned into a slave for a good cause, though I could see making an exception in your case."

"I have the riding crop and whip right here," Rebecca interrupted, pointing to the fancy items of correction sticking out of the end of her carryall now secured on her shoulder. Was Sloan flirting with Ash? She narrowed her eyes at the woman.

"Well, let's get going, Lady Vixen. Oh, and you got your mask, right?"

"Excuse me?" Rebecca stopped dead in her tracks.

"Yeah, we're all being given new monikers for the party. Yours is Lady Vixen and mine is Lady Zee. Don't worry, it'll be fun."

"O—kay." Sloan seemed to have adopted a brand-new persona. Or maybe this was the real woman? At the very least, the event was going to prove educational and take Rebecca's mind off what she didn't want to think about—if she could survive it without dying of acute embarrassment.

"You take care of Rebecca, Sloan. I'm counting on you to keep her out of trouble," Ash said, his expression stern, the look in his eyes concerned.

"Don't worry," Sloan about cackled in her over-the-top glee. "What happens in the Red Dungeon stays in the Red Dungeon!"

Rebecca rolled her eyes, but bravely trooped after the woman, giving Ash a final wave of her hand. He stood unmoving, his arms crossed over his broad chest. *Handsome as the devil, and infinitely more dangerous.*

Chapter Twenty-Two

If Cinderella's shoe fit perfectly, then why did it fall off?
— Anonymous

The drive from the castle to the event took longer than Rebecca expected. Sloan went on about it the prestigious Hill House, an upmarket private manor house she'd been to before, saying it was even more spectacular than rumors let on. The venue would supposedly add an extra luster to the hen party. Rebecca would have preferred it to have been held closer to home, making the drive less tedious, but her choices were to get out and walk or just go along with it. The image of Ash standing and watching her leave was still burned into her mind and a part of her would have done anything to go back and spend the evening with him. She had no free nights left.

"Here, have a glass of champagne. It will loosen you up a bit," Sloan said, digging the bottle out of the large ice bucket at her feet and pouring some into a crystal flute.

Maybe. She took the offering. 'Lady Zee' poured one for herself, then held up her glass. "To a night of delicious pleasurable experiences that hopefully give you a basis for some extra fun with your soon-to-be-husband, the Duke of Piers. Lucky you. Nabbing yourself a duke on first try."

"Yeah, lucky me," she muttered, then gave a sweet smile to soften the words.

"You do seem to be spending more time with the earl though."

"We seem to have some kind of karma, always running into each other at every turn, considering how large the square footage is in Castle Piers."

"It's an expensive abode." Sloan peered at her over her freshly refilled glass. "It would be nice if the family came into money to handle all that upkeep. You don't happen to be a millionaire, by any chance?"

"No, sorry. Only going to happen if the money in my wallet gets lustful and multiplies like the fishes and loaves at Galilee." The champagne was helping to settle her stomach. She held out her glass for a refill.

Sloan snorted the liquor through her nose, sending her scrambling for her bag. After wiping her face, she topped up the flute for her guest. "Well, you do bring other special gifts."

"Yeah. What? My ability to set a kitchen on fire?"

"No. I was thinking of your beauty and brilliant mind. You graduated university and were on the dean's list, according to your Facebook page, and you write novels."

"Flattery will get you everything."

"Good, because that's what we want."

"Sorry — we?"

"Oops, slip of the tongue. Ah, we're on the final approach."

The gothic structure, complete with looming gargoyles, rose out of the hillside, the lower floors barely visible through an oppressive stand of giant elms. An odd trick of the light made it appear to be crawling with thorns and bushes. Words from Jackson's brilliant novel came to mind. *Hill House not sane, stood by itself against its hills, holding darkness within; it had stood so for eighty years…and whatever walked there, walked alone…*

"Isn't it just to die for!" Sloan turned a face with too-excited eyes her way. The woman was over-animated, almost possessed by the idea of the house. *Uncomfortable* about summed up Rebecca's own feelings. *It just might take me as much moral strength to step inside as it did Eleanor Vance, the doomed heroine of* Hill House. *Is that another damn bell tolling?*

"It's something all right. I'll give you that. Bit odd for a hen party, don't you think? I was thinking a nice hotel and spa would be more relaxing." An understatement if she had ever indulged in one. The creep factor of this estate was a thirteen out of ten, like the old joke about how many people out of ten loved chocolate — thirteen of course.

"I think it's perfect. Spooky enough to get your blood flowing and it fits the theme of bondage perfectly. You know the original story from the novel, right? The woman being possessed by the house and it becoming her tomb? Sort of like that song, *Hotel California* by the Eagles. You know —" She began singing in a rather tuneful way, "'*Welcome to the Hotel California*' and that line about '*You can check out any time you like, but you can never leave.*'"

"Yeah, not comforting if that's the way you meant it." She shuddered. All cultural joking aside, under her bravado, a genuine sense of foreboding had awakened.

"Don't worry. You'll be perfectly safe with us. We just enjoy a bit of a thrill."

Is that a cackle?

"Why would someone deliberately set out to create a replica of Hill House?" The house was not growing on her. Every Spidey sense tingled, as though she was on thin ice. She set her flute aside, then rubbed her hands up and down her arms. She needed something stronger than the bubbly. Or more precisely, she'd like to just go home. *As new experiences go, this one sucks.*

"Don't know. But impressive, eh? I love your Canadian idioms. Always wanted to use that word."

Rebecca's heart dropped even further when the car glided to a final stop in front of the manor house. Shrouded by trees and greenery, the structure was a compilation of every horror mansion ever featured. It obscured the light, growing out of the hillside like a damn mushroom. The front façade stood three stories tall, a straight-up monolith that kissed the foreboding gray skies of the premature twilight. The building imposed light restriction on the ground around it, adding long shadows. Most prisons appeared friendlier. Even the one in Huntsville, Texas, where a cloud of bats come forth every night at dusk over the prison walls. Studying that institution had been useful for a book. *Note to self—cut back on so much spooky research.*

She pulled on her big girl knickers, as the British would say, and stepped from the car, holding tightly to her carryall. *Maybe I should have found a safer hiding place for the ring.* Because the Red Dungeon looked like the kind of place that would swallow it up and keep it for itself. She shook her head. *Stop it. It's just your writer's imagination running away with you yet again.*

"Good evening. Welcome to the Red Dungeon. I'm Lady Red. Please call upon me for anything you may require. Your every wish is my command." *Cheesy or what?* Their red-gowned hostess greeted them with an expansive wave of her heavily ringed hand, ushering them inside. A woman in her physical prime, she emitted a strong signal of complete confidence with her sexuality, her silk dress cut down to her navel, exposing full breasts, and a slit on the side showing off long slender legs. *Lady Dracula is more like it.* Rebecca suspected a great deal of two-sided tape was required to keep her intact.

"May I take your cloaks?" she asked. 'Lady Zee' immediately stripped hers off, leaving Rebecca the only one covered up. She looked around the foyer. *No one else in sight. Good and bad.* A large crowd would add a safety margin but they would also be party to what she was wearing.

"Okay." She reluctantly added her own covering to the pile over Lady Red's forearm.

The ambient temperature of the reception area would have been comfortable if her Spidey senses hadn't been jangling to beat the band. So would the atmosphere, if she was into lots of plush royal-blue carpeting with gold-patterned edges, ceiling-high engraved mirrors, oil paintings of hunting scenes, and old-gold sconces. Personally, she was more into hardwood floors, and scenes of wildflowers or Canadian geese flying over fields of grain on plain walls with a hint of color. The organist playing heavy-handed theatrical music — not helping. It reverberated in her body, making her even more jumpy, expecting Christopher Lee or Bela Lugosi to jump out at her from behind a secret panel and go for her neck. She rubbed her throat, touching her necklace talisman for courage.

"Lady V and all the other ladies are waiting for you in the parlor. If you will follow me, please."

They followed their escort, the thick flooring deadening the noise of their high-heeled attire. The house seemed to absorb sounds so efficiently that Rebecca couldn't hear another living soul in the place. Maybe theirs was the only party tonight?

"Is this place owned privately or can anyone rent it?"

"Not just anyone. It's very exclusive. You must be an approved member and know someone. Our guests require discretion to play in the dungeon. And since yours is the only party scheduled this evening, your group will have complete privacy to enjoy yourselves." Lady Red's smug expression added little reassurance.

Just how much goes on in this so-called dungeon?

"You have places like this in Canada, right?" Sloan asked, her over-bright eyes still worrying. *Is she on something? Meth, cocaine, life?*

"I would imagine, yes. But not establishments I would normally choose to frequent. I'm more a vanilla kind of gal."

"Maybe it's time to broaden your horizons. Let those timid Snow Bird Canadian wings loose to venture into new territory. Never knock something until you've tried it, my grand-mum always said."

Rebecca declined to answer, keeping her eyes open for exits and escape routes if it came to that. *Should have brought my own ride. But at least I have my trusty mace.*

"Ah, here we are." Lady Red opened the door, waiting for them to go inside before vanishing.

The parlor was an intimate room with subtle lighting. A small narrow stage stood in the center, projecting far into the room. Around each of a handful of tables in the perimeter of the room sat two or three women on high-backed chairs, making about a dozen women in total. Vanessa rose to greet the newcomers from the spot nearest the end of the prominent runway-slash-stage. She sat alone.

"Lady Zee and Lady Vixen. I'm your hostess, Lady V. I thank you for attending our little soirée tonight to celebrate the upcoming nuptials. Come, join me. Welcome our guest of honor, ladies. The bride-to-be, Lady Vixen. Lady Vixen is marrying the Duke of Piers this Sunday." She was already in character, the bondage outfit fitting her to a tee.

Polite murmurs of greeting followed the professor's announcement.

Lady V gave a loud clap of her hands and the room came to life. Men clad only in gold lame' shorts came strutting in from all directions, their pectoral muscles exceedingly well developed and their washboard abs to die for.

Holy shit! There is such a thing as eyes bugging out and tongues gagging on the floor. All the men were prime specimens from some kind of hot-studs-rental store.

Lady V leaned over and called above the loud techno music that had transformed the atmosphere from gothic to clubbing in—well—a clap of her dainty hands, "You get first dibs, Lady Vixen. Just nod or point when one takes your fancy."

"What do I want him for again?" The rules of this game might come in handy.

"Why, to discipline, my dear. A little spanking can go a long way to exorcise your inner demons."

"What if I don't have any demons?" She had to almost shout over the noise. A couple of the women looked her way.

The professor pushed back her head and let loose a good old-fashioned belly laugh. "Sweetheart, *everybody* has demons."

Her phone buzzed. She reached over to retrieve it from an inner pocket in her carryall.

Before she could answer it, Vanessa reached over and snatched it right out of her hands. "Absolutely no phones allowed. Red Dungeon rules. Break those at your own peril."

Beyond annoyed, Rebecca pressed her lips together, drumming her fingernails on the tabletop. The text had been from Ash. *What does he want?* The suspense of not knowing was murder. She had a sudden wish for him to be one of the men strutting their stuff on the runway. *Hmm.* The daydream was delightful, the best part of her day so far. Even the vision of lightly swatting his perfect ass while he was wearing those form-fitting briefs gave her pleasure. All her lady parts began tingling in agreement.

"So, who's it going to be? You have to choose first, before the others are allowed."

"Bit stringent, Lady V, don't you think?" She disliked being pressed into a corner. This woman was beginning to get on her nerves. Who was she to be calling all the shots? *Should have known this was a bad idea.* All she wanted was to get the hell out of there.

"If you'll excuse me, I need to use the restroom." She waved her hand around with some disdain as she got up from the table. "Don't hold anyone up on my account. I insist, have at it. I'm not in need of exorcising any demons."

Vanessa gave her a steely-eyed glare.

Rebecca sashayed to the door and pushed it open. Out in the corridor, she began sleuthing out a ladies' room. *Got to be one around here someplace.*

Lady Red glided up, spooking her by coming around a corner unannounced.

"Were you needing anything, Lady Vixen?"

"Yes. A bathroom."

"Of course. Follow me."

The woman walked her around a corner, pointing out with a long red pointy fingernail a discreet doorway, then vanishing for parts unknown. *Best guess, to the attic to hang upside down by her heels.*

The bathroom was as dimly lit as the rest of the place, but it still showed Rebecca looking hot in the full-length mirror. Too bad it was wasted on this crew. She imagined what her fellow Ringers would say about the get-up. She needed proof. *Damn it.* Her phone had been confiscated like a schoolgirl's. *Grrrrr.*

She used one of the stalls, then washed her hands. The sense of isolation in Hill House bothered her. Some things just weren't adding up, the demonologist professor being the main one. Rebecca had been so busy trying to get out of the wedding these past weeks, she'd not been paying attention to other vital clues.

First there was Vanessa breaking Rebecca's necklace, then insisting on taking her blood when she was rumored to be the descendant of the infamous demon guy. Then the vial had been about to be stolen at the party if she hadn't intervened, and the odd event of having it leak into the dresser drawer. The break-in at the church. The ceremonies in the graveyard.

Unease crept up her spine. Far too many odd coincidences to be ignored, especially adding in this unnecessarily weird and isolated location for a hen party. All the women fawning on the professor like a group of hypnotized cultists. And what else could that crew be involved in? She didn't want to call them names, but a terrible suspicion dawned. And the fact that Vanessa had dated Ash wasn't helping to ease things, considering how he had cooled towards her, if Rebecca wasn't mistaken. Maybe there was some kind of payback planned for tonight? Got her out to the wilds of England to torture her in some way for taking away the attentions of a man she coveted?

Oh boy. Was it just her writer's imagination at work again, or was there something to worry about?

First things first. *Calm down and think, Rebecca.* Asking to use a phone might alert them if they were up to something. Could she just slip out and run away? Hide in the woods? Steal someone's keys and drive off in their car? Out in the middle of nowhere, that wasn't the best option if the police stopped her and asked for the registration. Not to mention it would seem entirely odd behavior if nothing untoward was going on. Everything that happened did have another logical explanation.

Okay. The best thing to do was to stay sober, keep alert and watch for an opportunity to get back to the castle. Maybe while the others were busy with their own shenanigans? Would they leave for private cubicles, or stay as a group? Not knowing the rules was beyond maddening. But, realistically, what could they do to her? Everyone knew she was with them—if something happened they would be the most likely suspects. And the professor had a great deal to lose. Her career and her standing in the community.

No. She shook her head. *It must be my imagination.*

Shoulders back, she exited the bathroom, determined to put a brave face on it but stay vigilant.

She walked into the parlor, her mind seething with impressions, the music more a distraction than enjoyable.

"Ah, Lady Vixen, we're still waiting for you to make up your mind." The professor's voice had a cranky edge to it. Good. The woman needed to cool her jets.

"I thought it had been decided to go ahead without me." She gave Vanessa a pointed look.

"Sorry, no can do. You're the main reason we're here, and we want to see you *entirely* satisfied first. That you get what's already been paid for — by me. If you don't choose soon, you'll be letting down a lot of eager young women."

"Fine." One of the young Adonis males was strutting his stuff near their table, doing a lot of groin thrusts and such. She pointed at the man. "Him."

"Nice choice." Vanessa clapped her hands and the man approached the table, a wide smile on his handsome mug. His sandy-blond hair hung over his eyes quite fetchingly. At least in his own opinion, if Rebecca wasn't mistaken.

"So, what am I supposed to do now? Have you prepared a rule sheet or something useful for a novice?"

"It's entirely up to you. But I would recommend you show him who's boss first. Use your whip on that tidy bum. Get him to do something for you that you would like. Perhaps a foot massage or a back massage to relax you? You seem rather tense."

"Right here?"

"No, silly. In one of the prepared cubicles in the back. They're set up with massage tables and scented oils. You can go as far as you like. No restrictions in the Red Dungeon."

"And if I just want to talk?"

"Your loss." Vanessa shrugged her shoulders. "But at two hundred pounds an hour, seems a shame."

Rebecca squinted her eyes at the woman. "Are you saying what I think you're saying?"

The woman got up without answering. She pulled out a collar and chain from her bag hanging from the back of her chair and locked it around the man's neck. "There you go. He's all yours now."

The other ladies began clapping enthusiastically, chanting, "*Go. Go. Go.*"

Feeling like the worst kind of fool, and with as much dignity as she could muster, 'Lady Vixen' got up, took the offered end of the chain and led the young man to the back of the room. The craziest moments at Castle Piers paled in comparison.

She opened one of the doors and a red light above the frame turned on. *Figures.* She walked inside and surveyed the twelve-by-ten space. It bore a white massage table as promised and an array of small bottles on a side table, complete with a stack of snowy white towels. A small bar with bottles of premium alcohol stood at the ready. Soft elevator music was already playing and added a benign-ness that was proving helpful.

"What would my mistress like?" The man's deep voice made her jump.

"Ah, maybe a foot massage." No way was she getting undressed.

"Of course. If you would lie down on the table, please. Would you like something to drink?"

"Bottled water if you have it."

"Certainly."

She watched as the man efficiently twisted off the screw top lid of a sealed bottle of water and poured her a glassful.

"Thanks." She took the offered drink. "Are you doing this gig for financial reasons?" *Duh, why else, Rebecca?* Conversation was going to be tricky at best.

"You think this an odd choice, mistress?"

"Don't call me that. I'm Rebecca. And your name?"

"Slave Number Ten."

She shook her head vehemently. "No. You are *not* a slave." Was that a trace of disappointment in his eyes? Great. Now she was letting him down as well. She took a swig of water to hide her discomfort.

"Your every wish is my command. My safe word is *banana*."

Water snorted out of her nose as she snickered. "Of course it is. I'm sorry. I must be a terrible disappointment to you. But at least you'll get paid for doing very little."

"You're very beautiful, mistress. I look forward to giving you a foot massage. Would you like me to lick your boots clean for you as well?" A hint of excitement in his eyes and tone accompanied his question.

"Ah, no need. They're already quite clean, thank you very much. I just shine them up this morning at the castle. You know, Castle Piers, where I've been staying for the summer and where I met my fiancé. Nice castle, all the amenities of home." *Liar.* But she dutifully leaned over and undid her boots, tugging them off and tossing them under a bench well out of his reach. She hopped up on the table and lay back. Maybe a hand massage might have been a better choice? No. Bare feet were better for running than five-inch stilettoes. And if this got any creepier, she'd be running off into the sunset in record time.

Then the man began to work on her feet. And he was good. *Very, very good.* Her feet began to signal how good within seconds. He applied an oil giving off the fragrance of relaxing chamomile, and she began to unwind for the first time in days.

"*Oh, yes.*" The words involuntarily eased out of her as the man worked on her feet, rubbing the balls and soles and each little toe with tender loving care. *Oh my, lovely. Ah, what was that new sensation?*

She looked down to see he'd put her big toe in her mouth and was giving it an avid workout. Heat rose in her body in what had to be a full-on blush. *Who knew it could feel like this? Maybe this slave thing wasn't such a bad idea after all.*

She had to remind herself to remain alert even as her body wanted to drift away, stay in that happy sphere of wonderous contentment.

"Ah, how's it going down there? Are you tired? Need a break or anything?"

"No, mistress. You have lovely feet. May I go a bit higher and kiss your sweet knees?"

"No. Just my feet, thanks."

"If you want more massaging, you'll have to punish me. Or maybe if I take liberties, you'll have to punish me?"

She felt his hand creep up her calf and she shot up like a bullet from the table, standing and giving him the stink eye.

"Ah, we're done here."

"Have I disappointed you, mistress?" His shoulders sagged. What was a gal to do?

"Yes. You have." She grabbed her riding crop, the first thing she found in her carryall, and used it across her hand to test it. Quite tame, really. If that was what would make the 'slave' happy, who was she to interfere? She'd just had the best foot massage of her life.

The slave bent over the bench and presented his tight buns to her, stretching the gold fabric across them rather enticingly. Was she going to do this? Rebecca Fairfax of vanilla fame? Damn right she was. If she chickened out now, she'd never live it down when she got back home and shared this story with her beloved Ringers. She gave a light swat to the man's ass cheeks.

"Harder, mistress. I've been *very* naughty."

Obligingly, she gave him a harder swat, enjoying seeing the riding crop whistle through the air and land on such plush firmness.

"Only three strikes, that's my call." She wasn't cut out for this, but a bit of fun never hurt anyone, right?

"Then make it count, mistress." His tone begged for more.

She gave a nice final satisfying swat at the twin cantaloupes, and tucked the riding crop back in her bag. Now, she could say she'd done it once. Tried a little extra-light BDSM, pee-wee, if there was such a category like there was in hockey. *Hockey.* What she wouldn't do to be at a rousing game of their national pastime, enjoying a beer or two with friends. Life seemed so much simpler back across the pond.

"Would you like something else, mistress?"

"No. we're done here. But I thank you for the best foot massage of my life."

A shy smile lit up his face. "Thank you. Perhaps a glass of Chardonnay or champagne before you go?"

"No, I'm good." His face creased with disappointment. She ignored him and got half under the bench to locate her abandoned footwear, pulling them out. She jerked the ridiculous boots on. *Time to exit the dungeon.*

She tried the open door, but it had jammed or something. She turned back to address him. "Could you open it for me? It appears to have gotten stuck."

"Sorry, mistress. That's the one thing I can't do."

A loud bell tolled in the recesses of her mind.

"I'm your mistress. You have to obey me, right?" Worry lodged in her throat. What the hell was going on?

"No, you said we're done. And it's soon going to be time for the next part of the evening, anyway. I'm keeping the key right here until you're called for. Don't worry, the next part is fun too." He patted the waistband of his shorts, his expression smug.

She turned back and gave the door a kick with her foot. Hard. Then harder. A series of kicks went unanswered. She stopped and took a deep breath to steady herself.

"Goddamn it, let me out of here!"

"No one's going to hear you. These rooms are soundproofed and for good reason." The man's expression had turned from smug to devious. A hardness around his mouth and eyes gave her pause. "No one's letting you go free anytime soon. Might as well give it a rest."

"Why are you doing this?" she hissed into a face that no longer held one iota of charm to her.

"Doing what? It's just part of your hen party experience."

Right. She didn't buy that for one nanosecond. "I would imagine that kidnapping and confinement are just as illegal in Britain as Canada, right?"

"Don't worry. It's nothing that ominous. Just a bit of pre-wedding fun."

"Tell me what's going on. I have access to a lot of money. I can pay you more than they can — whoever they are and whatever amount they've offered you — I'll double it. No, triple it."

"You mean the Order of the Black Sphinx? No, I think not. The dark side always pays more than the vanilla creams of the world, darling."

"What on earth are you taking about?" Where had she heard that name before? Yes, Allman, the demon guy, had a connection to the ancient order. Damn it, why hadn't she paid more attention to her gut feeling and gotten the hell out of Dodge while there had still been time?

"I don't know what their plans are, *mistress*, but I'm certain it will be quite amusing. Unfortunately, no men are allowed at their ceremonies."

She itched to have that riding crop back in her hands. "You don't really believe you can get away with this? I'm getting married to a duke tomorrow. A lot of people are going to notice if I'm missing."

"I don't think you'll be missing that long. You'll make the wedding, darling." He shrugged, unconcerned.

She wanted to shake the truth out of him. Or whip it out of him.

"How long are we supposed to just wait here?" She began to rummage around the room, looking for a weapon. *Yes, the mace in my bag.* She sneezed for effect, then casually picked up the large carryall from under the bench and slid it onto her lap, as if looking for a tissue.

"Until they call for you. They're setting up right now, I believe. Then I hand you over and just leave. All the other slaves have gone by now. The place is deserted except for your party. Not that I wouldn't like to see the ceremony, but, as I said, it's strictly off-limits to males."

He pulled on a terry robe and sat on a chair, legs casually crossed, inspecting his fingernails. *Creep.*

She found the canister with her fingers and mentally prepared herself. While he was busy making sure his fingernails were perfect, she drew it out and gave him a healthy shot right in the face. *Bingo. Better than a whip.*

The air filled with the harsh odor of pepper spray fumes.

"Bitch!" A stream of foul-mouthed expletives followed.

She grabbed a hand towel and kept it over her nose and mouth to avoid breathing in the toxic fumes. When he was incapacitated and down on the floor, she reached into the waistband of his shorts for the key. No need to whip him — she suspected that was what he was after anyway, and she wasn't prepared to satisfy anyone keeping her locked in a room without her permission.

Unlocking the door as quietly as possible, she pulled her carryall close to her body, the pepper spray cannister in one hand. She stepped from the room, closed and locked the door against the man's shouts for help, and made a quick perusal of the parlor.

Empty. Perfect. Guess everyone is still busy getting their jollies on.

She raced across the larger room, her footsteps thankfully muffled by the thick rug. At least they'd gotten that detail correct.

At the doorway, she carefully peered around it, taking a quick look each way. Still deserted. She hurried down the corridor. *Not far now.* The foyer came into view and her heart rate speeded up. *Just a few more feet.*

A person suddenly lurched in front of her. She banged right into them, nearly knocking her off her feet.

"Where are you're going? The party's just beginning." *Sloan? No. Please, please, don't let her be involved in this bruhaha.*

"This party's not my cup of tea. I'm heading home. You should join me."

"Aww, don't be a party pooper. The best part is about to begin. Lady V and the others are waiting to bestow the honor of the initiation ceremony on you. Don't you want to become part of our little group?"

"No, sorry, I'm already part of a sorority, the Brass Ring, plus I'm all done in. Headache, you understand." Rebecca's fingers curled around the weapon still hiding in her bag. Though Sloan didn't look threatening, something just wasn't right. It might be harmless, but it might be something more. Ah, but she had an ace up her sleeve. Surely the Piers clan would forgive her giving up one piece of such a bountiful harvest if it came to that.

"Ah, Lady Vixen. We're just coming to fetch you." Lady V came striding in the front door, followed by a half-dozen women. It was then Rebecca realized everyone had changed into long black robes with matching hoods. *Beyond creepy.*

"We have need of your attendance at our moonlight ceremony. I promise it will be enlightening and educational, becoming an honorary member of our little group. You're a writer, so you'll enjoy it, I guarantee."

"Yeah, right. What's going on? You need more of my blood?"

"Ah, so you've figured it out." Vanessa narrowed her eyes, the charming smile dropping away like a discarded mask.

"Not rocket science, professor. What century are you living in anyway? If power's what you want, I got something to trade. Much better than mere blood."

"Trade? What are you talking about?"

"The ring of King Solomon that calls upon seventy-two demons. I followed all the clues and discovered it under the castle. It had been left there by the Knights Templar for safekeeping, then guarded by Freemasons, followed by the Order of the Golden Dawn and the Rising Sun. I believe you were on its trail as well, Professor. Sorry you weren't the one to find it. Instead, an amateur bested you." Rebecca shook her head, slowly. "That's the way it goes sometimes." Baiting Vanessa wasn't her smartest action, but maybe it would seed some doubts among her crew. Make the cultists realize she wasn't invincible.

"Let me see it." The words had a death ray attached.

Rebecca ignored the tensions rising around her. She reached in her bag and pulled out the jeweled box that held the sigil, but was careful to keep the mace hidden in the palm of her hand. She tossed the box to the woman. *Forgive me, Ash, but I have no choice.* She'd looked into the woman's crazed eyes and knew she was on shaky ground that could collapse at any moment.

"Here you go. Take a gander at this. I think you'll soon see that keeping me is redundant."

"Oh, *really*. You think I'm going to let you waltz out of here and report any of this?"

"What's to report? So, the door was stuck in the cubicle. No harm done. But I do want to leave — now. Cross this line, Professor, and there's no going back. I have no wish to partake of any more shenanigans this evening."

She hoped her words were enough.

Chapter Twenty-Three

We may have been star-crossed lovers, but together we formed a constellation, forever remembered by the night sky.
— T. Joshua

Ash paced the floor, unable to drive the image of Rebecca in the revealing costume from his mind. He had to see her. Tonight. Before the wedding. Tomorrow would be too late. The thought of any other man laying a finger on her drove him wild. And knowing she was staying in such a private location, away from the cares of the world, where he could just slip in and see her for a while – the enticement was too much. He turned and strode out of the door. He'd checked the map earlier. He could be there in an hour if he got a move on.

* * * *

"It's time for you to come along peacefully, or do you need more persuasion? The ceremony must begin soon, while the moon is at its zenith. This is all for your own good, you realize. A chance to embrace your roots, understand your heritage. I'd think you'd be leaping at the opportunity I'm providing."

That was rich. But all the bravado in the world didn't hold back the frisson of fear developing in the primal part of Rebecca's brain, then slinking like cold lead through her entire nervous system before settling in the pit of her stomach.

"Is that ring not enough for you? You're holding the find of the century. Only the Holy Grail or the Ark of the Covenant would garner more attention." She worked at keeping her tone level, not give in to rising panic.

"It's fabulous, I grant you that. But I need a *little* something more that only you can provide. And in exchange we offer you the fabulous opportunity to become a full-pledged member in the Order of the Black Sphinx, a coveted honor as only those invited unanimously can join." The professor's eyes glittered evilly when she looked up from caressing the ring she'd placed on her thumb, as the circumference was too large for a mortal's mere finger. She appeared drunk with power, her bevy of minions at her back. How had she gone so long without being found out? Or was this a more recent leap into the deep end of the pool? Something was off, some piece of the puzzle Rebecca wasn't party to.

"Care to share what else it is you need from me? As a writer, I find this kind of thing quite interesting. You know, how people intend to get away with detaining someone against their will? I've already made it clear I wish to leave." She said the words lightly, not wanting to push harder than she must. *Take it easy. Baby steps, with a suspected psychopath.* Or maybe this was a true mental illness, untreated. If so, the woman needed help. Professional help.

"Why, if you don't cooperate, we could just take you up to the top-floor balcony for a nice dive into the ground. You know, tragic partygoer-gets-drunk-and-falls scenario. Happens more than you'd think. And lots of witnesses to support the claim. Just kidding, of course! We need you alive and well. Now, let's go." Vanessa gestured with the hand wearing the outsized ring. "And no funny stuff."

Shock reverberated through Rebecca even as a part of her thought the woman had been watching too many old movies to come up with *that* line. *No funny stuff indeed.* This had gone from bad—hell—she couldn't even think of a big enough word to encompass what this new image of her plunging to her death had done to her. She swallowed against the hard lump tightening her throat and attacked, her only card left to play. "The rest of you, you agreed to this? Keeping me here against my will?"

The faces of the women remained vapidly unconcerned. That scared her more than anything. *What are they on – valium?* It was like being on the set of a *Stepford Wives* movie shoot with a lot of dead calm robots. If only her Brass Ringers were here. They'd kick butt for sure. *Good must win out over evil, right? Because, goddamn it, it has to.*

Before she could consider just turning around and skedaddling, a trio of amazon women were suddenly at her back. *Trapped.*

"Ever heard of the twelve-step program for she-devils, Professor?" she deadpanned to cover her fear.

"You'll keep your mouth shut if you know what's good for you and display some respect for the deep honor we're about to bestow on you." A steely warning in Vanessa's eyes accompanied her edict, her gaze flicking up from admiring the ring for a brutal split-second to underline her need for having the last word.

Her fellow members of the Order of the Black Sphinx parted like the waters of the Red Sea as they shepherded their queen bitch to whatever crazy event they were all invited to. Pyramids and Egyptology were looking a lot less alluring by the second.

She stumbled on the steps. Her escort hissed near her ear, proving she'd had garlic for dinner. "Keep up."

"Ever think of having a breath mint or two? Maye a piece of gum?"

"Shut up."

"Don't all prisoners get a last request?"

"You're not a prisoner."

"How do you figure that?" Rebecca twisted around to get a glimpse of the woman. Dressed in a black robe, her face was shadowed by the hood. "I didn't volunteer for this game."

"It's no game we're playing. We're deadly serious. Now *stop* talking. You're annoying me."

"I'm annoying you. Well, excuse me, sweetheart. I'm the one being led to the hanging, not you." Twigs littered the gravel path the women were following in single file, scrunching under everyone's feet. They were into the woods now, the cool of the vegetation making Rebecca shiver in her risqué outfit. Now she could use one of their capes, but so far, she'd not been offered one.

"No one is going to hang you. We're not barbarians."

"Oh really, what do you call this little ceremony you're planning? A stroll in the park?" The full moon hung in the night sky, ancient and ominous. It signaled that time was about up. Did she have any regrets? *Oh yeah, not jumping into bed with Ash every chance I got.* That man did it for her. Even just one night, one night not worrying about anything else — that was all she wanted now. And if she got out of this predicament alive, she was going for it, she promised herself. Grabbing that man by the arm and leading him right to the nearest bed. Or wall. Even the ground would do.

"Just shut the fuck up already."

"Quiet!" The professor turned, her expression dark and past annoyed. *Good. Why should I make it easy for her?*

The women ahead of her broke into two lines, curving around a small open meadow until they stood in a circle, joining with a few other women already in attendance. She was led into the middle. God, what did they have planned? It boggled her mind that she was in such a dire situation. What could she have done differently? A lot of things, if she'd only been aware. Fake engagements had a way of tying up a million or two brain cells. Surely they didn't think they'd get away with it? It had to be a ruse, a joke, a vast rift in the cosmos.

She'd seen better odds in Vegas. She counted twelve women — she'd be the thirteenth if she hung around. *Not going to happen.* She caught a slight movement out of the corner of her eyes, and more figures in black flowed in and around the group, mixing with the first tier. Reinforcements. Her heart fell further. She gulped, perspiration running in trickles down her sides, chilling her in the damp air.

A flash of light reflecting off a shiny object drew her full attention. *Oh boy.* Vanessa's right hand now held a ceremonial dagger. It must have been tucked in the folds of her robe. *I don't like where this is headed...*

Vanessa held the knife out in front of her, and her followers at one end of the circle parted, revealing a structure set up on the ground. Made of what looked like dark wood, it rose three feet off the grass, long and narrow, with room for a body to lie on top. Some kind of an altar, a place of ill repute in this context, no doubt. *If they think I'm crawling up on that thing, they have another think coming. This kind of shite never ends well. "I wanna see you be brave."* The words of the song fired her brain, helping her keep the panic at bay.

She waited it out, fingers clasped around the mace. *Please, please, let there be enough left for a good final dosing.*

The professor obviously loved theatrics, using Latin phrases and sweeping gestures in front of the makeshift altar. It was set up inside a pentagram marked out on the grass, now visible. It enthralled the rest of the members, judging by their stance. When Rebecca heard the words from her recent nightmare repeated, she started, nearly losing it. She disliked the unexplainable. Intensely. But maybe in the future, she might consider listening to her intuition a bit more?

When the professor turned back toward her, the ornamental dagger still clutched in her hand, Rebecca knew it was now or never. Like a gunslinger of wild west fame, she was just about to bring up her right hand, setting off a noxious spray of pepper right into the woman's face — at least she could take her down before she was swamped by the others — when a familiar voice interrupted her concentration. *What?*

She turned toward the voice. *Impossible.*

"Rebecca, it's me. Miranda." The woman slipped off her mask, revealing the beloved face of her friend.

"And me. Elin."

"It's all of us." One by one, her friends removed their masks. Lacey, Lily, Ava, Tessa and even Casey, who must have abandoned her archeological dig. Her heart filled with emotion. *What are they doing here? Who cares?* She was just so darned happy to see them.

"What do you think you're doing? Stop them! I — I am your high sorceress. You *must* obey. The spirits proclaim it." The professor's voice thundered across the meadow, but her followers appeared uncertain. Some clasped hands, others stood silent, unprepared to be challenged, to be surrounded. All the Ringers came forward, pushing through the line, gathering around her like in an old western when the covered wagons circled for protection. She took the same fighting stance as them, feet planted on the ground, arms raised ready for some Kung Fu action. All the self-defense lessons since high school were about to pay off. Big time. *Bring it on, ladies!*

And the sixty-four-thousand-dollar question — would the woman have the common sense or decency to stand down now?

"What is your problem? This is our good friend you're messing with," Miranda announced, not a woman to take any guff. Ever. Even from a suspected ghost when she was on one of her paranormal exploits. And never from any self-proclaimed sorceress from this lifetime.

"How dare you! This is my coven, my supporters. This will be avenged. I have the ring of Solomon! I can bring the wrath of demons down on your heads." The so-called sorceress brandished the knife around, shielding her body while threatening theirs.

"I'd drop that if I were you, lady," Elin said, exposing the taser she held in her hand, its green light promising action if the woman did anything rash.

Sweet.

"You will pay for this. That I swear." But Vanessa let the knife drop to the ground, obviously aware that none of her crew were backing her up. Miranda quickly moved forward, picking the weapon up off the ground.

Rebecca moved forward, confronting the professor. Most likely *former* professor once word of this event leaked out. "Hand over the ring. It belongs to the Piers family."

Vanessa backed up a step, but Elin held out the taser again. "Do as she says. Now!"

With poor grace, the woman threw the ring at her. She managed to catch it in mid-air. It felt warm and heavy in the palm of her hand as she closed her fingers around it. She tucked it into her cleavage to keep it safe and threw away the pepper spray. She'd lost her carryall in the kerfuffle and glanced around for it. But it had vanished.

Elin grabbed her attention with a firm nudge to her shoulder. "Go. We've got this. Ash is waiting for you. He'll take you home."

"Ash? For me?" She was too stunned to take the information in. "He's here?"

"Yes, you goof. He's over there." Elin pointed at the tree line, where Rebecca could barely make out a tall figure moving toward her. "He just arrived. He needs to talk with you." She gave her a nudge with her shoulder, but Rebecca planted her feet.

"But why are you all here? I mean—don't get me wrong I'm so glad you are—but how did you know?" *Who doesn't love the cavalry showing up at the last second?*

But being mystified to the why and how summed it up. Her eyes stayed focused on the figure in the distance while she waited for answers.

"We were invited, of course, for your wedding tomorrow, by Edward. He's been so helpful, filling us in on doings at the castle. It was going to be a *big* surprise. Then today we found out about the hen party, and decided to surprise you early. *Thank goodness.* And the rest is history. Now get out of here. Tomorrow's your wedding day and we want you to be rested and feeling your best. We'll see you back at the castle. Go!"

She backed away from her crew then, moving through the darkened woods in a trance. *Ash.* He was waiting for her.

Rebecca.

She ran straight into his arms, her chest heaving. *What the fuck is going on?* Nevertheless, he pulled her in tight, savoring her body next to his, while worry sent his stomach into hard knots.

"What's wrong, beautiful?"

She took control, grasping at his arms to tug him towards the car he'd just exited. A Rolls-Royce Dawn luxury convertible leased to impress potential backers of his brewing company. It looked like business partners weren't necessary now that unlimited funds were available, thanks to this incredible woman.

"We should go," she insisted.

"What happened?"

"You don't want to know." She shook her head. "It was all so crazy. Please, let's just go. I want to get out of here."

"Are you okay?"

"I'm fine now." She did sound fine, if a bit agitated.

But he was taking no chances.

He swooped her up in his arms and hurried back to the car, where he tucked her into the passenger side and went around to the driver's. He'd been taking the side road to the property when Miranda had returned his call, filling him in that they were surprising Rebecca at her hen party, and did he want to meet them there? Then the next call had been far more sinister, saying something was up and he should be prepared to take Rebecca home.

Now, he kept an eye on Rebecca as she struggled to calm down, taking deep breaths. It was enough just to have her by his side.

She put a hand to her breast, drawing his attention to her skimpy outfit. But now was not the time to seduce. He chafed at the bit, needing to let her know how he felt. He had never wanted her more.

"I can't believe what happened tonight." She shook her head, her tumble of blonde hair flowing around her bare shoulders in disarray. He longed to run his hands through the silky stands and hold her close. Preferably naked. And himself as well. He forced his thoughts away from the lustful image. He needed to know what had gone on tonight.

"Care to tell me about it?"

"Those women—they're even nuttier than your family."

"That's saying a lot."

She favored him with a smile.

"Yeah, well, you guys do have your moments. But I've come to find it all quite charming."

"What did the women do to you? It was just a hen party with an outrageous theme, right?"

"It was a hell of a lot more than that." She pressed her lips together tightly and shook her head. "They wanted to make me join the Order of the Black Sphinx."

"What? How can they make you do that?"

"They have a way of persuading you it's in your best interests. Like veiled threats and ceremonial daggers."

He gave her a look of disbelief. "Are you sure they didn't doctor your drinks or something? Give you hallucinations?"

"No, it was all too real."

"Okay, tell me everything."

And she did. When she got to the point of being locked in the cubicle, he just about lost it, ready to turn the car right around and confront the women himself. But she insisted they not go back, that her friends were taking care of everything. They'd most likely call the police and report the bizarre event. But one thing was for certain, the professor was stricken from the guest list. Rebecca insisted. That part made him shake his head. Rebecca never failed to amaze him. And if she was a gold-digger, well, he could come to terms with that. There was so much about her to admire that the how or why of things seemed less important now. The most important was that she was by his side.

"I just want to go home. Try to forget it ever happened."

"Do you think of the castle as your home now?" His heart softened. What a big a word that was. Home.

"Yes, I do. Your family, crazy and fun-loving as they are, have come to mean so much to me. I only have one humongous regret."

"What's that?"

She hesitated for a second, then gave a quick nod as if she'd made up her mind.

"Not taking you up your offer of jumping into the sack. When I was standing there, wondering if I was going to escape in one piece, that was what I wanted the most. To share a bed with you. If just for one night."

He swallowed hard, his hands shaky on the wheel. So shaky that he signaled a lane change and slowed right down, pulling onto the side of the road. The vehicle rolled to a stop. He didn't trust himself to drive.

A split second of eerie silence descended. He gathered the courage to turn and look at her. She stared back into his eyes, her true feelings shining in their crystal depths. A sense of destiny larger than himself rose, nearly swallowing him whole. He yearned to communicate his true feelings to this woman. This incredible woman who had changed everything for him.

"We need to talk."

"No more talking." She pressed a finger to his lips, locking eyes with his, giving him a look that scorched his soul. "I don't want to think or talk. I want to find the nearest hotel or bed and breakfast. Is that too much to ask—too selfish? I haven't signed the marriage certificate yet. I'm technically a free agent."

He touched her rounded cheek, gently swiping a streak of dirt away. He pulled a twig from her hair and tossed it on the floor, then tucked a stray curl behind a delicate ear. "You're so beautiful, you take my breath away." His voice was roughened by emotion.

Unshed tears glittered in her eyes. But there was hunger too. A hunger mirroring his own.

As he leaned down to kiss her, she rose off the seat to kiss him. Their lips met, the touch electrifying and real. *Heat. Passion. Need.* His body wanted this woman more than he thought possible. He wanted all of her, naked, writhing under his touch.

"Let me in," he spoke against her lips, each caress, each sliding movement an overture to what he wanted most. To have her giving and pliant in his arms, calling his name.

His tongue ravished her mouth, seeking why she was the one. Her taste, her touch, her softness, all spoke to him on a primal level he neither understood nor could explain. But he did know that *this* woman — this package of pure dynamite — was the woman he was destined to be with. If just for one night. Pain seared at the realization and he tamped it down. He had to. Otherwise his heart would break.

He kissed her lips, her cheeks, her eyelids, then trailed kisses down her neck to her breasts, exposed to his view by the daring outfit. Her nipples responded, pebbling tightly, arousing him further.

A sweet moan escaped her mouth and he increased the torture. The urge to devour her, claim her, sent his mind reeling. His cock lengthened and thickened with the urgent need for release. Uncomfortable, he shifted in his seat, trying to relieve the pressure, holding on to her as though he was afraid she'd vanish right before his eyes. Like she had been doing for weeks now.

But it was so much more than physical. It dawned on him with what brain power remained that it was as much about how she made him feel as it was anything. How she made him want to be a better man. He'd never had more than just a passing need for any woman since Samantha's betrayal. This was different. This made sense. This scared the bejesus out of him.

But he couldn't pull away. He pushed past the fear. Embraced the unknown, if just for one night. But as he thought that again, he knew one night would be too much and a thousand nights not enough.

He took a deep breath, pressing his lips against her full breast, paying homage. And praying that somehow, someway, this woman would be his, without him losing everything else he had. His family. His reputation. His life.

He pulled together what little strength of mind and purpose he had in reserve, even as he accepted an understanding of something greater than himself going on. They were lovers who were passionate beyond all reason. Like Romeo and Juliet. Cleopatra and Mark Anthony. Tristan and Isolde. But how could that be? How, in modern Britain, in the common of the everyday, could such an enormous passion arise? It confounded him.

Or maybe, just maybe, this was how it was? That when a man or woman found their true mate, everything changed? He had no way of knowing if that was the way of it, nothing to compare it to. Only that he felt it and it was real. And he would never be the same again.

He took a deep appreciative breath, seeking the lovely vanilla cookie fragrance wafting from her, the undertones of a woman's sharp arousal.

He gathered her closer, tighter to his thundering heart. It beat in tandem with hers. If only what she was experiencing was a fraction of what he was undergoing, she had to see, had to know that she was his now. His for all time. No. It was more than that. He was hers too. Now and forever. *May fate have mercy on me.* He could never leave her now. If she married his father, he was doomed to walk the earth in ghost form, a shell, a broken spirit. *Please, dear God, let me communicate all I feel to this woman so that she understands what I have to do.*

"Stop, you're squeezing me too tight," she jokingly protested, a sweet smile lighting up her face as she pulled away. "So, are we going to find that bed or what?"

"Yes. A bed."

She laughed lightly. "A man of few words, eh?"

He cleared his throat, started the car, his body tight from holding so much inside. "If I begin, I'll never stop."

She gave him a glance, her expression baffled. "You can say anything you want to me, right? You know that."

"Beautiful, what I want to say would take too long."

"We have all night, handsome."

"A lifetime would not be long enough."

Out of the corner of his eye, he saw her eyebrows knit. She began chewing on a fingernail.

"Nothing to say now?" he asked, working to keep his voice steady.

"Please, let's not make this more difficult. I just want to forget for one night. Can we do that? Just enjoy each other. Not worry about…anything else." She'd been about to mention tomorrow, he was certain of it. The thought of the day and what it meant made his stomach twist in pain. He pressed his lips together.

"Sure. I'll take whatever I can get." *And pray for more…*

She kept her face turned away, back to chewing on the nail, apparently fascinated by the passing greenery.

"How about a bed and breakfast? There's one close. Camomile & Camelot."

"Perfect. One should be soothed while revisiting that era, eh?"

The reminder of the fall of the three star-crossed lovers gave him pause even as he embraced the quirky 'eh' he found so charming.

When he turned onto the driveway leading to the business and she caught sight of the golden castle-like structure for the first time, giggles erupted, making his heart reel.

"It's awesome." Her expression quickened and she pointed at the turrets and spirals of the golden castle with its drawbridge for guests to walk along. She flushed, drawing his attention to the perfection of her skin, suffused with pink.

Keep your mind on the road, Ash.

He found a parking space in front of the establishment and turned to her. They locked eyes, the current that had been raging inside arcing between them. The connection burned, like a spark about to combust into flame.

His instincts took over. He gave a solemn nod. "Ready?"

"Yeah, I think so."

"If you're not. I understand." *Nothing* inside him would understand if she changed her mind, but he had to say and do the proper thing. Be the right man for her.

"I'm as sure as I'll ever be. But we must never, never, *ever* speak of this again. Right?"

He swallowed hard. Could he do this? Have his dream girl for one night only? Then walk away? Perhaps an earthquake or a tornado or a tsunami or even a horde of zombies that threatened all human existence would descend on the isle. Then they could make good their escape. Hide out in a cabin in the woods with no amenities. He didn't care. He just wanted to be with her.

"I want you any way I can have you." That was the truth.

"Maybe we'll be like that pair of lovers in that old movie, *Same Time Next Year*?" Though the words were meant to be taken lightly, Rebecca's voice broke, trying to manage the proper nonchalance. His heart squeezed for her. For them.

"I don't want to do anything but love you." He ran his hands through her hair, tugging her face close to his, touching foreheads. "I can't do that. Walk away and see you like this only once a year. Without barriers between us."

"What other choice do we have? Please, let's not talk anymore. Let's get a room. Make me forget, Ash."

She pulled out of his grasp and exited the car. He did likewise and came around to take her arm.

"How are we going to explain the lack of luggage?" she asked, peering up at him.

"Lack of luggage is the least of our concerns. How are we going to get away with your get-up?"

She gave a shaky laugh, looking down at her clothes. Or lack there of. "Like the hooker in *Pretty Woman*, I'll get dissed."

"If they dare to make you feel one iota less than you should, my God, I won't be held responsible for my actions," he growled.

"Calm down. No need to go all he-man on me. I'm sure they'll just think it was a costume party or something."

"They'd better."

Arm-in-arm, they crossed the drawbridge. *The portal to paradise.* He was barely holding it together, certain that at any moment, something, anything, would come along unexpectedly, tear them apart, making his worst nightmare come true. But it all went well, and soon they stood at the threshold to the suite on the top floor, the aptly titled *Lancelot & Guinevere Room*.

With a grand gesture, he kicked open the door, swept her up into his arms and carried her inside. A huge bed dominated the space and he headed directly for it. "I should shower," she said, even as her hands began to make short work of his clothes.

"Later."

His shoes thumped loudly hitting the floor. She tore off his shirt, then attacked his pants, pulling down the zipper. He struggled with her corset, groaning at how hard it was to get off. She turned around and presented her back where a string tied the whole thing together. He worked the knots loose and her breasts sprang free. *Finally.* For one glorious moment he stared at her. His wild woman, all honey-blonde hair and satin flesh. A feast for his starving eyes. She set aside on the night table an item she pulled from her bodice. He ignored it, his interest only in seeing and being with her.

"You're so beautiful."

"Not too shabby yourself, handsome." The twinkle in her eyes about did him in.

He pulled back and pushed off his pants and underwear in one smooth move. She watched his actions, her eyes growing rounder.

"You're very blessed."

"Thanks."

He tugged at her boots, pulling them off and tossing them on the floor. She unrolled her stockings in a gesture of seduction that made his body heat well past comfort.

"You're killing me." But he made himself take his time. If they only had one night, he wanted her to remember it. *Always.* He knelt, taking a shapely calf into his hands to run his fingers along the softness of her flesh up past her knees. He caught a glimpse of her skimpy black panties. One strip of thin lace was the only thing standing between him and her.

She smiled, her glance locking with his. She reached, caught the panties between her thumbs and tugged them down, revealing herself. All of her was the same—flushed, pink and ready for him. She licked her lips in an invitation.

He growled, kissed her leg and worked his way upward, keeping his eyes locked with hers. He wanted to see her, all of her, and know what effect he was having. When he hit the V between her legs, she rose, presenting herself to him.

He drank her. *Nectar. Sweet and salty.* And all hers.

When her body arched with orgasm, he held on, giving her all she needed, lapping all she had. He moved quickly, giving her no time to recover. Pausing to pull on a condom, he straddled her body and entered her in one swift indelible moment. Ash drove himself deep and her tight walls closed around him, squeezing him, making it hard to hold back and wait for her to build up to another orgasm. But in a matter of a few strokes, she was groaning again, seeking release. The pressure built inside him, the need for his own climax excruciating.

"*Oh my God*, unbelievable," he whispered, the tension exquisite and mind-blowing. Then he was spiraling into his own full-on ecstasy. Wave after wave of pleasure rolled through him, each larger than the rest, until they began to recede, leaving him on a distant shore.

They lay exhausted in each other's arms, holding tightly to the other, not wanting to let go. Their harsh breathing taking time to reside, he took a moment to pull the sweaty stands of hair from her lovely face.

"Wow, that, that was... I'm sorry, I don't have the words." Her eyes bigger and rounder and brighter than ever before, she stared up at him. Her expression alone convinced him she had felt it, the overwhelming sensation that they were a perfectly matched pair, a favored event of gigantic proportions. Even knowing he had fallen in love with her the first moment he'd laid eyes on her, all indignant and holding her ground in the tunnel, he still hadn't expected this. This wonder at their being together, sharing the gift of themselves.

"That must be a first," he quipped back. Giddy with life, no other word for it. Right now, if a unicorn — or any magical creature for that matter — ran through their room, he'd not blink an eye, assuming it belonged.

Chapter Twenty-Four

And remember, as it was written, to love another person is to see the face of God. — Victor Hugo

Rebecca propped her head against the nest of pillows, basking in the wonder of having just made love with the incredible man singing off-key in the shower for — what was it? *The seventh, no, eighth time. Somehow, we managed it. Kept real life at bay for hours.* Sunlight crept around the drapes covering the windows, announcing the new day.

Ash's cellphone beeped. She glanced at it, wishing she had hers, remembering that a certain witch had snatched it away.

He came into the room then, drops of water sparkling on his smooth chest, his hair damp from the shower. Nine sounded like a better number.

"Your phone buzzed."

He glanced at it, then picked it up, checking the number. His expression darkened.

"Who is it?"

"My father."

The words hung between them. The room darkened. Even the sun vanished behind the clouds.

"I'm going to tell him," he said. She looked at him in shock.

"No, he's got a bad heart. What if—"

"It kills him like this is killing me—us." His brown eyes smoldered darker than she'd ever seen them.

"We could hold off on our being together until—you know—things change."

"No." He shook his head. "That's not right. We have to make this right." He came closer, sat on the edge of the bed and took both her hands in his.

"You love me, right?"

She had never seen him so serious. "Did I not say it enough times last night while I was screaming your name? Of course I love you. More than I could possibly say, you know that."

"Then we face this thing together. We go back now and tell him about us. He has a right to know."

"No, I can't do that. I can't bear the idea of anything bad happening to your family because of us. I couldn't live with myself if it did. And all those people are arriving today— No, we can't chance it. I'm sorry."

They dressed in silence. She had lost her carryall in the woods, so there was nothing to do but dress in the same costume. When he tied her corset at the back, his hand lingered on her shoulder. She reached up and held on to the lifeline. He kissed her hand, then moved away.

"Time to go."

She remembered the ring and picked it up, tucking it back into her bodice. Somehow it had lost its luster. Ash hadn't even mentioned its presence.

As if in a dream, she walked with him from the room and down the hallway to the lobby. She ignored the inquisitive glances. What did it matter what she was wearing? They were about to break a man's heart, no matter which way this went. Better a broken heart than end a life.

The day had turned from bright sunshine to threatening rain in mere minutes, the dark clouds moving in from high over the ocean, ready to dump their weight of accumulated moisture on the land. The anticipation of the static-charged air pebbled her skin with goosebumps, making her shiver.

Ash pulled her close, draping his arm around her to keep her warm.

"I have something else to tell you."

"Hmm." Her mind was active someplace else, thinking ahead.

"I'm glad you won't be alone today. I'm happy you'll be surrounded by your friends." His quiet, resigned tone was tough to hear, though she instantly understood and knew she would do the same under the circumstances.

She swallowed. *A heart crying must feel like this.*

"Thank you."

"For what?"

"For being you."

He said nothing more, helping her into the passenger side of the car. He was right, they needed to save their strength for what lie ahead. The one thing she knew, it was going to be brutal, however it turned out. There was no way getting around that.

* * * *

Thirty minutes later they drove under the portcullis into the castle courtyard and parked. He turned off the motor, giving Rebecca a glance.

"Ready, beautiful?"

"Yeah, ready as I'll ever be. How are you going to explain our taking so long to get back here? A fiancée being out all night doesn't bode well."

"Just follow my lead. I got this."

He would be strong for her now, make it work. That was his job. Sometime during the best night of his life, he had assumed the mantle to keep her safe and protected. And he would honor it.

At least the rain had stopped, freshening the air. They walked side by side, not touching, into the castle.

"Where's Sloan? I thought she was with you?" the dowager asked. She was sitting in the Great Room with his father. They were drinking morning coffee from china teacups and they both looked up when they entered.

"It's a long story, but I don't think you should expect her anytime today. Or possibly ever."

"Such an unreliable girl." His grandmother tisk-tisked.

Ash cleared his throat. He'd deal with the whole Vanessa and Sloan situation later. "I have something I need to discuss with father."

"Sorry, no time for that now, son. The wedding guests will be arriving shortly. Rebecca, your friends are here and waiting for you upstairs. Ash, I need you with me."

And before he could turn around, his father had grabbed his arm and was hustling him out of the room. He was surprisingly strong for a man at death's door.

He turned to see Rebecca being led away by his grandmother in an equally firm grip. He groaned. How had it come to this? Just when he was prepared to step up and do the right thing...

* * * *

"Rebecca! Finally! We've got everything ready for you." Miranda turned from laying something out on the bed, catching sight of her. She was already dressed in a pretty party dress. Lilac lace in a close-fitting bodice with a full skirt that skimmed her knees.

"What are you doing here? How did things go last night?" Rebecca was filled with questions, eyeing her own wedding finery strewn about the room. Lacey and Lily popped out from the bathroom, dressed in the same becoming dresses. Ah, they were bridesmaid dresses. When had that happened? Casey and Elin, along with Ava, barged in behind her, similarly dressed. They did look beautiful, she had to admit, if surreal under present circumstances. *Well, time to suck it up, buttercup.*

"Fine. All is well. We just need to get you ready. Your hair and makeup need a bit of work. Thank goodness Lacey's a charm at such things."

"Come on. We need to get you showered and ready. There's no time to lose!" Lacey said, coming over and tugging her by the arm into the bathroom.

"O—kay."

She was given strict instructions to take a fast shower, then hustled out of the bathroom in her robe to be perfumed, pampered, made-up, hair-styled in a fashionable updo, and ready to be dressed in record time. *Kind of like a lamb to the slaughter.*

She stepped into the gown with the tulle skirt and allowed her friends to sort it out. When the veil went on and she caught a glimpse of herself in the mirror, her legs turned to rubber and she nearly collapsed back onto the bed. It was Elin who helped keep her on her feet. "Whoa, I'll bet you forgot to eat something, sweetie. Here, have this." She handed her a glass of orange juice. "It will tide you over until the ceremony's finished."

She dutifully drank it down.

"Better?"

She nodded, her throat too tight to speak.

"You look so beautiful, Rebecca. Wow, you clean up nice, girlfriend."

The door to the bedroom swung open, revealing Gracie groomed for the wedding. She fairly danced into the room, wearing the same style of dress as the others, though in a deep purple shade, denoting her status of maid of honor.

"You look so beautiful!" Rebecca moved forward to hug her. Knowing she was doing the right thing by the sweet young girl gave her an essential injection of courage.

Her friends, old and new, gathered round her in the mirror, a lovely pointillism painting brought to life. It was a gorgeous image, the eight of them in their wedding finery surrounding a vision in white. Her. She was more than thankful her friends had not questioned her decision, even if it had surprised her that they hadn't said a word, but had done what they had to do to pull off the day. *Best friends a gal can have. Ever.*

"Thank you, guys. For being here for me." Her heart swelled three sizes.

"Where else would we be on your wedding day, you goof?" Elin asked, her white-blonde hair pulled into a sleek chignon like all the others, though Miranda's locks were too short and just slicked back. Sophisticated and beautiful. She heard the tremble in her voice, and knew she was holding back — heck, they all were, judging by their expressions. A group hug ensued and a few tears spilled.

"Okay. We all ready?"

Everyone nodded.

"Then let's go get 'em!" Miranda spoke for them all.

* * * *

Ash fumbled with the knot on his black silk tie. The fancy monkey suit was stifling, and he took a few deep breaths in an effort to calm himself, staring at his pale image in the mirror. He had no idea how he was going to survive *any* of what was coming. In a few minutes he was expected to stand beside his father and watch him marry the woman of his dreams. Surely some sense of mercy was left in the vast universe for his plight? Maybe an earthquake or volcanic eruption could be arranged by someone in charge to stop this friggin' freight train? *I promise to behave for the rest of my life if you make this upcoming wedding not happen.* He knew it was too much to hope for.

"Have you got the rings, son?" His father had slipped into the room unnoticed while he had been trying to bribe fate.

"Ahh, sorry, no."

"Good thing I have them right here then." The cheerful tone of his father grated today, making him feel like the worst son ever for all he was going through.

If his dad could put the best face on it, with all he was facing, then Ash had to suck it up and get on with things. It wasn't the end of the world, right? *Hell, yeah, it is.* He ignored the voice and gave his father the best imitation of a decent son he could scrounge up from the mess he was inside.

"Thanks. I keep losing track of them."

"No worries. Okay, we ready? We need to get out there before the bride makes her appearance. We don't want to keep our beautiful Rebecca waiting."

"Dad, about that—" He had no idea what he was going to say, fumbling around in the dark recesses of his mind to come up with the words to fix what couldn't be fixed. He never got the chance as a loud knock on the door interrupted, taking his father's attention away.

The other groomsmen flowed into the room, one holding a giant magnum of Dom Perignon. Another held champagne flutes. The young men were all friends of the family. Surprisingly, Arthur, his best friend, was standing up with Ash's dad. Why? What was wrong with choosing a wife his own age? *Fucking mid-life crisis shit. Okay, gotta get a lid on this or I will screw this all up.*

"We need to make a toast." Arthur popped the cork from the champagne and sloshed it into eight flutes. "Here's to the groom who's won the most beautiful of brides, Rebecca Fairfax!"

"Here, here," a chorus of male voices said, each picking up a glass and saluting.

"Are we ready?" Edward asked, setting down his empty champagne flute.

"You bet."

"Then let's do this thing."

The men lined up and made their way through the French doors to the lawn where the ceremony was to take place. They trooped in military precision to the overhanging bower arranged for the nuptials, arranging themselves on one side of the altar, leaving the other for the women. It would be perfection, if this were any other wedding.

A couple of hundred guests sat in rows of chairs in their wedding finery, waiting for events to unfold, their chairs festooned with gold, purple and lilac ribbons floating softly in the breeze. A gold carpet runner lay in the center for the bride and bridesmaids to enter on. It was strewn with fragrant flower petals, as was the scented bower over the heads of the bride and groom.

He took a deep breath, standing beside his father. Love birds, confined in a crate, were cooing nearby, drawing his attention. *Good Lord, a lot of fuss and bother for a wedding.* Though on another level he got it — *for the right woman, a man will go all out.*

A few chords on an organ announced the pending arrival of the women. The first female placed her dainty satin shoes on the golden walk and began her slow procession to the front, followed by another and another. Then Gracie took her turn. His lips formed into a weak smile. She looked enchanting in her pretty lace dress. The music hit a thundering crescendo, announcing the imminent arrival of the bride. Everyone stood and turned.

Ash took a deep breath, his gaze focused on the exact spot she would be first visible. A vision in white appeared, her beautiful face through the thin gauzy veil beyond lovely. Exactly what a man wanted to see coming down the aisle toward him. The woman any man would be proud to wake up with every morning for the rest of his life. If only it were so...

She moved slowly, stumbled a bit and his heart lurched in his chest. Was she all right? But she righted her step and kept moving forward. Right up to almost beside him, one man between them. His father.

"Dearly beloved, we are gathered here today..."

White noise filled his ears, roaring so loudly that the minister's voice fell away. Then a line stood out, drawing his attention.

"If no one present can give just cause why these two people should not be joined in holy matrimony —"

Joined in holy matrimony. No. Holy Fuck. This is wrong. Panic filled him, his skin crawling with an army of ants threatening to burrow inside his flesh and eat him alive. If he let this happen, he would be drowned in sorrow. Forever. He knew it. Knew he would love this woman for all time.

"Stop! No, this is all wrong!"

The stunned silence was so thick a feather floating to the floor would have been heard.

"Ash, please, no, you can't do this. It's okay. It's the right thing to do." Rebecca moved enough around his father's body to confront him.

He took her hand, tugged on her moving her closer, pushing his father aside in the process. "Sorry, I must do this. Please, you must let me make this right for you — for us."

He saw her look of deep worry and squeezed her hand with reassurance. He turned to his father, who stared at him with astonishment.

"You know I love you dearly, right? You're my father. I can't imagine my life without you, or Grandmother or

Gracie. I've wanted nothing but happiness for everyone — even when I've been a hard case."

"Of course, son. But it means a lot to me to hear you say it. I love you too."

The dowager spoke up from a few feet away sitting in the front row, nodding sagely. "I've loved you since you were born, Ash. Even when you took it upon yourself to be the district's Lothario. At least you were the best at it."

He flushed. "I am sorry about my previous behavior." He felt Rebecca's eyes on him as he accepted responsibility for his past actions. *A man can't go back and change things, much as he wants, but he can move forward and do better.* "There is something I need to share with you. Something that has happened that I never expected to, not in a million years." He hesitated. The world was crashing in on him. His heart lurched in his chest and he swallowed hard. Would he lose his precious family over this? Would his father be all right? Could he even do this? *Please, dear God, give me the strength to do the right thing. Please, tell me how to do this...*

He straightened his shoulders, a belief coming from inside that a man has only one chance in life to make things right for his woman. And this moment in time, it was his to do. Rebecca was so kind she would have gone through with what she should never have been asked to do. This was his to fix. "I've fallen in love with a woman who means the world to me. A woman I can't live without, much as I've tried to." He turned to Rebecca, squeezing her hand in a simple gesture.

He bit his lip — there was no turning back now. He prayed that the news would not damage his relationship with his father beyond repair. But for this woman, he was prepared to risk it all. He had to. The choice didn't feel like his own, as though he owned it. It felt as necessary as breathing.

His father stood straighter, his eyes narrowed in thought, his next words shocking. "When did this happen?" He looked over at the dowager, as if for support.

"It's been happening since the beginning. I'm so sorry. I fell in love with Rebecca almost as soon as I saw her. Then at the Teddy Bears' Picnic, when I watched her being so selfless for Gracie, and wanting nothing but the best for this family by staying engaged to a man she doesn't love—I'm sorry for your loss, Father, but I can't let her marry you when she loves me."

"What about the fact you called her a gold-digger? That she came here hiding the fact she was hoping to do some research on our family line for the books she writes?" The duke looked him straight in the eyes, wanting to know the answers. He had never seen his father more serious. But at least he was upright, not clutching at his chest. He'd had no idea he was going to do this. It had just happened, something organic he could not have stopped for anything. But if his family paid the ultimate price—losing their patriarch—he had no idea what he would do.

Ash shook his head. "It doesn't matter anymore. I'm so far beyond worrying about that stuff. What matters is doing the right thing now by Rebecca. But if I lose my family over this..." He swallowed. Hard. "I hope you can all forgive me. I'm sorry for my past actions. About Samantha and all the women. It will never happen again. You have my word as a Piers. I would swear a blood oath if that helps."

His father waved away that too.

"And you intend to do right by her?"

"Yes, of course, sir."

"Then you have my blessing and the dowager's as well."

His grandmother beamed at him.

"Sorry, excuse me?" Stunned beyond anything he had ever experienced, he shook his head to make sure he was hearing correctly. Seeing correctly. He felt Rebecca's hand holding on tighter, darn near cutting off the circulation to his fingers.

"You've made me proud, son. Standing up and declaring your love for this fine, outstanding woman."

He blinked. The words did not quite register. "*What? Aren't you upset? You were going to marry her.*" His mind floundered, trying to make sense of events.

He glanced at Rebecca. She looked flabbergasted, her eyes wide and staring with disbelief at his father.

He checked out his father again. He looked fine. His color was good. No sign of any medical distress. Realization dawned. He'd been played. Hell, they'd both been played. A spark of anger rose beneath the overwhelming relief that filled him.

"Were you just pretending to want to marry me?" Rebecca's voice sounded squeaky. She'd found her way to the final door of the labyrinth around the same time as him, opening it wide and trying to grasp what had been revealed.

"It worked, didn't it?" His father's expression turned smug as hell. "I even called your Brass Ringer friends and got them on board. And of course, Mother knew from that first day."

"Of all the dirty, low-down tricks to play on us. When I think of the time I spent worrying about your health and well-being, my God! I have no words."

"Careful, son. You're getting what you wanted. The woman and the blessing of your family."

"Did Gracie know?" His father had the wherewithal to look embarrassed.

"No, but she'll be fine with this. She loves you both." Gracie gave him a look of stunned surprise, standing on the other side of Rebecca. Then nodded, even managing a smile.

Ash shook his head. But his father had a point that was impossible to ignore. His ruse had worked. Ash had changed, become a better man. And soon as he'd gotten over the anger, he'd thank him.

He took a deep, cleansing breath. Now was as good a time as any to step up, drop the charade and speak honestly.

"I don't know what to say. I never saw this coming. And I admit, I'm angry at being played, but at the same time I'm also relieved. I had no wish to hurt anyone. It would have broken my heart to be disowned by my family. To lose you all. You mean more to me than I can put into words."

"I know, son. You don't have to say another word." His father's expression softened.

"But I do. I need to thank you."

"What? Don't expect me to thank him for pulling a stunt like that," Rebecca muttered, though he could tell her heart wasn't into it. Judging by her expression, she was as relieved as him.

His father chuckled. "You got yourself some woman there, son. I hope you both will be very happy."

"And produce many fine offspring," the dowager added with a wink. "You know she has those fine birthing hips for a reason."

"Grandmother. Please."

Rebecca's cheeks turned a brighter shade of red. "You're way ahead of yourselves. There's been no talk of children or marriage. We're just starting out, for heaven's sake!"

The dowager waved a royal hand. "Semantics, my girl. Any fool can see where this is leading. I may be eighty, but I'm not blind."

Ash sighed. *Family. Can't live with them*, but he was damn glad not to be living without them. Then he remembered something. Then hadn't used protection last night in the wild need to be with each other. *What if Rebecca is pregnant?* Holy fuck, it was entirely possible.

"Would you care to marry the girl now, Ash? Everyone is waiting." His grandmother asked the question, her expression composed, a twinkle still visible in her faded blue eyes.

Marry. Right now? Going from almost losing the woman of his dreams to being asked to step up to the plate—well, life didn't get any better than this.

"Yes, I will." He swallowed. "If she'll have me?" His heart stopped, literally, while he waited for her answer.

Discombobulated, addled, shaken, thrown, undone, flustered, unnerved, rattled. Yup, they all worked. Rebecca was equal parts pissed and relieved, leaning toward the relief side of the equation as the seconds ticked by. How had she not had one inkling of this twist? She was a writer, for heaven's sake. *But, really, how could any sane person have seen this coming? Real life is not a book.* And yet, she realized her story would make a great autobiography one day. Chapters on finding ancient treasure and King Solomon's ring, being held captive by a madwoman—and even more crazy—

being played by a man who turned out to be the father of the man she'd fallen in love with. Course, she'd have to live the next forty or fifty years first to finish her story, but she was willing to wait.

"I have something to confess too," she spoke up, wanting the air clear before she addressed Ash. Not the least was they hadn't used protection last night, but what the family didn't know about that would be fine for now. There was something more pressing to get off her chest before she felt free to decide the rest of her life.

"Yes, dear?" the dowager asked as she hesitated. Ash squeezed her hand.

"I traded a valuable artifact I found with the gold for my freedom last night. I got it back — don't worry — but now the world knows, or will know, about Solomon's Ring. I'm sorry if this exposes the family to any unwanted press." She dimly heard the gasps and intake of breath of the wedding guests. They'd know soon enough anyway. She laid her hand against her chest where she'd hidden the ring in her bodice. It had brought her luck yesterday, and today the artifact had outdone itself. *Best luck of all.*

"Well, I'm sure you only did what you had to do, dear. Why, I remember once having been given a rare brooch by the King of Siam and I traded it for passage back to England. You know — needing to escape the harem. Tedious to be one of many wives, no matter if you are the most favored. A woman should have only one husband, and a man only one wife, in my opinion."

Everyone stared at the lady of the castle, sitting so regal and talking about exploits only she could manage to toss off with such aplomb.

"Mother. You never shared that story before. Good heavens — a harem. For real?"

"A wise woman keeps her secrets, dear. And it was a long time ago." The dowager leaned forward, shaking her forefinger at her grandson. "*If* she wants to stay mysterious and capture a man's attention. Don't understand all these modern girls." She shook her head. "Always thinking the truth has to be so plain and boring. Icing is important to the cake of life. You're a writer, my dear, you know of what I speak. Exploits need a bit of dressing up. The charm is not giving away what is embellished and what is fact. Correct?"

"Sounds about right," Rebecca managed. She chewed on the inside of her cheek to keep from laughing aloud. The anger had about vanished, replaced by good humor. But she was also scared to death. It was time to answer Ash.

Her hand trembled in his. Her beautiful eyes with their starbursts were wide open, dominating her face. He smiled at her, wanting to give her reassurance of his intentions. "Will you have me, Rebecca? Will you marry me this day?"

The world hushed, the people in the audience leaning forward, transfixed.

"I will."

His heart swelled with emotion. He took her hand to his lips and kissed it reverently. "Thank you. I thank you with all my heart and soul. With all that I am, I promise to be true to you, and no other."

The minister pulled it together then. "Please." He gestured. "Would you both come forward and let me do this right?"

Ash stepped forward, drawing Rebecca with him.

"Okay, where was I? Oh yes, one last time, if there is anyone present who has just cause —?"

"Stop the wedding!"

Everyone turned at the sound. *What the fuck?*

A woman in wild disarray came barreling down the aisle. *Vanessa.* What was she doing here?

"I want my ring back! Give it to me!" she screamed. And that was the moment when he noticed a gun in her hand. He moved in front of his soon-to-be-wife to shield her. If anything happened to her now...

Then everything moved in slow motion. His father, Arthur and the other groomsmen moved forward to put an impenetrable barrier between them and the crazed woman. No. That wasn't right. He had caused this. He gave his love a quick order. "Stay here." Then he moved out in front of the group, needing to be the one Vanessa dealt with, to keep the others safe.

"Vanessa, give me the gun," he said, trying to take her attention away from anyone else.

She waved it wildly about. "No! Not until I have the ring. Give it to me! Right now!"

"I don't have the ring. But we can get it to you. Please, drop the weapon." He took another step forward, reaching out.

"Wait! I have the ring." Rebecca came forward, tugging something from the top of her dress. She held out the heavy-looking golden ring on the palm of her hand, the sun striking the object, making it appear to glow from within.

Vanessa's eyes widened as she stared at it, then narrowed to slits as she beckoned with the gun. "Bring it to me."

Rebecca began to move forward, but Ash held her back, pulling the signet ring from her hand, warm to the touch from the heat of her body. He held it out to Vanessa, keeping her attention on him and away from his love. What this woman was capable of remained unclear, but holding a gun on a wedding party suggested she was in trouble. Deep trouble. What could have gone wrong? He'd known her most of his life and he'd never had a whiff of this kind of activity.

The woman's eyes followed only the trail of the ring he held out to her, her obvious lust for the object clear in her face.

"Take it. It's yours. Just go and leave us alone."

"You'd like that, wouldn't you? Stamp all over my heart, make me play those bedroom games, then marry this little do-gooder." She looked at him with raw pain and anger in her eyes.

He tamped down his worry, made himself stay calm. He could do this, keep everyone safe if he chose his words carefully. He moved in front of Rebecca, trying to keep the woman's attention focused only on him.

"I never promised you anything. You wanted it to be casual, to have no commitment or ties. Hell, you insisted on it, Vanessa. Be fair now." He moved a step closer. "You should have said if you wanted more. I would have listened."

"Fair? Ha, you don't know the meaning of the word." She moved a step forward, and he did as well. He reached out and placed the ornate ring on the palm of the hand not holding the gun. The hand that held the gun dropped, until it was hanging by her side.

Her attention focused on the ring, giving him a split-second to act. He moved in a flash and grabbed at the gun, tearing it from her relaxed fingers.

The gun now in his hands, his people safe, he felt a rush of anger at what could have happened. But a part of the anger was filled with the realization that he had played a part in this. Well, no more. He was reformed.

Never again would he expose his family to anything but the best for all the years of his life. God and country and his family had his word on it.

Two men came rushing up across the lawn, bookending Vanessa and taking her firmly by the arms. She didn't resist, seeming to realize the folly of it. He hoped she got the treatment or help she so obviously needed.

"Sorry about this. We were driving her to London and she jumped right out of the vehicle and must have run all the way here. Never expected anything like this to happen. We'll take her with us now."

"We would like our ring back," his grandmother's imperial voice rang out.

The man took the ring from Vanessa and Ash slipped it into his pocket.

"Thank you, gentlemen." Ash watched the men hustle Vanessa away. Relief was too small a word for how he was feeling.

The minister cleared his throat nosily behind him. "Excuse me, do you want me to continue?"

Chapter Twenty-Five

Being happy never goes out of style. — *Lily Pulitzer*

"Do you want to continue?" Ash asked her, his face worried and looking as if he was trying to bury another emotion. Hope. That was it. After what he had just done, saved the day, what other answer was there to give?

"Yes! I want to continue."

Cheers followed from her beloved Ringers, echoed in the loud clapping of the crowd that apparently also approved.

"Didn't expect that," Ash said with a rueful grin. "'We English are not known for such public demonstrations. But I am so thankful, beautiful. I want to be with you, in the worst way."

"Don't you mean in the best way?" she teased.

He nodded, his eyes alight with suppressed emotion. A wedding was exactly what was needed.

"Please, continue," she said to the minister, who was still holding his good book open to the proper page.

"Thank you. Now, where were we? Oh yes, the part about objections," the older, gray-haired man said. A couple of groans came from the wedding party.

"You can skip that part, Reverend, about who present doesn't want this wedding to happen, yada-yada-yada. Just get to the good part," the dowager called from her seat, bringing a few stifled laughs from the crowd.

"Of course." The minister pressed his lips together to hide a smile that still managed to quirk up the sides of his mouth anyway. "We will have the vows now."

She just needed to slide her somewhat embarrassing middle name by this crew and all would be well. "I, Rebecca *Wilcox,*" she whispered the second name, adding a louder, "Fairfax, take you, Ash Edward James Piers, to be my lawfully wedded —"

"Excuse me, what did you say your middle name is, dear?"

"Ah, Wilcox." She swallowed hard, wishing the minister would just get on with things.

Ash bent his head a bit to the side, giving her a questioning look. "The W. in Samuel's name stands for Wilcox. Did you know that before today?"

"No." She shook her head. "Not at all. Just never cared for the name. D'uh! I mean, okay if you're a male. Anyway, I want this wedding to be legal, without a shadow of a doubt, so I'm giving my full name."

The minister glanced from Ash to her. *Was that a tic in his right eye?* "Are we ready to move on or is this a game changer?"

"No, go ahead, Reverend, we'll check on all that later. We just might be distantly related is all. Nothing that would interfere with a legal marriage."

"Start again, Rebecca, please."

"I, Rebecca *Wilcox* Fairfax, do take you, Ash Edward James Piers, to be my lawfully wedded husband to have and to hold from this day forward, for better, for worse, for richer, for poorer, in sickness and in health, until death do us part."

"And I, Ash Edward James Piers, do take you, Rebecca *Wilcox* Fairfax, to be my lawfully wedded wife to have and to hold from this day forward, for better, for worse, for richer, for poorer, in sickness and in health, until death do us part."

He took a deep breath and something in the intense light shining in the liquid pools of his deep brown eyes gave her pause. "I need to say this." His voice cracked, and he cleared his throat, continuing, "I also promise to love you, cherish you, be faithful only unto you, and to hold you above all others for all the days of our lives. You are my wife — my life." He drew her hand to his mouth, kissing the back of it with warm lips, his tender expression filling her up with emotion. The breath stilled in her body, the moment stopping time.

Wife. Oh my God, this is for real. She let out a gasp, reality hitting home.

"You okay?" Ash asked, his eyes filling with worry.

"I—I'm fine." She swallowed, her eyes welling up with unshed tears. It was all too perfect.

"Then, by the authority granted me, I now pronounce you man and wife."

"What about the rings?" Ash asked. He felt around in his jacket pocket, but his fingers came up empty. He looked surprised, glancing at his father.

The man of the cloth groaned, blinking his eyes rapidly. "Ah, sorry, sir, yes, of course. Who has the rings?"

"I do," Edward announced, his voice deeper and stronger than she'd ever heard him speak. He seemed to be very much enjoying himself. Ash just shook his head.

"Then hand them to me, please."

Ash took the ring offered by the minister and slipped it onto the proper finger on her left hand. She'd never seen it before, but it fit perfectly. "With this ring, I thee wed."

Rebecca accepted the man's gold ring and slipped it onto Ash's finger. The fit was also perfect. This had been planned. *Thank the gods above.*

"With this ring, I thee wed."

"I now pronounce you man and wife. You may kiss your bride, sir."

"Finally!" Ash grinned at her, swept her into his arms and bent her backwards for a big finale. His lips were so warm, so enticing, so delicious. She clung to him, pressing her lips to his until she heard the distant sounds of a crowd clapping and hooting. *Hooting?* When she looked up, shocked that a proper English crowd would behave like that on a proper occasion — well, maybe not a totally orthodox occasion — her body tingling from the amazing kiss, she saw it was the dowager doing the hooting. *Of course.*

She glanced at her new husband and her heart felt about to burst. They were finally free to be together without any qualms or doubts. Free to be just them from now on. A couple. Married and sanctioned. By kith and kin. She breathed in his essence, his fragrance filling her with desire and need.

"You take my breath away, Ash, and you give it back. Thank you for being who you are. For being brave and standing up for the truth," she whispered, staring into his eyes, the words meant for his ears only.

He gave her a rueful smile, half cocky, half endearing. And all Ash.

The doves were released by someone in charge, flying free and making the crowd ooh and ahh over the enchanting sight. Well-wishers surrounded them next, offering congratulations.

"You should have told me, guys." Rebecca shook her head at her crew, needing to make the point.

"What fun would that be?" Elin asked, her eyes alight with glee, a glee reflected in all the Ringers' beautiful faces. They appeared far too smug, but it was impossible to be angry with any of them.

They made their way inside the castle, to the multiple reception areas with drinks and hors d'oeuvres provided by an army of uniformed servers. She spied Gracie and pulled her into a hug. "Are you okay, sweet pea, about everything?"

"Sure, why wouldn't I be?" she asked with a shrug of her slender shoulders.

"I was worried it might come as a shock to you?"

"Adults think they know everything." Gracie rolled her eyes. "Give me some credit. Like d'uh, who didn't notice."

Yup, twelve going on eighteen.

Her Ringers gathered around her, wanting a few moments before she and Ash circulated among the guests.

"I want to officially welcome all your sorority friends to our home." The dowager spoke with pride, joining the circle of friends, holding out her hand regally to each bridesmaid in turn. "I do hope you can all stay for a while. I must get down to work and find you all husbands. It would be my utmost pleasure. I have connections, you know. Why, look around you. Dukes and earls, and even high officials of the realm abound at this wedding." She lowered her voice and stage whispered, "the guest over by the chocolate fountain is from Interpol. And single—I personally saw to the vetting. I can match *any* of you with the man of your choosing."

Lacey began to laugh, giving Casey a pointed look. "But Casey and I are already married, though my sister Lily might need some help," she teased. "She's still single and looking."

Lily gave her a look of chagrin, hands on hips. "My twin forgot to mention that I've got a *thing* going on."

"A thing. Is that what they call it these days?" Ash's grandmother's eyebrows furrowed together.

"Lily won't share exactly what this thing is." Lacey pursed her lips. "Just says *it's complicated.*"

"He's not married, is he, dear? Because that's never a good idea if you want to be married yourself?"

Lily turned a lovely shade of cerise. Being a fair redhead had its curses. "No, nothing like that."

Miranda snorted. "I'm never going to get myself tied down to one man when there's a whole world filled with stellular specimens needing to be test-driven."

"Miranda! When did you get so militant?" Rebecca gave her a look of surprise. This was new.

"Since that rat Johnny left her for Sierra," Casey muttered.

"I'm sorry." Rebecca gave her a big hug.

"No biggie. Best to know now, right?" But Rebecca heard the pinch in Miranda's words. "If a man can't handle a capable woman who wants to get to the bottom of mysteries and prove them hoaxes, then he'd better get out of my way. Science over superstition is my thing."

Casey nodded sagely. "Johnny's parents had some kind of encounter with a ghost and didn't take too kindly to the knowledge that Miranda thought it all bunk."

"You're better off without him, then," Rebecca said. "But you haven't shared the dare yet. What's it to be, Miranda? Who's in the hot seat this time?" She didn't want this magical moment to end, and offered the request to delay it.

Everyone looked at Miranda. The time had arrived. She stood tall, rocking on her heels, her expression downright sassy.

"I call out Elin Johansson — ufology expert extraordinaire." Elin of fairy hair fame. A maiden right out of medieval history with an angelic face and cornflower blue eyes. The outside hid a heart of gold too, overlaid with some awesome Amazonian skills.

Elin groaned. "Why do I have the feeling that your winning means my world's about to fall off the rails?"

"Why, sugar, you can handle anything. Just bat those big blue eyes at any man and he'll help you carry out the deed in a heartbeat."

"Okay. Hit me with it."

"I think I've come up with a fun one that pushes the envelope. Drum roll, please," Miranda said.

A chorus of trills filled the air.

"Elin is dared to, tah-dah, sit on the lap of a strange man of her choosing for ten minutes. Why should I be the only one to suffer, right? I want to see you work your way out of that one, girlfriend."

Elin groaned. "You mad at me or something? I'm not even dating. I'm on strike in sympathy *with you*. Remember? That should earn me something."

"Of course it doesn't. But since Rebecca's been in England, she's learned a lot. You can grow from such an experience — if you let it happen." She gave Rebecca a look of fondness, including Ash in her smile.

"My choosing, eh? That means I don't have to be attracted to him or anything, right?"

"Up to you. But you can't set it up. He has to be a stranger."

"Fine. You're on. No biggie."

"Yeah, if he doesn't begin to follow you around like a puppy dog, you'll be lucky." Casey gave a knowing nod, checking with one hand that her chignon was still smooth and intact.

"I'll be smart and choose a guy who's not looking for a woman. Someone hot *and* unattainable. Maybe in law enforcement or the military."

"You might get arrested," Ava, the resident lawyer, jumped in with an objection.

"Good point. Safer to sit in a male stripper's lap."

"And no paying for it!" Miranda said.

"You didn't stipulate that up front, so it's too late to add any extra rules now."

She frowned, displeased. "Fine. But you'd think a Ringer would play fair. Rebecca did it. Found a real live duke to kiss."

"And look at the trouble that landed me in!" She laughed. "Well, before it was all made all right." She beamed at Ash now, her happiness bubbling over.

"Okay, okay." Elin put up her hands in mock surrender. "I'll play fair. Especially since it's a small thing anyway next to my Ringers wish. And I've changed my mind on what I want. No ordinary Fabergé egg for me. Plus, it's already been done. So instead, I'm heading off to recover a real crystal skull from a den of iniquity." A sense of false bravado accompanied her words.

Stunned silence.

Oh Lord. Elin had a secret that the world did not know about. Only the Ringers. This was a huge step for her, revisiting her past. Old wounds were hidden by her lovely face. Wounds that had never healed. *I'd thought she'd leave all that behind her forever.*

"Are you certain, Elin? You know, you can combine the dare with any adventure, right? It doesn't have to be such a drastic one." Rebecca was worried and not afraid to say so. The simple truth was that Elin had been raised in a cult for the first twelve years of her life, and had only escaped with the help of law enforcement, to find her way from foster family to foster family until the age of majority, when she'd taken it upon herself to get a degree at the University of Manitoba, working full time as well.

"I have to do this. It's time. Never going to properly get on with things until I make sense of the past. And I need to see if my little sister's okay in person. A yearly Skype session on her birthday isn't cutting it any more. Don't worry, I can handle them now."

Rebecca wished her friend sounded more certain. There was a fragility in Elin that defied her Amazon warrior creed, one she didn't let others see, but one Rebecca had been party to time and again when any tiny creature needed her help. The woman literally couldn't hurt a fly. She even picked up ants in summer off the floor and took them outside to set them free.

But she had to let her friend grow, leave the past behind by making peace with it. No one knew the whole story because she'd been tight-lipped about it for years. That didn't mean Rebecca couldn't worry, though. She looked over at Ash, listening intently to her beloved Ringers with an open mind. Rebecca felt more than blessed. No word quite fit the bill. Not honored, not exalted, not esteemed. Maybe cherished. Hmm, she'd get around to finding the right word eventually. Right now, she just wanted to live and love.

"If you'll excuse me. I have a new husband to see to," she said. *Husband.* The word sounded beyond amazing when it meant Ash.

She moved away from her Ringers to join him. He took her hand and kissed her fingertips, one by one.

She looked up into those chocolate brown eyes and the soft curls that always decided they were going to look charming, no matter how much product was applied. He was a gorgeous man. And best of all — he was all hers. "Thank you."

"What for, beautiful?"

"For choosing me. For being you. For loving me."

He took her hand to his lips and kissed the palm, sending delicious shivers racing through her. Her mind drifted to the night ahead, and all the possibilities. "Love is being devoted to another's heart, soul and body. I have officially dedicated all that I am, all that I have, to you. I want nothing more than to spend all my days with you, beautiful. Two hearts beating as one."

The poetic words and the look in his eyes caused tears to spill over. She let out a sigh of contentment she could no longer hold in. Her body was just too small. She trembled with it, the tide of it pushing her forward, blessing her with effortless momentum. The words on her lips came right from her soul, branding her forever.

"And I promise to cherish every precious moment we have together, Ash, come what may. I will love you all my days, and with all my heart, and for as long as we both shall live."

He nodded, sealing the deal with the most awesome of kisses.

Then another.

And another…

Want to see more from this author?
Here's a taster for you to enjoy!

The TETRAD Group:
Racing the Tide
January Bain

Excerpt

Day One: 5:13 a.m.

The bed trembled, its legs jerking and thudding about in a kind of macabre dance. Cole woke instantly. *Is this the big one?* The king-size bed shimmied and rattled a few more times, then settled back down, coming to rest slightly askew on the hardwood floor of his bedroom, the earth having released its rage. *Another fucking tremor.* He ran his hands through his sweat-damp hair, glancing over at the bedside table.

Five-fourteen a.m. He slid his gaze from the clock to the picture, as he did every morning, ready to administer his daily punishment. During the long night of sleeping intermittently, he had made up his mind, but now, looking at her face, he couldn't do it. He couldn't dishonor her memory in that way. *Especially not in that way. The coward's way.*

His mind zeroed in on the single event defining his life, the day haunting him every second the clock ticked. The day almost a year ago when he'd pulled into his driveway after a voice message he could make no sense of. Finding the front door ajar. Walking down a hallway so silent he could hear the pounding in his skull echoing his slamming pulse. Finding the bathroom door shut against him. One more obstacle. Turning the handle as slow as a swimmer in deep water, finding it unlocked, his throat tight and aching. The creak of the hinges. The door swung open. His vision darkening around the edges as he took in the horror of the scene. The heaviness in his chest that made him sink to the floor, gathering her into his arms. *No. Oh, God no. Not like this.*

His cell phone rang in the dead stillness of a house that had once been a home, jerking him back into the present. Swallowing hard, he picked up the phone from the table, turning his back on the photo of his wife and himself mugging for the camera in happier times. The words of his father haunted him. *'A real man never cries, son, no matter what'*. Did he mean even if the worst thing that could happen, happened?

"Yeah." He managed one sharp word.

"Hey, Cole, it's Jake. How's it going?"

Hearing his friend's voice ratcheted down his anxiety, put the cap back on his demons. Had it been only nine months ago that they had put Kastrati and his son away for crimes against humanity? The one bright spot in the past year had been the whirlwind operation involving Jake and his new wife, Silk. Teaming up, they had been successful in putting the Kastrati crew, a cartel that had been on his radar for some time, behind bars for trafficking in women and drugs.

Silk had borne the worst of it, when the son's senseless drunk-driving had left her sister and her sister's unborn child dead on the streets of LA. She'd even gone after the man herself when he'd been released on a technicality with the help of high-priced lawyers — she'd been waiting with a high-powered rifle across from the courthouse to take him down. And that was how she and Jake had met. Better than a dating agency, Cole supposed. A more awesome and skilled pair of operatives he could not hope to meet. Jake with his brilliant and fine-tuned military skills and Silk with her PI's investigative knowledge and dedication. She was almost as obsessive as he was about taking out the bad guys.

When he didn't answer right away, Jake asked with a hint of concern in his voice, "Did I wake you?"

"No. A fucking tremor managed to do that this morning. Seems the San Andreas fault is unhappy these days. Playing with us mortals and reminding everyone who's the boss. Other than that — I'm fine. How's the new family?"

He cleared his throat and focused on the present. He got up and padded into the living room to open the drapes, staring out at a world that appeared normal, on the surface, anyway. He knew better. A dark abyss lurked underneath, just waiting to swallow a person whole. *Not going to happen. Life is precious, even when crawling through hell.* Staying there kept Mathew's memory intact and he'd not give that up for anything. Someone had to remember his little boy. *Keep him alive.* And someone had to try to save others. Do what they could. *Choose me.*

"Great. Glad you're okay. We were wondering if you've got the time to come our way for a visit?"

"Sure, what's up?" He recognized Silk's excited voice in the background as she insisted, "Just ask him already!"

Now, it was Jake's turn to clear his throat. What was making his friend who had undergone the horrors of war nervous? "I had intended to wait until you got here, but you know our Silky. Well, here it goes. So, we're in the process of starting up our own company — The TETRAD Group. I think it could be right up your alley, Cole, with your need to rush in and rescue others, not to mention that your skills and abilities complement Silk's and mine perfectly. You know we shone as a team when we worked together to take down the Kastrati crew a few months back. Silk and I still talk about it all the time, thinking — hell yeah, we can do more. All of us, together, taking on cases for people who have nowhere else to turn. We can go and do things even law enforcement can't and yet have their support and insight because Quinn Malone's already on board with his far-reaching connections. I know you've worked with him lots in the past. He can bring a slew of abilities to the group, what with his undercover operative skills from working as a FBI agent and his former career as a lawyer. He knows the law inside and out, just like you do. Isn't that where you met? At law school?"

"Yeah, Quinn and I competed for top honors in our graduating class." *A long time ago and in a land far away.*

"What do you say, buddy, want to come to Vancouver and discuss it? Become one of the four founding members? Our aim is to help people who have trouble going to the local authorities — you know — do whatever it takes to make a difference and protect the innocent. Like you've been doing already. But with your tech savvy, hacking skills, undercover experience and understanding of the human mind, we would be unstoppable. Strength in numbers with a diverse range of overlapping skills brought into the mix from all of us. We'll stand together, strong and proud. Make a difference in this world that's desperate for more heroes."

Do I? Maybe this is what I need. A complete change. And working together on cases meant so much more could be done. He had an admiration for the like-minded, married pair of Jake and Silk. And he'd worked off and on with Quinn over the past few years, his contact with the former FBI agent proving invaluable to his own personal crusades when he'd used up every bit of knowledge he could throw at criminals allowed by law, and then some.

The guy was the best. Knew how to play the dual role of human being and undercover agent and not mix up the two. He always got which side of the law he was on. Cole understood first-hand how hard that could be, acting at being one of them without becoming one of them. Learning to live with duality. It was hard enough infiltrating a motorcycle club or a drug cartel, but when he'd taken it to a far more disgusting level to get close to the nefarious perverts of NAMBLA, the North American Man-Boy Love Association, and had to listen to their sickening conversations and self-justifications, well, that took it to a level Cole found he was unable to deal with, though Quinn had gone on a righteous crusade and brought the fuckers down. Even having to talk Cole off a ledge when he'd threatened to blow up the convention center where the group was holding one of its secret annual meetings. Cole had to admire not only his dedication, but his loyalty to the cause and to friends.

Hell, Quinn even had a sense of humor about his undercover work, sending one criminal to jail when he was posing as a drug dealer and having the asshole call him from there to ask him to "raise bail". He'd done that all right. Raised it to a million with the help of inside officials—not quite what the creep had meant. Though the time when Cole had posed as a hitman-for-hire in an online sting to take down a dirty lawyer looking for a revenge killing on a business partner and his innocent wife—that time had cemented the loyalty of their friendship when Quinn had smoothed things over with law enforcement. Things have a way of going awry when Cole worked a case driven by emotion, lack of sleep and an intense drive for justice. No apologies. *It's who I am.*

People said they looked alike, but Cole could never see it, at least not anymore since he'd lost so much weight and Quinn now outweighed him by a good twenty pounds. Sure, they both had dark, military-short hair and brown eyes, but that was where the similarity ended. Besides, his nose had been broken playing basketball—being so big and tall had made Cole a favorite on his college team. *God, those were simpler days.*

In a blink of an eye, the series of cases they'd been involved in flashed through his mind, pushing him to a quick decision.

"Sure. What the hell. I'll come up, see how things work out on a trial basis. Not much going on right now, anyway. Kind of between things. I can close up shop for a few days and not a soul would know I'm gone." He shrugged, staring out of his front window at a neighbor now watering his lawn. "I'll catch a plane tomorrow and text you the time."

"Great! That's great." The palpable relief in his friend's voice was nice to hear. Made him feel needed, something he'd not experienced for a long while. He ended the call and strode into his office, where he booted up his laptop to check out airline reservations. He found a flight with a layover in Denver and booked it. *God, I need coffee.*

His phone rang again. *So much for coffee.*

"Cole," Jon said before he could even say hello, the hard edge to his friend's tone unusual.

Hmm. What now? "Hey, Jon, I was just thinking about you. Great minds think alike. Just planning on calling you about dropping by and visiting tomorrow. I have a layover in Denver planned." Jon lived in Denver, had for the past fifteen years, since his daughter Sara's birth, his and Rose's only child. "How you doing?"

"Been better, but it'll be good to see you. How about you? How you holding up?"

"I'm okay. What's up with you?" A tightening of his stomach muscles made Cole straighten in his chair, all senses alert. He shut his laptop lid and homed in on the voice coming over the phone, paying careful attention to each nuance. In the psychology courses he'd taken, he'd discovered the subtle clues for what a human being wanted to share or tell a listener were there, not hidden at all.

"Sorry, it's just business. So much going on right now. Crazy busy—you know how it is. But you're going to be here soon, so we can talk then."

It was damn well more than just business. But it was also obvious Jon would never say whatever was troubling him over the phone. Cole would get to the bottom of it tomorrow, that was for damn sure.

"I'm okay. Got an interesting job offer I'll tell you about also, if you're sure you have the time?"

"Sure, we'd love to see you. You know how Rose dotes on you." Jon's voice softened, sounding more himself, when he spoke of his wife. A good woman, Rose. Cole swallowed hard, regret riding him hard.

"Okay, tomorrow it is."

Cole hung up the phone, his nerves on edge. He went into the galley kitchen, filling a cup with instant coffee and adding hot water from the special machine that kept water hot or cold all the time. He drank it standing over the kitchen sink, surveying his neglected backyard that had used to be his pride and joy. The bright red swing set he'd sweated over a few years ago needed a coat of paint, its rusty surface beginning to lean. *Yes. Past time to move on and do more.*

Home of Erotic Romance

What's hot this week from TOTALLY BOUND PUBLISHING

Sign up for our newsletter and find out about all our romance book releases, eBook sales and promotions, sneak peeks and FREE romance eBooks!

https://totallyentwinedgroup.us7.list-manage.com/subscribe/post

About the Author

January Bain has wished on every falling star, every blown-out birthday candle and every coin thrown in a fountain to be a storyteller. To share the tales of high adventure, mysteries, and full-blown thrillers she has dreamed of all her life. The story you now have in your hands is the compilation of a lot of things manifesting itself for this special series. Hundreds of hours spent researching the unusual and the mundane have come together to create a series that features strong women who don't take life too seriously, wild adventures full of twists and unforeseen turns, and hot complicated men who aren't afraid to take risks. She can only hope the stories of her beloved Brass Ringers will capture your imagination as much as they did hers when she wrote them.

If you are looking for January Bain, you can find her hard at work every morning without fail in her office with two furry babies trying to prove who does a better job of guarding the doorway. And, of course, she's married to the most romantic man! Who once famously replied to her inquiry about buying fresh flowers for their home every week, "Give me one good reason why not?" Leaving her speechless and knocking her head against the proverbial wall for being so darn foolish. She loves flowers.

January loves to hear from readers. You can find her contact information, website details and author profile page at https://www.totallybound.com

www.ingramcontent.com/pod-product-compliance
Lightning Source LLC
Chambersburg PA
CBHW020215260626
47156CB00002B/384